love after never

EMPIRE BAY BOOK 1

MELANIE KINGSLEY

Love After Never © Copyright 2023 Artemis Girl Publishing LLC

Copyright notice: All rights reserved under the International and Pan-American Copyright Conventions. No part of this book may be reproduced or transmitted in any form or by any means, electronic or mechanical, including photocopying, recording, or by any information storage and retrieval system, without permission in writing from the publisher, except for the use of brief quotations in a book review.

This e-book may not be re-sold or given away to other people. If you would like to share this book with another person, please purchase an additional copy for each recipient. If you are reading this book and did not purchase it, or it was not purchased for your use only, then please return it to your e-book retailer and purchase your own copy. Thank you for respecting the hard work of this author.

This is a work of fiction. Names, places, characters and incidents are either the product of the author's imagination or are used fictitiously. Any resemblance to any actual persons, living or dead, business establishments, organizations, events or locales is entirely coincidental.

The author acknowledges the trademarked status and trademark owners of any products referenced in the work of fiction, which have been used without permission. The publication/use of these trademarks is not authorized, associated with, or sponsored by the trademark owner.

Warning: the unauthorized reproduction or distribution of this copyrighted work is illegal. Criminal copyright infringement, including infringement without monetary gain, is investigated by the FBI and is punishable by up to 5 years in prison and a fine of $250,000.

love after never

Even the blackest souls need love...

Seedy underbellies and dark depravities don't scare me. I've seen the worst and survived.

But I've *never* seen a man like him before.

Gabriel Blackwell, the raven-haired demon of the underworld,. He's the sickest bastard of them all. He might also be a murder suspect.

If I'm going to do this job and see him behind bars, then I need to use my wits. I do not need to let him slide beneath my defenses the way his hand slips under my shirt.

I can't stop myself.

And if I don't, then I won't make it out the other side of this case. My life hasn't been anywhere close to easy.

He wants me for his own. And a piece of me, the chaotic and traumatized part I barely acknowledge, wants him back. I'm not sure which one will be harder to resist.

18+ Romance. Love After Never is a full length dark romance with enemies to lovers themes, featuring a psychotic tormented hero and a badass heroine. Contains darker themes and lots of steamy scenes. The first in the Empire Bay duology.

a note to readers

The following story contains mature themes, strong language, and sexual situations intended for adult readers. Those with triggers are encouraged to proceed with caution. Triggers may include: extreme violence, strong language, dubious consent, and sexual situations.

ONE
layla

THE FLEETING ORGASM is the first one I've managed to chase down in weeks. There and gone in the span of seconds with the shrill ring of my cell phone ripping me out of the fantasy.

"Sinclair," I growl into the phone, stilling my movements on top of the male beneath me.

I slam a palm down to the middle of his chest when he resists, bucking against me in a clear demand for me to continue. Weeks of this bullshit back-and-forth and lying to the beta beneath me about being absolutely great...only to have it come to this?

My glare has brought down stronger men but this one pays me little mind.

"We've got a situation," the voice on the other end of the phone says. Simple. Harsh. "I need you to get your ass out of bed."

I know what it means.

"How do you know I'm in bed?"

"Because no matter how much you hate it, you are a

creature of habit, and it's about that time. You're not going to want to waste time. Layla...this one is bad."

"*How* bad?" I ask my partner.

I keep my answers short now. Curt. Still crouched above the Sub with my legs on either side of his hips, an inch separating my cloth-clad core with the erection he's forced to keep in his pants.

Forced until I give him permission to release it.

The Sub I've been playing with for weeks groans underneath me and shifts his hands up to my nipples. He grabs the globes of my breasts and squeezes.

"Please," he begs. A world's worth of need in one syllable. "*Please.*"

His groan turns into a panting and whispered plea. Mental note as I smack down on him to get him to stop: If I keep playing with this Sub then I'll need to restrain his hands. He should know better than to touch without my permission. It's one of the rules we set out whenever we first started playing with each other.

"It's bad," my partner replies simply. "Get your ass over here, Detective."

"Where are you?"

The Sub groans. "Are you going to talk on the phone the whole time I'm here?"

I've been calling the Sub *Bill* because I know it's not his name and it's another level of control between us. Or so I thought when we first met each other.

He agreed to play by my rules when we got into this relationship of sorts, but if he's going to push boundaries then he's got to go. I don't have time for a Sub who doesn't know how to pay attention.

The whimpering man annoys me. Especially when the whines are coupled with the grabbiness of the hands. A good Sub knows when to touch and when to lie still. This one? Everything about him screams *newbie*.

Too new for me, and I realize there won't be a next time for him. He's reached the end of the line with me.

My partner sighs on the other end of the phone. "I'll text you the address. Get here as soon as possible."

"I'll meet you there."

He clicks off without another word and I toss the phone into a pile of laundry.

"Bill" is red-faced from trying to control himself. The whimpering is gone but the panting reminds me of a dog.

Weak. Pathetic. Not a dog, but the man.

"We're done here, friend."

I slap my palm down over his cock a few times but there's no way I'm getting off now. And the sensation of having my orgasm stolen leaves me pissed off. It leaves me beyond frustrated when I think of how long it's been, that none of these men have been able to give me what I want and need.

"Can I come?" Bill asks. His blue eyes are wide and he's searching my face for an answer. "Please. Let me come. I'm so close, baby."

I climb off of him rather than give a verbal answer.

Now those blue eyes narrow into thin lines of frustration tinged with a hint of violence. He quickly tamps down on the latter. "What the fuck?" Bill bursts out. "That's not fair. You're leaving?"

He starts to push up off the mattress as well until I hold out a warning hand to still his movements. "I'll make the punishment ten times worse if you don't lie there. Don't touch yourself or you won't come," I tell him.

Playtime is over for both of us.

Already thinking about the case, I turn the Dom/Sub

part of my brain off and Bill ceases to exist under the weight of duty.

We've got a new murder.

A new crime scene to investigate.

The whole of me, seconds ago attuned to pleasure, now shifts into deadly purpose.

With my back to Bill, I slip out of the black-and-green lingerie and into a comfortable, functionable sports bra. A simple cotton tank follows, and a pair of well-worn jeans all shades of midnight and navy, with a dark zip-up jacket and black construction boots to match.

I toss my hair into a ponytail while Bill watches. He's still on his back on the mattress, making it a point not to touch himself.

"Get dressed." I bend at the waist to pick up his clothes and toss them to him.

"You really are serious," he mutters under his breath.

I pat my jacket, going through my mental checklist. Keys, cell, badge. Shit, I need my gun.

"Yes, I'm serious," I tell Bill on my way to the gun safe in the closet. "I've got to go and there's no way in God's blue hell I'm leaving you here in the apartment alone."

The safe beeps and the lock clicks open as I wait for him to get dressed as well, confusion twisting his face, and when he's done I take him by the hand.

"What about me?" the man asks.

Not bad looking. I never look at their faces though. I only look at the potential and what we can bring to each other in this sick game I love.

"Next time," I promise.

It's a lie.

We both know it's a lie.

Seconds later I've tossed him out of the apartment and

locked the door behind us both. Bill seems pissed at me and he walks backwards, staring me down.

"I've never been involved with anyone like you before." He's still sporting an erection and rubs it suggestively. "It's so fucking hot."

"You never will again."

"When can I see you?"

I stalk ahead of him, leaving him no choice but to follow me down the hallway toward the stairwell. And once we're in the car park of the apartment building, my key fob unlocking the sedan, I turn to him and sigh. "Don't bother calling me. Go find someone else to take care of your needs. Another Dom. Someone who doesn't give a shit that it takes so long to train you to do this right."

Maybe he'll learn a thing or two with a better teacher.

"Hey, that's not fair." Bill's pissed and he has a right to be. "Hey! Mistress—"

This situation takes edging to a completely new level and I'm too far into my cop headspace now to give a shit.

"Sorry. Take care."

Sliding into the front seat, I flash him a barbed smile before I crank the engine and peel out of the parking garage, leaving a trail of exhaust fumes and dust behind me to keep him company.

I've seen men and women in my department take bullets to the chest and bleed to death. I've seen bodies on the street that look more like roadkill than actual human beings. I've held the gaze of a woman with a needle in her arm while she silently begs for death to take her.

Bill's suffering, while nothing to make light of because we all know how rough it can be to have an orgasm withheld, is nothing in comparison.

My cell pings and a glance at the screen shows a text from my partner Devan with the address.

"27th and H street," I mutter out loud.

It's not too far from my apartment, either. Not the worst area but nothing good. You'd never tell your grandma to move in and take up knitting there.

The sun hides behind thin gray clouds and turns the sky to a sick shade of yellow, broken only by the towering spears of buildings. Empire Bay, New Jersey, is sick. I'm sick too, and neither of us seems willing to change any time soon.

Maybe it's because we've both made peace with our lot in life and the place we occupy in time and space. The city will always be a haven for the fuck-ups and the go-getters. I'll always carry my trauma right there in the open and live my life the way I want. Take what I want.

Cities come with anonymity for some and a host of problems for most. I'll always fight for justice for the small ones this city stomps beneath its feet. Right into the dirt where the people of good society say they belong.

People like my dad.

His face flashes through my mind, but not how he looked when I found him. I remember one of our game nights, *before* he dragged the bottle out of the liquor cabinet, where he'd actually been laughing at a joke I'd made.

I flip the blinker and take a left turn—right into a line of backed-up traffic.

It's always fucking busy on this end of town.

I force myself to settle. The killing calm morphs into something darker and far more dangerous, the icy pool at the center of my being born of necessity and tragedy. The will to survive.

I pull to a stop two blocks over from the scene in the

only parking space I find. Parallel parking is a skill I've never mastered and I nearly bash into the mirror of the car behind me when I tug too hard on the wheel.

Stupid nerves.

I can't slip again.

Sunglasses in place, I cut through the crowds on the sidewalk and try to blend in. Stalking forward unflinchingly until I reach the yellow-and-black hazard tape surrounding the scene.

The tape is already in place, thankfully, and very necessary with the crowds gathered to take in the mess. Red and blue flashes turn the metal of the nearby security bars to neon, the bars that keep the businesses to the right and left of the scene locked tight until nightfall.

Through the crush of bodies and the chaos—

There. Something inside of me stills.

My stomach dips and swirls until I rein myself in and force my nervous system under control. There's an arm outstretched in a pool of blood with fingers clenched in a position of perpetual reaching. Whether it's for something in this life or the next, I have no fucking clue.

Another body, another murder, and it's up to me to make a quick arrest.

I take a deep breath but it stalls in my lungs when I glance up at the glowing red sign. Then it takes everything inside of me not to fall apart.

I'm frozen at the edge of the caution tape with my gaze trapped on the flickering lights of the convenience store behind the body. On the store sign that reads SAM'S. Soon even the edges of the red lettering blur into a mishmash of shapes and shadows.

It shouldn't still affect me.

I've gotta get it together. Have to maintain control and pretend—

Pretend like another group of officers didn't investigate a similar murder, beneath a similar sign, the night my dad was murdered.

TWO
layla

MY FATHER'S HONEY-SWEET LAUGH, *so at odds for a man of his size, enveloped me as much as the hug. He stooped to my level and those massive arms cradled me to him.*

He laughed a lot when he stayed away from the bottle. He hadn't had a single drop of liquor that night. Which made this a special occasion. I didn't know the reason why but I liked it. I wanted him to stop drinking.

To say the words.

Three words he'd only said to me once.

"But Daddy!" I whine, tugging at his jacket. Desperate for him to listen to whatever was on my mind.

"Count up to 100, my girl, and time me. I'll be back before you're done."

He was just going out to the convenience store. I remember telling myself that over and over as if it would somehow make my racing heart calm. He was going out for some cookies and chips and he'd be back before I knew it. A game. We were just playing a game.

Except something inside of me felt sick and I had no idea why.

I still hear the conversation with Dad not in my head but like it's happening in real time. As though he's still there whispering in my ear and telling me to count down. The sensation sends shivers through me. Talk about having someone walk over your grave.

This is not the same story.

I have to tell myself that on repeat. This is not the same story and not the same murder.

But they're all the same, aren't they? Death comes for everyone in the end, even if the means to get there are different.

I wish I'd parked closer so I have a door to slam to mark my arrival. Drama and noise is so much better than shaking my head and coming to, hoping no one saw my little disconnect.

Reaching down to my belt, I wrap my fingers around the frayed leather edges of the holster keeping my badge front and center. I hold it up for the cops standing watch at the edge of the perimeter.

"Stand aside," I tell the one on the left as I stifle a groan. "Detective coming through."

Of course. Of *course* I'll have to deal with Frick and Frack today.

"How the hell do you always get a heads-up on these deals, Layla?" The douchey detective who already has his notepad in hand sniffs, his gaze almost a physical touch as he scrapes it from my head to my toes. "It's some kind of fucked-up radar you got."

"Well, I don't have my dick in my hands 24/7, Jerry. It makes me easier to reach." I flash him a smile dripping with false charm.

I probably get laid more than he does. The shrink I used

to see says I use sex as an escape, but what the hell do shrinks know, anyway? I manage just fine now.

"If you want my dick in your hands, then you only need to say so."

"If I want to pet a rat I'll go to the pet store. Sorry, Jer." I narrowly resist reaching out to give him a little pat-pat-*slap* on the cheek for emphasis.

Jerry has his cap snugly on his head and tilted to the side. Might as well have a flashing arrow pointing down at him telling the world he's a Grade A douche. Anyone who knows him finds out the truth soon enough. He's one of those guys who peaked in high school and has spent the rest of his life chasing the same glory.

His brittle blue eyes bore into mine on my way past but he knows better than to stop me. Rather than coming up with a retort, Jerry only scoffs.

"You smell like you've been left used and wanting more times than you can count," his partner Clint replies in the silence, doing the dirty work for Jerry. "You should let off that O and do us all a favor. You get pissy when you don't finish."

Clint thinks he's funny.

He's only been on the force with us for a year and he's still trying to make a name for himself.

He sniffs at me, close enough to run his greasy nose along the whorl of my earlobe.

I ignore him.

I ignore Jerry when he lifts his hand for a high-five and the two of them dissolve into the middle-aged-man version of a giggle fit. Those two dickheads are the only ones who laugh. Which is punishment enough in my eyes.

Especially when a hard knot makes itself known in my

torso and my pulse hitches. The vic's arm is back in view now.

Bystanders on the left side of the scene are already pushing against the ropes and one of them has gone so far as to duck underneath with his cell phone in hand. Snapping off pictures or video of the body like someone hadn't lost their life brutally.

"Move, I can't see!" one of the bystanders calls out.

My already highly strung patience snaps as I turn on Jerry and Clint. Furious, fuming. To the point where I'm surprised smoke doesn't start to curl from my ears and nostrils. "Maybe instead of coming up with idiotic one-liners, you can secure the fucking crime scene like you should. Anyone can wander in here."

They treat this gig like it's a joke. Their attention gets so entirely focused on themselves and feeding their egos, feeling like big men in charge of their tiny crumb of the world, that they let bystanders get close. Too close. I flash my teeth at the guy with the camera and he backs up a step, running into the side of the building and dropping his phone close to the pooling blood.

Too damn close.

Mucking up evidence, when finding the tiniest shred of DNA might make all the difference.

Jerry scoffs and the edges of his mustache bristle. "These people see death every day," he reasons. "It's nothing new for them. The scene is secure, Layla. Let them have a little fun. Not like they're getting past me."

My hands clench into fists at my side.

"Hey, L! Over here."

Devan Bishop's voice cuts through the haze in my head and I turn toward him. He knows exactly where I'm coming from and why Jerry bothers me and why an unsecured crime scene has me seeing red. The same kind of thing happened with my father's murder, except *I* was the one who pushed past the tape and compromised the scene.

Devan called for me just in time, too, before I can further get into it with the ass-fuck twins. I've got to let Jerry's shit go and focus on what's actually important.

My gaze flicks from the sheet-covered victim to the tall, quiet man standing on the opposite side of the scene that Jerry and Clint secured.

"We were here first, Detective McGee. Which means we don't need you playing security guard," my partner Devan tells Jerry. "Get back in your car and scram if you're not going to be helpful. Captain Ashcroft gave the case to us."

No one messes with Devan. His height means he's taken much more seriously than I am. I barely top five foot three.

Bright blotches of red color Jerry's cheeks at the comment. "You need me here."

I swallow over my smile to try and keep my expression neutral. "No, actually we don't."

"I'm going to try and get it anyway," Jerry blusters. Pissed off and mustache twitching like a fidget spinner. "It's ridiculous how you two think you can waltz right in and take over any high-profile cases that come through the precinct."

I straighten my shoulders, heading to Devan's side. We both ignore Jerry. Soon enough his voice fades into the rest of the background noise.

"What do you think?" I ask Devan. "First impressions?"

Devan's got the figure of a backstreet fighter, all length and wiry strength. He keeps his black curly hair shaved short and tight to the scalp. His chocolate-brown eyes simmer in barely contained irritation which disappears even as I watch. "Typical shit, L." His dark skin colors with frustration. "It's nothing good. My first impression is senseless violence."

He's the only one I let get away with any kind of nickname. And only Devan because he'd taken a bullet for me during a case too many years ago to count.

My stomach churns.

"Guy manning the register said she came in looking flighty, flaky. Scared. She fiddled around, asked to use the bathroom, changed her mind and bolted," Devan continues. "She went out, he heard arguing. And finally boom." He mimes someone pulling the trigger of a gun. "Right here on the street, clean through the head. Crowd claims they didn't see anything."

Poor thing.

I search around for one of the crime scene techs and grab a pair of gloves from them, peeling the material over slender fingers. Pulling back the sheet is always a crap shoot because you never know what you're going to find on a vic even when you know the specs.

This one has her eyes open and her features frozen in a mask of pleading terror. The knowledge of her impending death. The hole is straight between the eyes and out the other side, with pieces of skull and brain matter coloring the sidewalk like chalk.

I move down to the jacket, pulling apart fabric to check the pockets. Then the ground around the body.

"There's no lighter," Devan tells me gently. "I already checked."

I nod, shrugging. "This is also one too many cases on our plate. I don't suppose we're in a position to push it off on someone else, after what happened with Jerry?"

The knot inside me is still there, and when I tune in to

the reactions of my body, my heart is skipping every other beat.

"Nope. At this point, we're going to have to shuffle some things around and make it work." Devan searches my face and whatever he sees there has him nodding. "You good to let it go?"

I peel the gloves off and toss them toward a nearby bag of trash, ready to head out with our guys when they clean the scene. "Guess so. It kills me to let those freaks step in, though."

"Make their day," Devan agrees as he straightens.

He hates it just as much as I do.

"Okay, Jerry and Captain Jokes-a-Lot," I call out loudly. "It's all yours. We're taking a pass."

I touch Devan on the shoulder as I walk by and head back to the car.

The knot doesn't loosen all the way back to where I parked, not when I slide into the driver's seat and hold the steering wheel tight enough to crack it. Staring out the window.

A knock at the window has me jumping even when I see Devan's familiar features. Obligingly I roll down the window and stare at him until he gets to the point.

"You know, chasing ghosts is going to get us killed one of these days." He leans his forearm against the roof of the car. "I don't know if I'll always be there to have your back. Not that I plan to leave but just stating facts."

"I know." I blow out a breath and work hard on smiling, for both our sakes. "As long as you're not telling me you want a new partner?"

I work harder still to try and hide my disappointment. Everyone I trust leaves eventually. It's a fact of life. I should really accept it.

"No. There's no one else I'd trust. But at the rate we're going, we won't make it much longer on the force." Devan has the matter-of-fact tone of voice that lends itself to delivering bad news. There is no sugar-coating in those rich syllables, only truth. No matter how hard the truth might be to swallow. "We're going to burn out before too long, L."

He's right. Devan is always right and he's the only person in this world I care enough about to heed. Which makes him very dangerous for me.

Rather than get philosophical, and because we both have things to do, I salute him and throw the car into drive. I need to take the edge off, now, or I'll lose it.

THREE
layla

THE NOISE of the city brings me nothing but peace.

Wide-plank pine beneath my ass provides a way to ground myself. Sitting cross-legged on the floor, I stare out the window of my bedroom, the bed still disheveled and without a distraction by whatever his name was. Left to the quagmire of my own thoughts.

The open window lets in the sound of life. Shouting and laughter. Car horns and sirens. Barking dogs and screeching tires. From this vantage point, Empire Bay is nothing but buildings reaching into the grayish-peach heights of the sky above. There's very little character since all of them are more than four and five stories. If I stand at the window and stare a few blocks over, I can make out the distinctive glow of a fast-food place, a couple of laundromats, and the corner store where I go for snacks.

I twirl my Glock 22 in my hand, its weight familiar. The handle gleams.

Another murder and another dead end. Devan isn't wrong about our caseload. We've taken on more than we can really handle although we do our best, both of us driven by a deep-seated desire to help people and escape our own demons.

Except Ashcroft won't let us off this one, and I know that no amount of wishful thinking will accomplish it.

Scoffing at myself, I reach for the bottle at my side and take a sip of the whiskey I'd picked up on the way home. Cheap whiskey helps with the grounding. Keeps me from lulling myself into a deep sleep with its flavor rough enough to sharpen my attention rather than soften it.

I cock the gun and unload the bullet in the chamber, the magazine only half full.

Another sip.

Count up to 100 and time me. I hear his voice in my head.

I cock the gun again and unload the next bullet.

I'll be back before you're done.

The whiskey burns.

Squeezing my eyes shut, I cock the gun a final time and click off the safety at the back of the pistol grip.

Murder after murder after murder. My *life* is murder. I've solved too many damn cases and they never go away for me. It makes me and Devan a good team because we share the same unrelenting stubbornness that makes each case personal. In a way that so few people do these days.

But no lighter on the last one.

Much to my eternal disappointment, no matter how Devan and I search, there is never a lighter on our vics.

I cock the gun again and let the bullet drop before flicking the safety back on and dropping it to my side. Head between my legs, I blow out a breath and suck in a deeper one, holding it until my lungs burn and seize and my head spins toward the ceiling.

One hand wrapped around the neck of the bottle, I reach with the other toward the slight weight buried in my pocket. I know every groove of the fucking thing. It rests in my palm as if it belongs there, as much as I hate it.

I flick the lighter and watch the flame erupt before letting go and starting all over again. The light of the flame materializes as a phoenix burning, succumbing to the heat rather than rising out of the ashes. Twin swords form an X behind the phoenix and the fire is stylized, blue, more like ice than flame. The pommels of the swords are ivory roses.

My throat goes raw. I'd screamed so loud that night. *I counted to 100. I counted to 100. I counted to 100!*

It's not life, the one I'm living now. Nothing besides a bland existence of rinse and repeat and it doesn't seem to matter how many people I help. I look for the next one, the next case to close, but it's never enough. All those lives changed and perpetrators brought to justice...when is it going to be enough for me? When will I ever find the satisfaction?

I bring the flame to my hand like maybe the heat will burn away the memory of blood everywhere that night.

The cell phone bleats from a foot way, vibrating against the floor as it rings. I let it go to voicemail. There isn't anyone I want to talk to right now. Devan knows to text me two times in quick succession if he really needs something once I clock out for the day.

We joined the force around the same time and although we'd each gone to separate districts for our first beat, our track records made our current captain in this district consider the pairing.

Neither one of us looked back.

The slender golden-skinned woman and the slender dark-skinned man. We're a sight with the height difference, and we've both learned to cultivate our image when we approach people. Or for intimidation.

The cell rings again, and again.

"What?" I finally answer, my breathing heavy; I've gotten too deep into the memories. It's the damn murder at a convenience store tonight. It looked too similar. Except it missed the lighter, the one my partner knows I have to immediately scour for like an addiction.

"Devan said you might need me, that you're going to a dark place, so here I am, baby girl. I'm here for you to use! Or just to amuse you."

"I'm not going dark," I assure her. Then I glance at the bottle of whiskey. "I'm skirting the line, but I'm fine. I promise." I smile even though she can't see me. "It is good to hear your voice, though." Slowly I uncurl my legs and stretch them out in front of me to work out the kinks.

Taney chuckles and the sound is designed, perfectly cultivated, to cause anyone who hears her to shiver deliciously. "I know you, Layla. I've been your friend for how many years now?"

"Five," I answer automatically. "Longer than anyone else. You are my rock, Taney."

Except for Devan.

"Exactly. Bullshit a bullshitter one more time and see what happens," she warns lightheartedly.

"I appreciate your concern but—"

"That's it. Me. Your friend, who is concerned about you. Who loves you unconditionally. And I'm sure it's not a stretch to say you're probably holed up by yourself in your apartment when it's better for you to be around people." Her voice takes on a wheedling quality. "You know I'm right. You need people!"

"Ugh, people." I groan dramatically.

"Normally I might let you off the hook but the club is

hopping tonight and the energy is good. I think it would do *you* good to come," Taney finishes.

I think about it, monitoring myself for any hesitation and only coming up against my razor-sharp thoughts. "I'm not in a good mood for people-ing, Tane. I'd only bring the vibe down. I'm not fit for company by a long shot."

"Please?" She doesn't exactly plead but she's not going to make it easy for me to back out, either. Not when she's made up her mind.

She's the type of hard personality I appreciate because she refuses to flake out. Taney sticks to her guns, maybe even to her detriment at times.

"I feel you resisting and it's giving me a headache," Taney continues. "And clearly I haven't been sending you Subs you like, so the best thing to do would be to come and pick one out for yourself."

"I hate it when you bring logic into my dominant heart."

Taney blows a wet kiss to me, audible even through the phone. "I love you, too," she says. "Be here in less than an hour and you'll have your pick."

* * *

I've never found the thumping of EDM or the ultra-loud boom of the club appealing before. Walking in after the day I've had, I finally see the allure. The thrum lights the blood and makes it easier to forget the masks we wear for the outside world or the people we pretend to be to fit in with society. The bass helps lower inhibitions to allow any dark threads of pleasure to come out and dance in the light.

Or, rather, the muted glow from bulbs designed to mimic candles.

The underground club isn't on any map and good people won't be able to give you directions. Black velvet lines the walls and the carpet beneath my feet mutes any sort of footsteps. Making my approach silent. The air is heavy with roses and sweat and sex.

It's like a homecoming, in a way, because there are others here who feel the way I do.

The club offers all sorts of dangerous activities for both sides of the coin, the submissives and the dominants like me. At least here, Taney is right. I'll find willing men. I've always trusted her judgment as my friend because this is her playground. I never come here to play myself.

How in the world did I let Taney convince me?

Oh. Yeah. She knows what buttons to push, and because I love her, I cave. She called to express concern and offer a solution, knowing my guard drops for her. The same as the others in the main room of the Velvet Underground.

The dark hallway opens up into a large circular room lined with fabric and benches. A main stage dominates the back end of the building, with several women on the stage and in cages dancing to the pulse of the music. The benches are lined with bodies in various positions of sex and sexual acts.

A few tables decorate the main floor where patrons can sit to enjoy a drink and take in the sights. Everyone here is dressed in lingerie or something that passes for it, flashes of skin accompanied by leather and lace. It's a patchwork of sin with the odd splash of color as people crowd the floor. They mingle and fuck and network and drip lust like some people drop chips on a poker table.

I'm standing at the start of a fun house with the mirrors on display. Nothing here is what it seems to be, and underneath we're all made of the same stuff, regardless of what you see on the outside.

A shiver runs through me. The drive over here demolished the last of my buzz from the cheap crap whiskey but left a hollow empty space in my gut. The dancers on the stage and in the cages twist and writhe under the glow of the lights, with their skin oiled and assets on display.

That's why we do this, I muse, striding forward and pushing down the hint of discomfort. To be free. To show the world that we are unafraid to own ourselves in this way. It's a show of bravery but I, for some reason, have to muster up bravery tonight.

"My darling Layla!" Taney winds her way through the crowd and wraps her arms around my neck. She's pocket-sized, which normally brings her face directly in line with my chest when she's barefoot and I'm in boots. Tonight she teeters on sky-high heels. "Look at you, all gorgeous. Smelly, but gorgeous!"

"I didn't change after work," I murmur against her ear.

She might be short, but Taney got the lion's share of girth in the breast department. I look flat-chested in comparison. Tonight, her dirty-blonde hair is wild around her head and she's wearing a collar. Taney's dressed in a black-and-purple corset ensemble, and the silver clips keeping her thigh-high stockings up match the silver of the dog collar. I'm out of place in skinny jeans and a black tank top, if only because I don't have my legs or tits or ass out on display.

Once she pulls away, my arm still around her waist, I stare at the collar. "Seriously?" I gesture with my chin toward the dog tags jingling at the front and the shiny lock on the side.

Taney shrugs. "Not all of us like to be the *big bad*." She

winks. "I've got a sexy Daddy holding the other end of my chain tonight. Oh! By the way, there's a hot new Dom who's come in a couple of times. He's about to go on stage tonight and I thought you'd want to take a look."

"Pass." I hold up a hand to stop her. "I'm not interested in men who get off on dominating. Don't they do that enough in everyday life?"

"Some of them," Taney admits with a laugh.

I'm only partially joking because my mind immediately shifts to Jerry and all the detectives I've had to work with who are exactly like him. Including a few women who take one look at me and make an assessment, who feel like they need to push me down because apparently I'm a threat just by being good at my fucking job.

I do my job better than any of them. What they don't know is the extra hours I put in to *be* better. Unlike them.

"I know you're not into that kind of thing but give him a chance. At least watch him play. When I say this Dom is hot, Layla, I mean hot." Taney angles me toward the stage, and when she stares at me her eyes are so very blue, resting on my face with nothing but firm affection and trust. "He's a fucking *scorcher*."

"Fine, you've convinced me," I say with a laugh. I acquiesce because it's her, but it's also this place, this atmosphere.

"When you see this guy..." Taney trails off and shakes her head. "You are going to cream your jeans."

"Remains to be seen." I keep my arm around her waist, linking the two of us together, and damn it but she was right. I needed the company. More specifically, I needed her company and the energy she brings to the table. The crowd in the club is popping, yet it's more subdued than expected.

Until the lights flash and dim, drawing everyone's

attention to the stage. Most of the seats are already taken, but Taney hisses at a couple on a red velvet chaise a feet away from the stage. They make a hasty exit and leave the seat free for us to commandeer.

It's too dark to see if there are stains on the fabric but I'm willing to bet there are. Taney settles at my side, crossing one leg over the other and revealing more of those toned legs.

"This is one show you won't want to miss," she murmurs.

We turn in tandem to watch two women, clad in nothing but strips of silk with black leather accessories, stride past us and disappear down one of the hallways toward the private rooms. There's smoke in the air that winds around people dancing, women tossing long hair over their shoulders, men jerking their hips.

It's all bare skin dripping with sweat. Dripping with life. Vitality. Energy.

It makes me dizzy.

"So you put us in the splash zone?" I joke, my lip curling.

Taney grins. "Trust me on this. He's fabulous."

"What's his name?"

"Um...I think he goes by a stage name, but I can't remember it right now."

Enter our nameless Dom, striding across the stage wearing only a black thong strung across his hips and giving the audience a very good idea of what he's packing. His muscled chest is bare and also covered in oil, and unlike some of the dancers and patrons, he's not wearing a mask.

Judging from his profile, he has the type of face that should be chiseled in stone and commemorated. Sharp cheekbones, a strong jaw, an equally proud nose. Long dark hair flows from a dramatic widow's peak and frames his face, his eyes dark and filled with challenge.

Black-and-green tattoos in a tribal pattern decorate his neck and his shoulders. He's got leather cuffs around his wrists but I'm willing to bet they hide more patterns. Rather than detract, the designs only add to his charisma.

Taney is right again.

He's fine fine fine. And doesn't he know it, too?

FOUR

layla

HIS GIANT EGO is evident in every stride he takes, prowling toward one of the meeker looking girls dancing on the stage. She gives a yelp when she sees him eyeing her.

He grabs her by the back of the neck and bends her over in front of him, her legs straight and her ass arched up for his scrutiny.

Taney shivers at my side. Her attention is glued to the stage.

A certain low burn kindles between my legs, like the ghost of the orgasm I lost earlier today.

While the audience watches breathlessly—me among them—the nameless Dom who looks only a few years older than me peels the woman's underwear down. It pools at her knees and he turns her ass to the crowd to show them how wet she is already.

The woman locks her knees, arching her hips as the Dom slides two fingers inside of her, then a third, working her until she starts to shake.

As much as I usually hate watching a man dominate a woman this way, I'm captivated. By the inked swirls of tattoos and the play of golden light across his pale skin, by the fall of his black hair. By the way he moves.

He's a predator, pure and simple.

Yet for some reason he's hooked me through my lady parts.

In the next heartbeat, the nameless Dom has got his dick out and his hand strokes up and down the length of his massive erection. He shoves the black thong aside, drawing a foil-wrapped condom from it and sliding it inch by tantalizing inch down his length. The audience holds its breath collectively, watching him slide his dick along the woman's dripping slit, especially the bulbous head of that already-hard cock before he shoves it into the submissive woman panting in front of him.

No real foreplay and no warning.

He grabs her around the waist and shifts both of them so that their sides face the audience and we're able to watch every slow thrust. Every punishing jerk of the Dom's hips as he enters her again.

Again.

Again.

There are chairs on the stage for more play, and the meek woman has no choice but to hold on to the back of one as the Dom pumps into her, hard enough to have her eyes roll back in her head from pleasure.

He's why the place is filled tonight.

He's the reason why so many have stopped their own play to watch him fuck. He pulls out of the woman so that only his head remains inside her pussy before surging forward and making her shriek. The sharp sound of pure pleasure and feeling echoes in my ears and Dom Daddy reaches out to spank her ass. Her tits. He squeezes her nipples and her wails take on a keening quality.

He reaches around to place his index fingers at the corners of her mouth and holds her tight, like the bit in a bridle, as he slides in and out of her channel. Time slows around us and the seconds are measured in each harsh inhale from the man, each lusty sob from the woman he's working over.

I can't look away and I can't make my mind work the way I need it to.

Gods, this is *hot*.

There is something in the way he moves, the way he tilts his hips and works her body, leaving no doubt as to his control. Over her and the situation.

The man is...something special, and I see it even with my irritation. He's lean and muscled, with a thick dark goatee that lends the appearance of a bruiser, adds to the stage persona that I don't think is a creation but his real self.

His bottle-green eyes are icy yet confident when he rakes them across the crowd.

He pisses me off.

Frustration tangles with desire inside of me.

Not for any particular reason other than the arrogance clinging to him as tightly as his sweat. He's someone who has built up a reputation based on looks and ego. Sure, he's got a big head on both counts.

He's got raw sex appeal but nothing more.

Yup, an arrogant prick who knows he's good with his body.

Fine he may be, but he's the type of guy who's soured me on male Doms in general.

Ink flashes on his back when he turns to give the audience a better view of his ass and the pussy he pounds into.

My heart stops dead in my chest, breath catching and eyes going wide.

There are more tattoos. The stark black lines of the design cut across the muscles of his shoulders and his spine.

But it's the same design as the one in my lighter.

Down to the last detail.

His tattoo is a phoenix burning, the same twin swords with the white rose pommels and the blue stylized flame.

Fuck me.

This man with the magic cock has something to do with my father's murder.

The thumping of club music matches exactly the Dom's tempo of his performance on stage, and as the girl screams, finishing all over his dick, I bolt toward the stage area. Ignoring the way Taney calls my name.

I'm stomping my way up the steps, hiding in the curtains near the edge of the stage as the rat bastard pulls out, evidence of the woman's pleasure slathered all over the condom, and stalks away like he's just won some prize. Leaving her alone and trembling.

The audience goes wild, but he ignores it as he makes his way offstage. He doesn't see me there when I grab his elbow and yank him toward the open doorway behind the curtains, a small changing area for the girls to use whenever they need a break or some privacy.

"*You.*" His name isn't important. The tattoo is, and his connection—whatever it is—to my father. "I need to talk to you."

He stares down at me and, maintaining eye contact, reaches over to a side table to grab a towel, swiping it across his face. Turning so that his half-mast dick still wrapped in the condom bobs right in front of me. Like he wants me to gawk at it.

Stifling a growl, I grind my teeth and maintain my hold on his opposite arm. I force my gaze to his face and his emerald eyes, still glinting with the last hints of pleasure and a dark light that screams a challenge.

I wish I'd brought my badge.

I wish I had my gun.

My stomach does a lazy flop under the weight of his gaze.

"If you want a piece of me, then get in line, sweetheart." He rakes his eyes over me once before he sniffs, dismissing me, lazy contempt written across his face.

"You can keep your tired-ass dick to yourself. I have questions for you," I say. *Focus.* I've got to calm my ass down.

I slowly uncurl my fingers from around his forearm and take a step in the opposite direction. The Dom slides the thong down and off and kicks it aside, flicking the condom away before reaching for a pair of silk boxers. He draws them up over his hips, not even bothering to clean himself.

At least he's put his business away. I've got to make sure he can't escape or try to avoid this conversation.

I can't tear my gaze away from the tattoo on his back. *It's him. This is it.* He's either the murderer or he knows who did the deed. The design is unique and the lighter custom-made. Everyone in the department agrees.

Where had the Dom seen the design to get the tattoo donee if he wasn't connected to the case?

I will my heart to stop pounding so hard, otherwise I might pass out. My chest tightens, muscles clenching with adrenaline and the desperate need to kick this man's ass.

Whoever he is.

"If you're not here to fuck, then get out of my way. I'm busy." He glances over his shoulder at me. "Too many clothes on, anyway, and a flat ass."

I glower at him. "Who do you think you are?"

He leans in closer and flashes teeth. "Didn't you hear? I'm fucking Thor."

"I don't want your stage name." I jog to close the door behind us and block the exit with my body. "What's your real name?"

"What makes you think I'll give it to you? Especially if you're not here for fun." He seems to find my snarl amusing, if his grin is any indication.

"Name. Please." It pains me to add the last part.

"Who do I think I am?" he repeats. "You want answers and you're not willing to give me anything in return? Too bad. Despite the flat ass, you actually have a whole vibe going on." He uses the towel to gesture to my ponytail. "I kinda like it."

Rather than waiting for him to make a move, I get in his face, pushing a hand against his bare chest. "You're going to answer me."

He looks from my palm to my face and loses all hint of his smile. "What are you trying to start?"

I want to do a lot worse than a little slap. I want to knock his head into the floor and watch tears leak from the corners of his eyes.

My dad...

I'm not letting *Thor* leave this room without getting my answers and leaving him with some bruises. How's that for something in return?

"Sweetheart..." He smirks. "You don't want to do this."

"Your *name*."

His arm snakes out before I'm aware of the movement and suddenly his fingers are wrapped around my throat.

"What are you?" he asks.

"I'm a cop."

He barks out a laugh and squeezes my neck to the point where breathing becomes difficult. "Well that just makes me even less inclined to tell you my name."

I kick out at him, hoping to land a hit to that dick and not expecting him to anticipate my movement. The second I go to slam the side of my hand to his elbow, to get him to let me go the way my self-defense instructor showed us, he's already got my back to the wall and my feet several inches above the floor.

"Let me go!" I hold his wrist, kicking at nothing.

"You want a name? Might be one you already know. Gabriel Blackwell." His eyes narrow. "*Sweetheart*."

Black spots dance across my vision and I gasp, struggling to breathe. "I'm not your goddamn sweetheart."

"No, you're just a nuisance." He squeezes a bit tighter.

"Gabriel, stop!"

"Get fucked. Might do you some good." He suddenly drops me and I stumble, sucking air into my lungs.

I'm not about to let him walk out of here without talking to me. Despite the dismissiveness of his movements and the look on his face, I step into his path and hold out a hand. Making contact with his sweaty chest again.

His eyes darken further and for a second I'm raw, scared. Then I grit my teeth and throw his arrogance right back at him.

"We have to talk. There are things I must know."

"*Move*," he grunts.

"Not until you answer some questions for me." My

heart is racing hard, pulse thundering in my ears and a small chill working its way up my spine.

"What part of get fucked do you not understand?" He stares at me intimidatingly. "Or has it been so long you don't remember what it's like?"

"I might not have a badge on me now, but there are ways of making you talk and I'm sure I can get you into the station in a second." I snap my fingers. "Now, are you going to play nice or not?"

Before I know what's happened, his hand is again at my throat and he shoves me a second time, the back of my head slamming into the wall until those black dots become swirling stars.

"I said," he repeats, "get fucked."

The look on his face sends my stomach spiraling down into an abyss. I'd wanted a fight. Picking one is second nature at this point, especially when he'd been semi-physical before we even got to the juicy meat of the conversion. Pushing me aside is the fastest way to piss me right the fuck off.

"Who are you really?" He gives me such a hard look I have to swallow over the out of place lump in my throat. "Who the *fuck* are you?"

Handsome, even if he is an arrogant prick. All that dark hair and the giant specks of gold in his eyes...his looks promise to not only break hearts but crush them beyond recovery. My chest aches and it has nothing to do with his hands on me, reminding me exactly who is in control.

Gabriel steps closer and slowly I draw in a breath, bringing with it his scent. There's sex, of course, the musk of his sweat, and the smoke from the club. There's also a hint of bitter spice.

The scent cradles inside of me before reaching out with

searching tendrils to find the empty spaces and fill them. All of a sudden I'm trembling and it's not from fear.

I buck against him, hating the way he dominates me. Unfortunately it brings me in closer contact and my body reacts. The attraction flashes in blinding light, carnal. Absolutely greedy and hunting.

He knows it, too.

Humiliation brings unwanted color to my face. He wants a reaction out of me, and he isn't even going out of his way to provoke one. Like hell I'll give him what he wants. He's staring right through me, with one side of his mouth quirked in pure amusement. It's worse than the sensation of being laughed at outright.

"Layla," I say witheringly. "Sinclair."

"*Layla.*"

He steals my breath with the way my name erupts from his tongue. Those eyes go darker yet and I'm not sure if that is very good or very, very bad. His smile lines deepen into a hardness I know better than to push against. Even with unbidden lust invading my body.

Against my stomach, his cock twitches and reminds me that he's still hard under the boxers.

Gabriel smirks and the weight of his expression sinks until I feel it like a physical presence deep in my gut. "Next time you think about pushing me, *Layla*, you'll remember what it's like to feel my hands around your throat. And when I fuck you, you're going to cry out my name, and you're going to like how it feels to beg."

Damn him. My eyes go wide and my heart thunders an irregular beat.

Whatever effect he's going for...he's accomplished.

Remembering who I am, I slam the side of my hand

against his wrist hard enough and with just enough pressure on his joint to get him to release me.

"Go to hell."

I don't trust myself not to retaliate and push him a little bit further. Especially when Gabriel tilts his head to the side to study me.

I spin on my heel and leave the room, back down the steps and plunging into other bodies on the main floor of the club. I storm up to the bar and hold up three fingers. "Shots," I demand. "Hardest stuff you have."

The skin on my neck where he held me helpless brings my awareness back to him. The spot almost burns.

The bartender, a kind man with a rapidly receding hairline, sets three shot glasses full of yellowish liquid in front of me and I down the first. Then the second, and the third. I slam a couple of twenties down on the counter beside the empty glasses and walk out of the bar. It took too much time to get to the exit and when I push out through the doors, I can finally breathe.

"Tough night, huh?"

The Sub keeps to the shadows, his preference evident by the collar around *his* throat. Not as thick as the one Taney is wearing but enough to let me know his place and what he expects from this night. He grounds the butt of his cigarette beneath his feet and stares at me.

I crook a finger toward him. "Come play with me." It's a bad idea, and more than likely I shouldn't have gone past the alley with the strange Sub.

It takes so little effort to hail a cab and have the driver take us back to my place. The Sub stares at me with overly bright eyes but nods his head and agrees to the arrangement. It's not fair, for either of us, but it's the nature of the game.

And the force of Gabriel Blackwell's eyes sticks with me for the rest of the night.

The worst part is that a large piece of me, the one I've shoved down deep, wants nothing more than to go back to the club, get to my knees in front of him, and prove him right. I'm not sure if that's better or worse than bringing the Sub back to my apartment and continuing to chase the high I never seem to find.

FIVE

layla

THE CRAWLING sensation covers my skin in a way I haven't felt for months, *years*. It's the kind of itch that led me to realize my dominant tendencies in the first place. The kind of itch that only subsides when I close a case, and even then I'm half a step into relief before the itch returns.

Even getting off with a Sub only alleviates the feeling for a moment, never cures it.

From my place nestled in the shadows across the street from the Velvet Underground, I fix my gaze on the front doors.

The innocuous club doors with their beat-up iron hinges and wood painted matte black hide a world of sin inside. Four bouncers line the main hallway inside and make sure only the right type of fucked-up people make it onto the club floor.

I've been in the same nest for the last four nights, staking out the club on my own time. Devan is only a speed dial away in case we get a call on any of our active cases, but I've let Jerry grab the last two that have come our way.

So many of them are in a state of limbo with no forward

motion on the horizon.

And Jerry, being the type of person he is, sees my giving up the new casework without a fight as a sign he's won.

Like he's somehow become the big dog on campus again and is striding ahead of the rest of the rat pack. The king of rats. It must be lovely to live on Delusion Island. For the rest of us in the real world, there are bigger things to do than stroke our pathetically small egos.

It leaves me free to carve out some time to follow Gabriel, to see who he is and where he goes, the people he interacts with. The best place to start is the club.

Every piece of me is on high alert as a couple pushes out of the front doors, him with the leash in hand and her at the end of it. The swift click of her heels makes way too much noise on the sidewalk and the man lets out a gruff laugh promising more fun to come.

My phone dings two times in quick succession and I glance down at the message from Devan.

Are you still out? I'm worried about you. You're not answering me.

He's incessant when he wants something. I should never have let it slip about my off the books stakeout. But I know Gabriel Blackwell is worth looking into.

He's got dirty feelers all over the city, I'm willing to bet, and the only way I'm going to get a chance to look into him legally is to see if he gives me something to go on. Some shred of evidence where I can bring him in and question him the right way.

Where there are other people around to keep me in line.

I shift, pain shooting up my knee and into my hip from staying in one position for too long. I don't need Devan's protection. Or his concern. I know how to handle myself and I've been doing it pretty much on my own since I left home. Twenty-five years of life made me into a traumatized but competent adult who takes her responsibilities seriously.

Where the hell is Gabriel?

I glance up sharply at the sky when the first soft patter of rain dots my face. Well, shit. I've got barely any cover here.

Using one hand to cover the phone, I type out a quick message assuring Devan that I'm fine before turning off notifications. I just want to find out who the hell Gabriel Blackwell really is and get back to my life, hopefully with a better understanding of the murder that changed my life all those years ago.

He's got the answers. I know it.

It takes another hour of waiting in the drizzling rain before the front door swings open and Gabriel himself swaggers out alone. I've seen him with women, with groups of people, and always a car picks him up each night.

Somehow I never manage to follow the car, getting lost in the tangle of downtown traffic.

Tonight, he's got the collar of his jacket tugged up tightly against the September wind and his hands in his pockets. His black shirt is unbuttoned to the center of his pecs. He takes a look around and, seeing nothing, saunters down the sidewalk toward the side alley where the club takes deliveries.

A flash of excitement zips through my system. This might be the break I desperately need.

Maybe my luck isn't as shit as I think.

Corner him, I tell myself, inching out of position and straightening. My muscles protest from the movement after so long spent in a single position and I crack my back. Find out what I want to know, and then get back to work.

What do I want to know? And why does it feel so imperative for me to figure it out from him?

I push the thought from my mind. The lighter. I want to know about the lighter and how and why the design matches the tattoo on his back. I'll find out about that and be done.

Gabriel glances up at the sky and the ominous clouds bubbling overhead, promising more than just the soft drench of rain. Finally he strides to the left and I make my move. Making sure to keep my distance and follow him as he traverses the street. He walks right into the alley along the side of the club. Every instinct in me is screaming not to follow him.

A different sort of insistence has me overriding my intuition. Follow him, get my answers, figure out what he knows and be done.

Be done.

I'll never be done.

I round the corner—and he's waiting for me. Slamming right into his chest, I barely have a chance to react before he shoves me down onto my ass. Off balance, I catch myself at the last minute and rear up, intent on ramming my head into the underside of his jaw. Fighting back.

His hand wraps around my wrist and he steps out of the way before I can make contact. Pivoting on the ball of my foot, I swing around with the opposite leg to knock him in the knees. He stands at least six and a half feet tall and most of him is rock-hard muscle. Unyielding and unbreakable. I figure that should make him slow to react, especially when I train every day for an attack.

But Gabriel is a step ahead of me at every turn. Each punch I throw his way is countered, not retaliated.

He covers my mouth with a hand and slams the back of

my head into the building hard enough for me to see entire galaxies this time.

I claw at his skin even as he slams my head to brick a second time.

The world goes black.

* * *

It's a slow spiral back up to consciousness, and the moment my wits wake, I'm greeted with pain. A sharp ache from the back of my head all the way through my skull until my teeth throb. I crick my neck from side to side, even when the pain deepens. *Holy fuck.*

There's got to be an ostrich egg back there.

I try to feel for it but discover that ropes bind my hands to the arms of a wooden chair.

It's not the first time I've woken up tied, but this time it seems the binds are tighter. My reaction time is slower.

I don't recognize the basement space. Dull gray cinder block walls are devoid of decoration and there are no windows. The floor is stained concrete with a drain in the center of the room.

My mouth goes dry.

The first time I woke up in such a position, it had been a game of cat and mouse between me and a boyfriend. One where I realized quickly that I never wanted to be on the receiving end of a Dom/Sub relationship. *I* hold the cards, *I* maintain control, and all is decent in the world.

That night, I'd ripped out of the fuzzy handcuffs, kicked the chair aside, and left, not even the buzz of alcohol in my veins enough to get me to give said boyfriend another chance.

Now, I don't have the luxury of walking away.

Rather than panicking, I push those sensations to the side and focus on what I can see. The ropes are rough and the knots professional and well done. There's only one exit.

There's also a man standing in the corner with a knife sliding beneath his fingernails, pointedly not looking at me.

"Took you long enough to wake up," he murmurs.

Gabriel.

"Did you sing me lullabies while I was out?" I ask sweetly. "Probably the best sleep I've had in months."

I refuse to give him any sign of distress or to struggle against the ropes. I already tested them; they're immovable.

"I bet you have a lovely voice," I joke darkly.

He won't look up at me yet, just continues to fiddle with the knife in his hand until it catches the dull sickly light from the single bulb overhead.

"Want to tell me why you've been tailing me?" he asks.

"Nope."

"You clearly want something from me. If you're that horny, you only had to follow through when I asked you the other day." He grins at me, a flash of white teeth, his long dark hair hiding half of his face. "I won't even punish you too badly."

"Having to spend time in your company is punishment enough. And look." I jerk against the ropes. "You know me well enough already to know I have to be tied down to be able to tolerate you."

"Are you always such a stone-cold bitch?" he throws back.

I force myself to shrug, hiding my wince at the movement. "Sometimes. On Tuesdays I like to really go for broke. Too bad it's not Tuesday."

We stare at each other for a long moment, with neither of us willing to break. Finally Gabriel pushes away from the wall and stops in front of me only a few feet away and close enough for me to remember the way he smelled at the club.

My stomach is back to flip-flopping madly at his presence.

"I don't take kindly to people who lie to me," he warns.

I cock my head to the side. "Did I lie? Is it Tuesday after all?"

"Purposely beating around the bush is as much a lie as anything else. Let me make one thing clear, *Detective* Sinclair. I've got the power here. And you've got nothing."

He must have gone through my information. I keep my badge and my ID in my back pocket and I don't need to squirm to know they're not with me anymore.

I struggle against the ball of ice in my chest, which only threatens to melt when Gabriel steps right into my personal space. The knife dangles limply between his fingers but there is nothing unintentional about him. Every move he makes or does not make is deliberate. Calculated.

"Why are you a bug up my ass, Detective?" The hint of a cruel smile plays over his full lips. "I've done nothing wrong. Nothing you'll be able to pin on me, anyway."

I'm willing to bet he hasn't been on the good side of the law his entire life.

"You've been watching and following me for the last four days. I want to know why. Not such a hard thing to answer."

"My business," I answer simply. "Official police business." I jerk against the ropes again but only once. "My precinct isn't going to take this lightly when I write up my report and include details of this abuse."

The look on his face threatens to undo me, even when he holds all the cards. Playing by his rules would be the smartest thing to do but...

I'm no Sub.

Just because this man is the Daddiest Dom I've ever seen does not mean I'm going to bend or break for him.

"Let's see you use that knife as well as you use your dick," I add. "Quit playing around."

He glances down at the knife. "This is just for comfort." He flips it up in the air, his anger barely restrained before tossing it at me. It lands in the wooden back of the chair way too close to my shoulder for comfort.

"I'm going to rip you apart," I tell him conversationally. "As soon as I get out of this chair you're going to wish you hadn't fucked with me."

I run my tongue along my teeth, fixated on the glint in his eyes. The specks of brown and gold there that stand out against the rich texture of green.

"Threaten me all you want. I'm not averse to foreplay."

I jerk back. "Foreplay?"

Surprise.

Gabriel reaches into his back pocket and opens the lighter. *My* lighter. The one I keep in my jacket. Everything inside of me tenses when I see him holding it, the metal dwarfed by the size of his palm.

"Where did you get this?" he asks.

Panic freezes my tongue and no words come out, my eyes widening as I watch him ignite the flame then extinguish it.

"You've got the finest set of tits I've ever seen, by the way," he continues. "I hope you don't mind. I did a little exploring while I waited for you to come to. The tits make up for the flat ass."

"You goddamn son of a bitch!"

"I've been called worse." He flicks the lighter again. "Where did you get this?"

He might be hot, might know exactly how to use his looks like a weapon, but there is nothing but fury inside of me. And that fury makes me spit at him.

It lands on top of one of his perfectly polished shoes and Gabriel only tracks the trajectory and notes the landing.

"My dead father's body," I say venomously. "I'm the one who found him and the lighter was placed so carefully on top of his mutilated chest. All right?"

"That's not possible." Gabriel's answer is quick. "These lighters—" He shakes it. "—they're only used for hits sanctioned by the Black Market Syndicate."

The what?

"Would you know if your father had a hit out on him?" he continues.

"What? No. My father was a drunk but he wasn't into anything illegal."

Gabriel's eyes flicker, holding both a promise and a warning that he is reaching the end of his patience with me. Annoyance at his overbearing attitude threatens to consume me.

Not to mention terror at what might happen if I push him too far.

"Dad was a jackass on a good night, but he loved me. He did his best when it was just the two of us, and there's no way he would have been involved with any of the cartels in Empire Bay."

Yet someone cut him down viciously and too soon.

Drugs?

I've never even heard of the Black Market Syndicate.

"This lighter is a calling card," Gabriel continues. "A way to claim the kill when it's called for by Broderick Stevens."

I stiffen at the name.

At least it's one I know, and not for anything good. Stevens is one of the biggest drug dealers out there but also the one with his fingers in every pocket like a fucking Gotham City politician. He works the underbelly of the city like a pacemaker, ensuring every beat is to his tune.

Shock ripples through my bloodstream along with a healthy dose of adrenaline. I've had my eye on Broderick Stevens for years but I haven't been able to pin him for anything.

Not one single crime.

And I've never heard of the Black Market name linked to him, either.

"You do not want to mess with Broderick. Do you understand me, Detective?" Gabriel slides the lighter into his pocket and shakes his head. Disgust narrows his eyes, as though he's taken aback that he told me anything in the first place. "So you'll stay under the radar and keep your mouth shut unless you'd like your friends and family to find you floating face down in the Maddock River."

"Listen, you piece of shit." I lean forward. He's been called worse names in his life, I'm sure, and I've heard more creative threats. I'm not scared of him. Even when I should be. "I'm expected at work at sunrise. And I've never so much as missed a day in my entire career. Unless you want every officer we've got on your ass, you're going to let me go."

Gabriel looms over me, his breath hot on my face as he grabs the knife and flips it in his hand. Rather than tucking it away the same as the lighter, he runs it down the side of my neck. The tip digs into my skin, dragging, a breath away from slicing me as he trails it between my breasts. Slowly. He cuts through the fabric of my tank top, down, across my belly button before pausing with the knife point on my hip bone.

"The way you tremble at the blade, I can only imagine what my cock will do to you," he whispers.

Lord.

I'm not the melting type but there's something about those words and the way he handles his blade. I know he's right. As if the display on the stage at the club had been...foreplay.

I glance up to meet his dark gaze, my tongue flicking out to wet my lower lip.

"Nothing to say, Layla?"

He holds the knife in his left hand as he bends and slices.

Right through the rope around my ankles, following up with the ones at my wrists and freeing me.

I grip the sides of the chair when he brings his mouth a breath away from mine. "Deny you want me," he whispers. "Tell me you would rather eat dirt than let me inside of you. Do it."

I say nothing.

Because then I'd be admitting that I've thought about it.

How it would feel to ride Gabriel Blackwell.

I keep quiet even when he nips at my lip, drawing it into his mouth and sucking on it. The heat curling in my lower belly blossoms and expands so that my entire body seems engulfed in flames. Goosebumps erupt along my skin.

Gabriel notices. He sees everything. A dark chuckle heightens the prickles on my skin. "Stop me, if you can."

I'm powerless as he captures my mouth in a kiss. His tongue demands entry and I open for him, tangle with him, lose my breath and my wits as wetness pools at my core.

He grabs my wrists to keep me from touching him as he dominates me and devastates me at the same time. The kiss is everything and I'm not sure where he leaves off and I begin. There is no mercy in a kiss like this. There is nothing but heat and predatory intent. I know where he's going with it. And if he's as good with his tongue as he is with the rest of him, then any woman he chooses to possess is a goner.

He suddenly breaks the contact and I'm left breathless. "Stay away from me," he warns. "Stay away from whatever leads you're trying to sniff out. If your father had this on him, then he was a big fish. Even *they* get snared when Broderick wants it done."

I can't move. But neither has he, his hands close to my hips with the knife still balanced between his index and middle finger.

"If you fuck like you kiss, then I'm going to be disappointed," I tell him. A huge part of me wants to fight him just for the sake of the fight. To see if I can knock him down a peg or too. But it's nothing if not shortsighted.

His eyes darken.

"What does that make you if the sigil is tattooed permanently onto you?" I ask.

My breath catches as he grabs my neck, taking a cloth out of the waist of his pants and wrapping it around my eyes. He covers my mouth and forces me to inhale whatever chemical he's splashed on the cloth. My senses dull with whatever he's used and I'm about to black out when he whispers in my ear:

"*I'm the goddamn reaper.*"

SIX
gabriel

MY COCK GIVES an indignant twitch as I close her car door, making sure it's locked before I leave the hot as hell detective in her little POS Ford Taurus. She parked down the street from the Velvet Underground as if a little distance should keep me from detecting her.

Fat chance. Her presence is electric.

Not that I ever let myself feel it for too long, but my cock does and he isn't one to give up before he's had his say.

I want Layla.

There's no denying the primal kind of lust that rises inside whenever she spews hateful words in my direction.

All her long dark hair just begs for me to wrap it around my fist while I work her sweet little pussy. Her almond-shaped eyes, the golden dusky skin speaking to her native heritage...and that's not her. That's just the face. Just the facade.

The fire in her eyes she uses to cover up the dead places inside of her...it's something I understand.

Fuck.

She needs someone like me in the club with her and she

has no idea how badly. Needs someone to show her exactly how delicious it can be to let go when you're with someone who knows what he's doing.

I cast one final look back at the Ford and the unconscious cop in the driver's seat, her head lolling to the side and her eyes closed, and force myself to start walking in the opposite direction.

Cozying up to a detective with daddy issues is the last thing I need. Unless I'm ready to die.

No one will bother her here, I hope.

She should be safe until she wakes up with a massive headache.

I grab the cell from my pocket and hit redial on my last missed call.

"Where the fuck were you?" the person on the other end asks after two rings. His voice has a gravelly timbre. "You *never* miss an appointment. Care to explain?"

"Losing a tail," I respond.

The weight of the day presses down on me and erupts as a sudden blinding headache. Pushing against my temple does nothing to alleviate the pressure.

"Who is it? Someone who needs to die?" my boss asks.

I shake my head although he can't see the movement.

"Tell me and I can eliminate the threat. It must be bad if it's taken you this long to accomplish."

"I took care of it," I assure him. The first lie I've ever told Broderick.

Why?

Why do it for her? *Layla*.

It's the way she shivered when I choked her, not out of fear but out of desire so thick I practically smelled it on her. How I ran my knife over her and her skin heated. Not from fear, not like the club's little girls, but from twisted passion.

She has no idea what her body is capable of. And it intrigues a dark corner of me to want to introduce the stick-up-her-ass detective to the darker side of lust, so much further than she's already pushed herself.

What will she do, what will she be, with the right kind of encouragement? With a man who knows exactly where to touch to coax it out of her?

Which means I need to be careful around her.

I don't fucking want to be, though.

I want to see what she'll do if I let my control slip, even just a little, how she might weather the storm.

Those pretty pink lips of hers always seem to demand a punishing kiss, just as the rich annoyance in her chocolaty eyes makes me want to drag her down into the abyss with me and ruin her.

I want to see if I can coax out all her filthiest desires. The ones she refuses to admit even to herself.

"Just get your ass up here. You're already late." Broderick snaps out the final demand before hanging up.

There's no way I'm willing to test the big boss's patience.

I knew what I was getting into when I signed my life away to the devil himself.

I stalk the streets, needing the fresh air even with the rain. Winding through alleys and several blocks as I always do on my way to HQ. The humidity has risen in the wake of the rain and the thick air forces its way into my lungs. The chill I expected earlier, from the bite in the wind, has shifted into muggy heat.

The end of September and we're dealing with the first Indian summer of the season.

Not my favorite weather.

Not when sweat coats my skin and makes killing a chore rather than a joy.

Another block and I keep my focus on my feet, one in front of the other. People step off the sidewalk into the street to avoid me. The faceless threat they don't have to look at to feel inside their skin.

Soon those filthy streets washed with heartache and stress and strife as much as rain give way to cleaner cement. Larger trees and more space between buildings. They're shorter here with the occasional three- or four-story, though most are wider than they are tall.

I stop in front of a disgustingly luxe complex with a ten-foot iron fence around the property and pristine white gables. The white stands out in stark relief against the gloom of the sky and the dull red brick.

Money can accomplish anything if you have enough of it.

Broderick Stevens plays this city like a guitar. He's got more than enough.

When I first got involved with the Black Market Syndicate, Broderick held our covert meetings in a warehouse he owns near the water. Now I've proven my worth many times over.

I'm allowed into his private residence.

I push my way into the front lobby area of the private complex and incline my head at two of the men dressed in black with ear pieces discreetly tucked into the curve of their right ears. Neither of them moves towards me.

The elevator doors slide shut soundlessly and I press the button for the floor beneath the penthouse. That entire floor is Broderick's private office.

I use the seconds to slick my hair back, mentally

composing myself for this meeting. It won't be pretty. They never are.

Each one of them follows the same agenda and they always leave me with a bad taste in my mouth.

The elevator doors open up to a foyer composed of seamless marble and all-white walls, the starkness an assault on the senses rather than a balm. I'll never admit that it's worked on me a time or two before I got really fucking good at raising my defenses.

I stalk forward to his office and close the door behind me.

This is opulence at its finest. The boss has a real taste for all things luxury, from the finishes on the crown molding to the gold leaf filigree on the ceiling mural. It straddles the line between tacky and old-Versailles.

Rather than Broderick himself waiting for me, his second-in-command stands in front of a merrily crackling fire in the black stone hearth.

"You're late," Antoni gripes.

I swallow over the litany of curses I'd like to throw his way and lift my gaze to the man's face.

"I took care of things," I tell him sharply. "And I don't answer to you."

"Well, tonight Broderick has decided that you do." His grin widens. "He handed the end of your leash to me. And I need you to take care of a new mark. You'll find all the information you need on the desk."

Antoni's face is cast in firelight and shade, making it impossible to know an accurate age. There's only the sparse dirty-blonde hair, the glint of a beard, and his hands clasped behind his back.

He makes no move to the desk. It's not his place.

Rather than get into the pissing contest I'm itching for, I

grab the manilla envelope and stuff it inside my jacket. I won't take the thing off despite the humidity and the heat from the fire. Principle.

"Got it," I assure him.

"Oh." As I'm leaving, Antoni tosses me a lighter and I reach out and pluck it from the air on instinct. "Broderick made this one a priority," he says. "Don't fuck it up."

"I never do," I bark out.

I'm too damn good at my job.

And knowing the types of idiots Broderick targets, this new mark might be a priority but it's going to be as easy as pie.

Alone in the elevator, I read the name and the location of the mark. And flick open Layla's lighter to start burning the contents of the envelope after I have the information memorized.

Back to the east side of the city. A few blocks over from the club, where the man works at one of those consumer cellular places.

It's not up to me to ask what he did or why Broderick thinks he deserves to die.

I wasn't lying when I told Layla about my profession.

The reaper.

The one the big boss calls in when he needs someone eliminated, whether they're a threat or he's simply bored. Not my call. I just do my job and I do it well.

The mark is closing up the shop for the night by the time I make it there, standing in the shadow of an awning and watching him fiddle with his keys. In his thirties, the guy stands at about my shoulder if I have to guess, glancing over *his* shoulder to see that he's still alone in the street.

Like I said: too easy. Finding him like he has a flashing

neon light over his head. Tonight's mark doesn't even give me the opportunity to stalk my kill. It's a pity.

Distracted, I follow the man down the street, my thoughts in several directions when they need to be in one.

Which means the sooner I get this over with, the better.

The man trips over a crack in the sidewalk and yelps. I use the sound to cover my approach and slam him into the alley between buildings, holding him against the wall. My knife is out in one move and slicing down the man's face before he even has a chance to understand what happened to him.

Then his eyes land on me, go wide, and he starts to shake.

The pain registers when I lean close and smile. "I'll make you a deal," I murmur. It's the same deal I give to all of them. Sometimes they take it. Sometimes they don't. "Taking the deal means one scare, where I just sliced you, to remember that I'll find you no matter how far you run."

A lot of these lowlifes piss themselves in the end and want to run. I've only ever had to hunt down one person who tried to come back. A lot of them are content to take the money I offer them and get the fuck out of Dodge to start over fresh somewhere.

They take the money and they disappear permanently.

The ones who don't take the offer?

I slice them and dump them somewhere. Either way, they're never heard from again, and that's all I care about. That's all the boss cares about. Nothing else matters.

I'm no saint. Not even close. But I give them one chance because Broderick doesn't get to be judge and jury all on his own.

I remove my hand from the guy's mouth, waiting for him to yell out for help and pleasantly surprised when he does nothing. I've got my features covered by the mask worn by all Black Market Syndicate operatives when we do business. A black turtleneck and pants, coupled with gloves, disguise every piece of me that might be recognizable.

"Disappear. Leave the city," I continue, the tip of the blade pressed to his jugular. "I've got cash. Take it and I don't want to catch you here again."

The longer the mark looks at me, the more the fear in his eyes dissipates into something sly. He knows who I am. Even more surprising.

"Why should I?" he sneers. "I'm willing to bet whatever petty cash you try to throw at me today isn't anywhere near the payload I'll get when I cut the rug out from under Broderick."

Wrong answer.

The guy clearly has no intention of going.

I won't give him a second chance to reconsider.

"Fine." My smile flashes right before I slice clean through the skin and muscles of his neck. A giant red gash leaks blood.

I butcher the mark, stopping only to make sure we're far enough into the alley that there will be no eyes. No one cares what we do. I butcher him, leaving pieces behind and the lighter on top of the pile of flesh.

He had his shot and he blew it.

SEVEN
gabriel

PARANOID.

Obsessive-compulsive.

Superstitious.

Whatever term best fits for the way I have to make sure I'm never followed, I have a routine burned into my brain so fully that I barely have to think about what I'm doing anymore.

I lay trails no sane person will be able to follow, changing my appearance just enough through different expressions and posture and clothing so as not to arouse suspicion by anyone who passes me on the street.

These are all part of the gig as I make my way back to my apartment.

My sanctuary.

Home, and the only one I've ever known because I had to fight to make it for myself. No one else is going to do it for me.

My muscles twinge in protest and my feet ache. Another long-ass day and even the joy of death can't erase the toll it takes on me physically.

The apartment complex swims into view against the cloudy sky when I turn the next corner. There's no doorman here and no one to watch with prying eyes and report my movements back to the big man in charge. I drag my ass upstairs.

There are multiple locks on the door and I throw them all open before compulsion has me locking them behind me, one right after the other, and then the top-notch security system primed and ready to alert me to any intruders.

Then, like clockwork, I check the apartment. There are no hiding spaces here. Even the closets don't have doors.

One room, then the next, my footsteps wooden.

No personal touches either. Nothing I can't leave behind if I have to pick up and go.

That's the way it's always been, the way my mama taught me.

Not even a plant in the window.

What kind of place does Layla have? I bet she's got a secret soft streak inside. Probably has a couple of stuffed animals on her bed that she doesn't let people see.

I slap myself on the side of the head.

Stupid thoughts. A product of exhaustion.

In the bathroom I shrug out of my jacket and let the multiple knives and guns drop to the floor.

I should shower.

I should do a lot of things that would make me a smarter man than I'm acting.

With the clock pushing three in the morning, I peel off my clothes and drop them in a basket to burn later. I rush through the shower without pausing to rest and let the water wash the grime away.

There's no excuse for the sins stamped on my soul.

And there will be so many more before I'm out of this

game, whether by my choice or someone else pulling the trigger.

I usually take a beat to rest in between marks. At least to enjoy the damn shower and to sit on the tiled bench and let the endlessly hot water soothe away the aches and pains.

Right now, I'm too curious to rest.

Curious about the detective. And her dead father.

Who is she?

Who was he?

How are the two of them linked to my boss and the Black Market Syndicate?

From first impressions, I gather that Layla has no idea who killed her father and left the lighter; more than likely he died before my stint under Broderick. No doubt, if he'd died as a mark, no one offered him the kind of deal I usually make.

Would her father have taken it, even if it was offered, and left his daughter behind?

Whenever I'm given a mark, usually that person does not necessarily deserve to die. They're only those who have crossed the line somehow. I offer them their life, to leave and hide away and never come back, or they're done. If they take my offer, then I consult my target list of rapists, lowlifes, and molesters who deserve to die and I butcher them in place of the mark.

Where would Layla's father have fallen on the spectrum? Did he deserve it...or not?

There always has to be a body.

And if I take someone else in place of the mark, then I slice their face until they're unrecognizable.

I'm never asked for proof.

I've proved myself in the sheer number of kills I've made and the problems I've helped alleviate for my boss.

I've established a position where I'm high enough to get rich and situate myself above reproach. It's worked out well for me so far.

Except now a damn detective has caught my eye.

The smart thing to do would be to kill her before she becomes an even bigger thorn in my side than she is now.

Fuck her. I'd like to, no matter how she infuriates me.

She's a little spitfire who thinks she's stronger than she actually is, especially when she's delicate enough to be breakable. They're all breakable no matter how big or brawny. But Detective Sinclair...if I'd had less control, I'd have carved her into pieces easily. I wonder if she knows that her emotions bleed through when she talks about her past.

She had a lighter, though, which brings her much too close to Broderick for comfort.

I grab a bottle of shampoo and squeeze a dollop onto my palm, working it through my hair. I'll go back to the club tomorrow night and ask around, see what I can find out about her.

Besides noticing the chip on her shoulder and knowing the way her skin smells, I'm working blind.

I don't like waiting.

For anything, least of all information

I've got no internet in this place, no landline, nothing beyond my burner cell. It leaves me unable to research on my own, and if I can't, then I'll have to go directly to a source who can give me what I need.

My steps drag on the way to bed.

Tomorrow night, I tell myself as blessed sleep claims me.

* * *

Once night falls and the doors to the Velvet Underground are unlocked to the public, I head for the discreet stairs painted black to match the walls. The stairs leading up to the owner's office.

Jade is smart enough to know when she's got a fucking detective in her midst, which begs the question—why has she allowed Layla to run wild in the place? It's clear to me that the night she watched me onstage wasn't her first time here.

Too comfortable.

Not with the surrender but with the sex, and the blonde at her side...a friend.

She's a regular even if she never comes on stage to play, and if she's a regular then Jade has to know what Layla does for a living. The woman owns one of the most notorious sex clubs in the city. She sees things no one else sees. She'll *especially* know if one of her patrons is friendly with an employee.

I open the office door and walk right in.

"Christ, Gabriel. Don't you fucking knock?" Jade glances up from her desk. Her shaved head shines in the dull glow of the overhead chandelier.

I shut the door behind me and flip the lock to make sure no one interrupts us.

She knows my real name. We've done this dance around each other before but it still makes me uneasy that she does. *Even though I gave it to Layla.*

Putting those thoughts aside, I shove my hands in my pockets. "I think we both know I come and go as I please."

I bring her more money than anyone else who likes to play for the public and I only ask for freedom. I don't even take a cut of what Jade rakes in when I perform. Because I perform for me, not for anyone else.

Ice-chip blue eyes stare at me long and hard. Jade takes her time rising from behind the desk and straightening the lapels of her suit jacket. Like she's some kind of legitimate goddamn business owner rather than what she actually is: an opportunist.

She saw a need in the market for people to explore their darkest depravities and she found a way to monetize it.

"What do you want?" She cuts right to the chase. "You itching for another performance?"

"There's a woman. She was here the last time I was onstage." I flash a grin that doesn't reach my eyes. "She's friendly with one of your girls, the one with the lion's mane hair. Pretty damn hard to miss with looks like hers. Who is she?"

Jade shrugs. "Her name is Taney. Why? Has she caught your eye?" she asks, arching a brow.

She's purposely misunderstanding me, a little piece of information I file away for later. "You and I both know I'm not talking about your employee. The woman who was with her. She's a regular."

"I have no idea who you're talking about."

"I think you do."

Jade is tight-lipped but she has a look in her eye.

I take a step forward and crowd her between the desk and my body.

She's on the wrong side of forty but keeps her body in decent shape. The cut of her jacket and skirt only emphasize the swell of her hips. Beautiful, yes, but distant. She keeps her private life private and her tastes minimal.

"Why do you want to know?" Jade asks. "What's the nature of your curiosity tonight?"

"None of your fucking business."

"I'm not sure what makes you think you can come into

my office uninvited and demand information from me without giving me something in return," she says coyly. "You want to know about the dark-haired woman with Taney? Fuck me for the info and you've got yourself a deal."

I want to roll my eyes.

It's not the first time I've been offered the same terms. By Jade, by other women.

People like her, people like me, use their beauty like it's a negotiable commodity.

But Layla?

She doesn't act like she's pretty.

She doesn't act like she knows her worth in the least. Which might be why she's hooked me.

It's kind of sad how often it comes down to either me leaving empty-handed or emptying my dick into someone. I don't particularly care where I chase my pleasure as long as the terms are clear before we start.

More often than not, I agree, since I get what I want on two counts: release and information.

Right now I want info on the detective and Jade clearly knows something. It's a simple enough exchange.

So why does it cause a sinking sensation in me?

"I know something you won't be able to find in any online search," Jade continues like it will somehow sweeten the deal. She smiles at me and lifts a hand in the air. "Deal won't last forever, though. Five seconds."

A quick fuck and I'll have what I came for.

Holding eye contact, I reach out to press my hand against her collarbone and physically maneuver her back against the desk.

I lift her onto the edge and part her legs, stepping between them, shoving her skirt up to her hips until I have a clear view of her panties. She's already soaked through them and wetness trails down her thigh.

"You're so hot," she whispers, searching my face. "Too damn handsome for your own good."

And smarter than people like her give me credit for. I've learned to use my looks as currency.

I keep my hold on her upper body, slowly shoving her down until she's on her back. With the other hand I peel her panties down and yank them off of her legs before stepping between her thighs and quickly unbuttoning my fly.

"Is this what you want from me?" I ask.

I flick a finger along her slit and slide moisture on every part of her pussy.

Jade licks her lips, craning her head enough to watch me finger her.

"It's always what I want from you. You know how good you are." She stares at my half-chub, hardening to full mast as she watches. "Do your worst," she says breathily, her face flushed.

"Oh, that's not a place you're ready to go."

For all her attitude, Jade isn't equipped to handle me. She and all the other girls in the club, the ones she employs and the ones who sign a contract with her to perform for the audience, have only met their own edge.

They have no idea what it's like to throw yourself over completely.

Because I'm not entirely fucking stupid despite my death wish, I grab a condom from my back pocket where I keep a few stashed and rip into the package with my teeth. Spitting out the piece of foil. Unrolling the latex down the length of my cock and keeping my clothes on.

The balance of power is with me, and even though I'm

getting what I want in the end, Jade is getting something better: a fantasy lived in reality.

Her eyes widen and her mouth opens when I press the tip of my dick against her pussy. I thrust inside in a single motion and she gasps, her body forced forward with the impact of my intrusion. She wraps her legs around my waist, her hands clawing at her desk until she finds purchase.

I won't let her touch me. Won't allow those roving hands against my skin.

I'm merciless, thrusting into her ruthlessly, each slam of my pelvis against hers causing her to cry out. I'm in control, and it's just another performance for me—a means to an end.

What would it be like if I could really let loose? All those chains keeping me contained gone as I lose myself to a woman? I never thought it was possible.

But I'm beginning to wonder if it might be. *With her.*

If it were Layla beneath me, I'd let her use her fingernails to claw at my skin. I'd work her over to the point where she begs for release. She'd be a wild ride, I imagine, one of those animalistic women who are too messed up to hold back and you know there's an equal chance of coming or dying.

I grip Jade by the neck, choking her as I chase my own orgasm. She grinds her clit against me, changing the position of her hips just enough to grab her own release, and I follow a moment later. Grunting as I spill into the tip of the condom.

Seconds later I pull out of her body, buttoning myself back into the confines of my pants condom and all.

Jade clears her throat and sits up. She wipes her eyes and straightens her skirt down. "Her name is Layla

Sinclair," Jade tells me. "She fancies herself a Dom and comes in here sometimes when her own Subs aren't doing it for her. Out for fresh meat, I've always said. She's never performed though. She started coming here under the guise of investigating her father's murder. David was his name. David Sinclair."

Her smile turns viperous.

"You said you had new information I wouldn't find online?" I push. There's more behind her smile than Jade lets on.

"She's more fucked-up than you realize. I suppose it happens when your mother is raped. Layla needs so little provocation to spiral out of control. I wonder if she carries the burden of her mother's suicide with her. Would make her good at her job, I'd think. She works for the 9th precinct over on Birch Street."

Orphaned, and in the worst circumstances.

"All of this I can find online," I snap.

"She's never caught her father's murderer. It drives her even more than what happened to her mom." Jade shrugs. "That's all I've got."

I walk out of the club only a single step ahead of where I'd been when I arrived.

Years he's been in the grave. Years, and Layla is still out there trying to find his killer and maybe atone for the sick beginnings of her life, like it's somehow her fault she is the way she is.

It's a twisted mental labyrinth I can understand.

* * *

Back at my apartment, I sit on the edge of my bed with a couple of my leather journals. My own sick and twisted way of repentance, I suppose, because I've kept the names of the dead immortalized on paper.

I know better than to think it will somehow absolve me of their murders, since that's how all those victims were remembered. By how they were found.

Not that guilt ever comes on too strong. Most of them deserved death.

I don't remember killing Layla's dad David Sinclair, and his name doesn't ring a bell. I don't have any entries with the last name Sinclair. That means nothing in the grand scheme of things, though.

I sit up straighter and the journal slips from my grasp. Was her dad some piece of shit I picked up for another to take their place?

I'm recognizable. There are only a handful of other reapers in Empire Bay and none of them as high-profile as me. I don't leave my victims the way David Sinclair had been found according to Jade. But I'd been messy in my early days. Maybe…

But no.

Who else worked for Broderick at the time? Who could have made the hit for him and left the lighter?

The sun breaks through the windows to the apartment and I haven't made any more progress. On the off chance that Layla's last name is different from his, I search again. There's no Davids at all in my list. Which makes me sure I wasn't involved.

Who else would have left a lighter at the scene, then, if I'm the only reaper with access to them?

EIGHT
layla

MY HANDS SHAKE as I bang out the keywords for my internet search on my work laptop. "Reaper" + "Broderick Stevens" + "Black Market Syndicate." As if something is going to magically appear this time when it did not the last time I checked five minutes ago.

Here's crossing my mental fingers I'll get a hit on the work database.

It's the first time I've actually had the name of the drug ring running this city.

How messed up is that?

Anger is a living and breathing poison in my veins. Especially when I received no hits typing in the name I thought he claimed as his own: Gabriel Blackwell.

I don't think he lied about it, although there's no reason for me to actually believe him outside of a gut feeling.

I didn't find so much as a birth certificate online for the dude. The man is a ghost.

Oh, there are plenty of people with the same name out there but none of them are him. Of course, Taney only knows him by his stage name as Dom Daddy Thor and nothing else. She only knows he's *fine*.

She wasn't able to tell me anything other than women and men line up around the corner when it's rumored he'll come to the club. They're all itching for a piece of him.

It's not the piece I want.

Rather, not the *only* piece I want.

I drum my fingers on the desktop. I'd like to carve him up for what he did to me, for making me wake up in my car with the most blindingly painful migraine of my life and my badge and ID gone. Confiscated along with Dad's lighter as if Gabriel has some kind of right to it.

Just like he feels he has a right to warn me off of my search.

Well, fuck him. Not literally, of course. I wouldn't touch him if his cock contained the cure for cancer.

"L, you've got to chill." Devan sets a bottle of water down next to me and takes a seat across from my desk at our shared workspace. "Hydrate. You look pale and you never look pale."

"I'm not actually hungover, but thank you. You're the best mom a girl can ask for." I bat my eyelashes at him but Devan knows to roll with the jokes. "What would I do without you?"

"No, you're not hungover, but you are high-strung and that's never a good thing with you." He glares at me and folds himself down to balance both elbows on his desktop, bringing us to eye level. There are no mementos for either one of us beyond the perfunctory things. A framed commendation letter and a red squeezy stress ball for Devan. On mine there is only the water bottle and a ring of condensation, along with the laptop.

"I'm definitely high-strung today," I concede, because

there's no point in fighting with him. "But don't worry. I'm not going to let it affect my work."

He's not about to let me off the hook easily. "You couldn't even answer your phone last night."

The look he gives me says I know better than to ignore him even when I'm on a mission. And I do. I can't even answer him because he's not the one I'm mad at, and I know if I say too much, I'll eventually explode.

"If you tell me what you're looking for with this guy then maybe I'll be able to help you," Devan continues.

"I'm sorry," I say, cutting him off before he says anything else. Before he's so damn nice that I have a crisis of conscience and spill everything to him. "It's personal. Please just let me do this." I grab the water and unscrew the cap, and take a drink. "Thanks."

Devan sits quietly, staring at me for the longest time before he bobs his head in an imperceptible nod and leans back into his chair.

"Sure," he says lightly. "However you want to play it." He blows out a breath and slaps his hands down on his knees. "It's not like I don't have a shit ton of other things to do."

"Sinclair! Bishop! I need to see you both in my office. Now." Captain Ashcroft stands in the doorway to his office and snaps his fingers at the two of us, a clear summons.

"Uh oh," Devan mutters.

"*Uh oh* is right." I flash him a grin. "Looks like we're in trouble."

"Close the door behind you," Ashcroft instructs as he walks around the side of the cluttered desk, the top filled with pictures and plants and trophies from some of the interdepartmental summer picnic games held every year. No one does the potato sack race like Ashcroft.

His is a clear and direct contrast to our workspaces.

"What's up, Cap?" Devan asks. He slides his hands into his pockets. He's the picture of ease, even though I note the way he stands with one shoulder cocked lower than the other. He's tense, prepared for a verbal tongue-lashing or whatever else this impromptu meeting will entail.

Our captain isn't one to ever let the outside world know how tired he is, or how much a case impacts him. He's got one hell of a poker face, one I've always done my best to emulate when things start to feel too heavy. Today, though, he's revealing stress. The lines around his eyes are deeper than usual.

Ashcroft throws down some photos on his desk and Devan and I lean closer. All dead women with knife slices across their bodies. One after the other until all three are face up side by side. They're eerily similar to our vic in front of the convenience store the other day.

I grimace. "Jesus Christ. Thanks for the warning, Captain."

"Oh, cut the shit. You two are just about the only ones in this entire office who I think can handle this right now." Ashcroft pauses. "The right way, at least. I need someone qualified who isn't going to fuck this up or puke every time they go to a crime scene. I think these are linked to female victim the other day. You know, the one you tried to push off on your colleagues."

That explains why we hadn't succeeded. He hadn't let us.

"Serial killer?" Devan wants to know.

"All the makings of one," Ashcroft agrees. He sucks in a breath, holding the air in his cheeks. "We've got four similar murders now and a fifth called in about fifteen minutes ago."

I force myself to push aside any queasiness and take a closer look at the pictures. If it is a serial killer, there will be clues, indications that point to the same perpetrator.

The bodies weren't arranged in any kind of pattern that I can discern off the bat. Each knife mark was clean and decisive, done at an angle that suggests a left handed killer.

Gabriel uses his left hand.

I saw it when he used the knife on me.

"I'm sending you two to investigate, so here's the down and dirty. Each one of the women in those photos was a hooker, by all accounts. And each one was tied to a cocaine bust this precinct has done in the past. We don't know much about our current crime scene as forensics is literally on their way now, but my gut is gnawing at me that they're connected."

"Could be acid reflux, Cap," Devan jokes with a shake of his head.

No one is laughing.

"I've already got an ulcer and an irregular heartbeat," Ashcroft admits gruffly. He shoves the other two photos toward Devan while I continue to study the first. "I don't need more problems. Find a link and get on top of this."

I turn my back to him and snarl at the pictures of the poor girls. Odds are good this wasn't done by someone on the same level as the hookers. There's a possibility they were killed by someone who wanted what they had without having to pay for it. Or if they really are connected to a cocaine ring, then perhaps for some of the goods.

My guess? Joy killings.

Someone with money. Rich people are sick fucks. All of them.

"I want you two on the scene as soon as possible. I'll

reassign any of your outstanding cases that might impact your time on this one," Ashcroft says.

I grab the pictures and the case files to read in the car while Devan drives to the scene, knowing better than to argue with Ashcroft that we can handle our cases. There are too many at this point for us to give our full attention to one in particular. If the captain wants us on this, then we've got to prioritize.

"I might have a lead on this one," I offer, dragging open the passenger side door.

Devan says nothing until he has the key in the ignition and the engine to the old car gunning. "Care to share with the class, L?"

The way the girls are cut up, slashed, and their connections to the coke ring all remind me of my dark boy. He does like to play with knives, after all. And he has definite ties to the ring through his association with Broderick Stevens.

All of which I tell Devan on the way to our new scene.

"You're sure about that?" Devan asks as we arrive. "You sure it's not just because of what happened between you guys at the Velvet Underground?"

I freeze, my hand on the seatbelt. "Have you been following me?" I demand.

My partner unfolds himself from the driver's seat, slamming his door behind him before he walks around to my side and wrenches mine open. He bends until we're face to face.

"I told you," he replies. His voice is serious, deadly. "You're the only one I trust to have my back. You understand that, right? Which means you've got to trust me to have yours."

My gaze drops to the area just beneath the collar of his shirt to the quarter-sized scar where the bullet had gone through his chest instead of mine. Aimed for my head but he's tall enough that it hit him near his collar bone and narrowly missed his heart.

I swallow back a sudden lump. "I do. I do trust you. But you don't have to worry—"

He cuts me off. "When you went radio silent two years ago and I found you about to blow your fucking brains out, yeah, I'm going to worry, Layla. So I know where you go. You're a creature of habit whether you want to be or not."

I shiver. Devan never uses my first name. I'm always *L* to him, or Sinclair when I've pissed him off enough that he's not fucking around anymore.

"I know your history and I know you were staking out some dude there."

My instinct is to rip him a new asshole, or give him another scar to match the one he got for me. I do neither of those things because the look in his brown eyes is so damn earnest, a part of me I can't afford to allow to melt begins to do so anyway.

"Nothing is going on there," I assure him. "Blackwell is a bad dude. I went to follow him for another possible lead and maybe it's a good thing, because now we have a direction to investigate for this case."

"Fine. I just know this is bothering you." Devan reaches out to still my hand before I can unfasten my seat belt. Not a sexual thing, but very much a big brother thing. He knows I have no one. We're the same age, give or take a few months, but he wants me to be safe. He cares.

"Your girlfriend won't like you holding my hand," I tease to take away the tension in my chest. Not from sex. From emotion.

"My girlfriend, as you call her, worries about you just as

much as I do. Especially since you've blown her off for dinner the last two times she's asked," Devan chides.

"I'm fine, okay? I'll let you know if there's a problem. But I think we need to consider Blackwell for this crime."

Devan only shrugs. "We'll see. I think it's best if you keep away from the club for a while. Take the heat off of yourself while we investigate."

He means stay away from Blackwell.

"We'll see," I repeat smugly.

We head to the scene of the crime, and it's not exactly the killing calm that is keeping my hands from shaking but a kissing cousin of it. It's a matter of turning off those pesky emotions and focusing on the little details, the pieces of the puzzle that it's up to me to fit together. The body is only that: a body. The former hooker is nothing but a sack of meat while I look for any patterns, any similarities to bring me back to a central point: What links her to the others?

The same slice marks across her chest, done from a left-handed angle. The blade is more than likely the same size as the one that made the other wounds but I won't know for certain until our tech has a chance to study them.

Devan stands at my side for the first few minutes with his pen scribbling quickly across his notepad. Standing so much taller than me, he has literally a different angle on the scene. We make a good team.

"Hey," I tell him after some time has passed and we've made our preliminary examination. "I'm going to the club. Are you okay taking the notes back to Captain?"

He huffs and gives me a look. "Seriously? It's like you're not even listening to me. You need to cool down and start researching."

He's pissed at me, I can tell.

"If it makes you feel any better, the owner won't let the

two of us in there at the same time and you reek of good cop to my bad," I say. "It's logical to head to the Velvet Underground and start laying out traps. See what people know."

Devan softens a little. "I expect you to call me in an hour."

I mock salute him. "Ten-four, good buddy."

Bad cop. Right.

Bad everything. There isn't a space in this city where I feel comfortable walking through the door like any normal person. Nowhere except Whip, and even there I'm apart. The saber-tooth tiger in the middle of a pack of wolves who think *they* are the predators. Only Gabriel Blackwell can understand. And I'm not sure whether I want him to be at the club or not.

I walk in the front door just as the sun starts to set beyond the horizon, working out the kinks in my shoulders. It's a good place to pick up details from loose lips and see if I can lay a few careful traps with people who spread rumors like candy. See what and who I'm able to shake loose.

I hate starting at the Underground but this crime isn't the only reason I'm here and I know it, even though I hate to admit it. I want to see Gabriel again. To see if he's feeling generous with info. See if he tries to kiss me again.

The crowd is sparse this time of day but there are bodies moving on the stage. The music pulses, low and upbeat. I pick a seat at the bar that gives me the best vantage point of the room and I watch several males strut around the place in various stages of undress.

None of them are Gabriel.

The thought of seeing him, after he turned on me in person, brings emotion I refuse to confront right now. Or ever. No matter how badly a small part of me wants to see him, I know logically that if he is anywhere nearby, whether on stage or in one of the main playrooms, I'll walk out.

"Layla? What are you doing here so early?"

Taney strides out from the employee lounge and wraps her arms around me. I hug her back.

"Surprised to see me?" I ask.

"Sure am. What are you doing here? And without libation!" Today Taney wears a slick silk dress the color of water, the fabric tight enough to look poured over her skin. It emphasizes the glint of her hair and the dark eyeshadow slicked over her lids.

"I'm on the job," I tell her in an undertone.

I've done a loop around the room but I still don't see him.

Taney nods in understanding. "Anything I can do to help?"

"You're an angel, but no. You keep out of the way. I shouldn't be long." I'll make a loop of the upstairs rooms, keep out of Jade's way, and be out before anyone gets suspicious.

A Sub I've played with before catches me when I'm halfway to the stairs to the second floor.

"Please, Mistress." He drops into a bow, his chest bare and glinting with oil. "*Please.*"

I curl my lip as I stare at him. The line between a Sub who was a visibly weak man and dominating a man who thinks he isn't a Sub is a hard line to walk here. And the truly submissive ones aren't my style. They don't scratch the itch I use sex to sate, so in the end it's a waste of time.

"Pass." I push him in the shoulder to get him out of my way. "You're not worth my time."

"Fucking bitch." His hissed insult only assures me I've made the right assessment.

Like I've ever made a mistake before.

The weak ones curse when they don't get their way. The Doms who actually want to submit act differently.

The upper rooms yield nothing and I don't see Gabriel there, but I nod at the upper balcony where Jade watches the floor every night. The two-way mirrors of her office allow her the best view in the house but no one catches a glimpse of her unless she allows it.

I'm lucky the woman lets me wander through the club as myself and not as a Dom. It's not a secret that some leads will be found here.

Better play nice and pay my respects to keep it that way.

One drink. One drink to give in to the temptation to stay, then I'll talk to Jade and head back to help Devan with his research.

One drink.

And the road to hell is paved with equally good intentions.

NINE
gabriel

LACK OF SLEEP is a health concern for normal men.

It's a fucking death sentence for me. There's too much at stake if I'm not working at optimal capacity. Too many threads to grasp to let any of them slip.

I close my eyes and it's not my palm that's wrapped around my cock. It's Layla, panting as I touch her, the look in her eyes as much loathing as desire. The combination is better than any sort of blue pill and I wonder what kinds of hateful things she'll tell me once I slide between her legs.

Because at this point I'm sure—it's going to happen.

I'm entirely too caught up in her and it's going to get me worse than dead; it's going to compromise my ability to do my job. More assholes on the streets. More psychopaths running wild.

And the delectable detective at the center of it all with her enticing mystery.

I need to leave it alone and stop fantasizing. I'm not the fantasy type. It doesn't matter as I stroke myself to completion, coming all over my own chest and working myself until the last bit of jizz drips out.

Cold hard reality is the only world available. People are shit, their motives are fucked, and a little kindness is normally wasted on the unworthy. The lighter, the symbol, the Syndicate...

I push to the side of the bed and grab a towel, wiping myself clean.

The burner phone on the nightstand bleats out a text alert and I glance at the screen. An address, from another burner number. Pushing aside my exhaustion, I focus on the number and memorize it before deleting the text, stretching my neck from side to side.

This distraction isn't good.

The building pressure needed a release, though, an outlet. Fucking Jade did nothing to help the knots inside of me. Even my balls are still tight. I need sex or death, somewhere decent to bury myself.

The latter will be more accessible, considering the text.

Another mark.

This one doesn't have to be a statement, at least.

Pushing up from the bed, I'm feeling a thousand years old. My bones ache and my muscles cramp. Mechanically I shift to the closet and press the button keeping my weapons hidden. The panel slides open. Coat, check. Knives? I slide them into special holsters built into my belt, around my ankle, under my arms, and at the small of my back.

Not even the barest minimum of excitement for this kill, which isn't normal for me.

It's got to be Layla I sink into before this is done.

The thought gnaws at me and I shake it right out of my head. I push my hair out of my face, behind my ears. I've never needed a specific pussy before. Just a willing one. It makes no difference to me usually, and I've got no damn clue why it does now.

Getting old.

Getting *too* old to keep fucking around like a guy in my twenties when I'm thirty-three.

It's easy enough to drive to the specific address from the text, glancing in my periphery at the abandoned gas station. I pull to a stop and stare at the pumps. The entire place has fallen into disrepair, the owners either foreclosed or unwilling to do anything with their investment.

More than likely the owner would rather not be known.

It needs to be condemned or torn down. There are too many hiding places, inside and out, dual alleys providing plenty of cover. Taking a breath to steel myself, I stare at the building and mark the exits, the chain keeping the front door locked and the plywood covering a broken window.

So this isn't a butchering, then. It's a meeting.

Why hadn't I been told?

My stomach drops and the headache is back, flashing behind my eyes and in my temples to let me know exactly what my body thinks of the change of plans. It's nothing good. I circle the block and weave in and out of the side streets barely wide enough for the sleek car.

I grab the cell from my passenger seat and dial in a familiar number I only use in case of emergency. The call rings once before it's answered, and silence greets me from the other end.

"Is this legit?" I ask.

Broderick groans. "Just go inside," he tells me gruffly.

That's all I'll get out of him, along with the clear impatience at his time being wasted.

"New project, huh?"

"It checks out, Blackwell." The call clicks off.

The boss isn't big on words. At least not with me.

It's as though even on his secure line, he's unwilling to chance staying on too long. At least I know the instructions are good now. *You can never be too careful.*

My gut is knotted and my head filled with thoughts of a forbidden brunette.

I park out of sight to monitor the gas station from a distance, needing to put some faces to the people I'll be meeting tonight. Any apprehension disappears as I fall into the usual routine. Watch, learn. Get a leg up on everyone else. See between the lines to the unseen.

I've got no fucking clue what this is about or why the boss wants me here.

Protecting his investments, potentially. As his eyes and ears on the ground? Certainly.

Fuck me. Work has never felt like work before.

I've always been good at what I do, since the first mark for a drug ring I got into half by accident and half out of necessity. These meetings? I'm being pushed somewhere and I don't need Broderick to tell me that.

By the time the last car arrives, I'm ready.

I walk up to the back door loosely gripping the gun underneath my jacket. The man in glasses guarding the entrance looks weak, expendable, but in this line of work, the weaker they sometimes force themselves to look, the more lethal they are...especially given the way the man's jacket hangs as though he's also loaded up in case things go south.

"We've had our eye on you," the guard grumbles as I walk up. "You do good work. It will be good to have you working with us."

I push past him and say nothing. The last thing I want to do is give any information away, especially shit I might be tricked into giving away.

Are these new bodies Broderick has brought in?

More geese in his flock?

It's hard to say.

There are only two people on the inside and both of them turn to face me at my approach. Their footsteps have left trails in the dust; the only light is from the streetlamps outside, the interior just as dangerous as the exterior.

The door slams shut behind me and the man on the right shifts, a smirk lifting his horn-rimmed glasses. "It's good to see you, Mr. Blackwell. Come closer."

"I'm fine where I am," I tell him.

Only a sliver of surprise shows on his face. Eventually he jerks his chin in acknowledgement and reaches into his jacket in a way that has me instantly on edge. "We've got something to show you. Take a look and see what you think."

He pulls out a folder and tosses it to me. I let it drop to my feet, glancing between the two of them before bending at the knees to pick it up, not taking my gaze from them. Whatever this meeting is...they're better prepared than I am. Which reeks of a setup.

The folder shows pictures of the bodies of three women and all of them slashed the same way I do things.

The way I'm assuming whatever others there are like me who work under Broderick have been trained to do.

"Well?" I ask them, gripping the photos tightly.

"These are not our doing. Three bodies, at least, and now a fourth. We've got no images of the most recent killing yet," the guy with the glasses says. "But our source on the inside said there was a token left behind on that body. One of the Syndicate's. Yet none of these are ours."

A token?

Shit, the lighter. The token that indicates a warning to others that a death is linked back to us. But if these kills aren't ours, then someone must be posing as a copycat, which means they aren't hits at all but a message.

A chill slivers up my spine and buries itself between my shoulder blades.

Also...source inside *where*?

These guys must be another team working under Broderick now, one I've never interacted with before. One with *sources*.

I flip through the photos again, noting details and names and dates typed on the backside of each. "I'm guessing this killer is the first on my list?" I ask.

"The killer is already dead," Horn-Rimmed Glasses says. "Broderick himself took the pleasure."

I can stand a lot of things, but thinking about the devil himself slaughtering someone makes me realize this may be bigger, much bigger, than my initial impression. Thinking about these men working under Broderick, all the secrets and lies, it makes me sick.

My mask fits firmly over my features to keep them apathetic, indifferent, and distant. I contain my surprise the way I always do.

"Why do you need me, then?" It's a simple, straightforward question.

The men glance at each other once and the exchanged look tells me more than they want me to know.

No one is going to tell me shit if I'm not careful. These types don't reveal more than they think I'm allowed to know. I stay quiet and wait for them to continue.

"You've hunted trash for the ring before. We want to know who is really behind the killings. The killer is only a piece at the bottom of a pyramid. We're interested in the man at the top who poses a threat to Broderick. Who sent the man out? And why was he told to make it look like your style?" Horn-Rimmed replies.

My headache grows from a dull throb to a full-out icepick in my temples. "That shouldn't be too hard for anyone to find out. But why me?" I hold up the photographs. "You can put anyone on this. It's menial."

There's a world of intrigue and connections lurking beneath the surface of the Black Market Syndicate. The more I do, the less likely it is I'll lose a piece of me or two along the way, and that's the way it's always been.

Now I'm being taken from contract killer to some kind of tracker and I don't like it.

"We were told you wouldn't ask questions," the other man grumbles.

"I don't normally have a fucking rogue in my game messing things up," I retort. "I'm entitled to a little curiosity."

"Broderick says you'll work with us, at our discretion, which puts you on a need to know basis going forward," Horn-Rimmed says with dull finality. "You're lucky you're good at what you do. You've taken more of my time than I blocked out for this meeting with your hesitation. Find our real mastermind. That's all."

Just like that, my leash has been handed off to someone else and they're tugging hard, exerting their dominance.

Horn-Rimmed and his buddy walk away, giving me their backs, and I know better than to call after him. To demand answers I'll never get. Not even if I push my gun into his mouth and cock it. Instead, I wait until they're both out of sight before I leave the gas station and head back to the car.

What I do, the rules I break, puts me in danger. I accept the terms. I knew them all when I got into this gig. But it makes me wary.

I'm careful.

So fucking careful that no one will ever find out how I do things. It doesn't make the feeling of eyes on me any easier.

And now these women...

I've never had a problem following blindly before. And a part of me wants justice for those poor victims of circumstance. The other part rages against the disgust of having to act like a detective.

Like Layla.

I sprawl in the driver's seat of my car with the folder on my lap. According to the notes on the back, these women were all hookers who wound up dead in some kind of connection to our cocaine ring. Supposedly. Someone took a lot of time to make sure these deaths led back to the Black Market Syndicate. They all wound up dead and mutilated and for some reason *I'm* supposed to find out who ordered the hits?

Why me?

I'm not a cop.

I'm a goddamn reaper.

The bleak reality of the situation hits me like a blindside to the back of the head. Detective... If there's a lighter on any of the scenes, then I know too goddamn well who is going to be involved. She'll be drawn to the cases. She'll have no choice.

My cock twitches and I gape down, incredulous. "Now?" I ask my lap.

Sleep first, I tell myself. Sleep, then off to the Velvet Underground for a quick fuck and some light BDSM, and then *maybe* a visit to see the detective. Somehow. It's not a promise but it's the best compromise I'm willing to make for the dick that can't take a hint. She might be off limits but I've always been partial to tastes I should not have. They're sweeter, better than any other. The forbidden fruits hanging low on the vine within tempting reach.

If I'm good enough, I can make the detective squirm again and get some information out of her about these murders.

* * *

Once night falls, I get dressed and head out.

It takes all of two seconds to know that Layla is seated at the bar of the Velvet Underground when I walk in. *Waiting for me?*

It's a nice thought but completely delusional.

Immediately, my plans change. She's the first step in this whole mess, the first lead to pull to set myself free. Back to my life. Back to my old routine. I'll figure out what she knows, use her and break her, and then release her back to whatever fucked-up trajectory she has for her life.

She lifts a hand to ask the bartender for her tab. I stare across the room at her until she turns, meeting my eyes through the crowd and realizing exactly how close I am to her. Her scowl is a thing of beauty to behold. The unwelcome sliver of awareness pulsing through me?

Not welcome.

Layla pushes off her stool with determination etched along every line of her body and face.

Turning, I head back to my SUV parked out front and wait until she follows me out, ignoring the gut-punch of adrenaline at seeing her.

It's time to play.

TEN
layla

MY CHEST IS ODDLY tight and my breasts ache with something similar to desire, but the need runs deeper. It's so much deeper than anything I'm ready for or want to handle. Especially being at the club and seeing...him.

How *ridiculous*, I chastise myself on my way out the door.

It's so fucking stupid to have these kinds of thoughts for a man who tied me to a chair and threatened me with a knife.

A killer and probably a psychopath.

At the very least a sociopath.

I slam a twenty down on the bar top when the bartender takes too long to get me the tab. I'm clearly delusional in the worst kind of way, convinced that Gabriel Blackwell has something to do with my case at work and coming back to the Underground in hopes of seeing him.

Except it paid off.

I want to see him for the case, I tell myself, *only* the case and nothing more. Now he's spotted me and he knows I'm going to follow him out. It's ridiculous how fast I'm out of there, trailing behind him close enough to choke on his proverbial dust.

I'm out the door and into the sticky oppressive night where a black SUV sits at the curb. The prickling sensation along my neck and spine has me reaching for my gun in the holster on my hip.

The window lowers with a quick hiss of sound and I can see Gabriel behind the wheel, gripping it tight enough that his knuckles turn white. My heart thumps against my ribs once, *hard*, a very firm clue that it's smarter to keep my distance from him. He's deadly, bad for me. A killer who makes my skin tight and my insides hot in a way I've only chased until now.

"Get in, Layla," he growls.

"There's no need to be a shit about it." I open the passenger door but hesitate to climb inside. "Can the attitude, Gabriel."

I say his name with venom and he glances around, making sure no one else is close enough to hear his real name.

"That's Daddy Thor whenever we're here. Now get in. Stop fucking around."

I oblige without hesitation at his dark command, showing more of my hand than I should at this point and knowing it's a bad idea. He sees how he affects me and we both know it. At least at the club there are people around and a slim barrier that keeps us from getting too close to each other. Crossing too many lines in my hunt for answers.

Alone in a car with the man...who knows what I'll do? Or how he'll respond?

It doesn't matter if I trust myself or not. The door clicks closed behind me, the lock thrown before I have the seatbelt across my chest.

Tonight he's dressed in another black-on-black ensemble, and combined with his messy hair and barely trimmed facial scruff, he's playing his part well. Jeez. The man is delicious looking. He's like something conjured out of a wild wet dream and designed specifically to get under my skin.

I never thought I'd be attracted to psychopaths, and definitely not ones who delight in domination. Yet here we are.

My skin grows tighter yet, hotter than a bonfire, when Gabriel pulls away from the curb and takes off down the street, giving me a delightful view of his profile. The lights turn green for him, another miracle. Neither of us speaks.

What am I doing here? Really?

If he doesn't have a lead for me and this is all just a game, then being alone with him is an even dumber idea than I thought.

I grip the seatbelt.

There's no way out of it now.

The stubble along his jaw is a new addition, I think as I covertly study him out of the corner of my eye. He looks rougher than I remember from the last time we were this close. The collar of his coat—why is he wearing a coat with this humidity?—hides most of the tattoos on his neck from view. Those vibrant green eyes focus entirely on the road ahead and he does not release his death grip on the wheel.

The quiet unnerves me. The tension in the car thickens with each mile until my throat closes.

Too many parts of me tingle being this close to him and caged in the steel prison of the SUV. My leg threatens to bob; I slap a hand down to make sure it stays in place.

This is the closest damn thing to feeling alive that I've felt in a long time. *Too long.*

Gabriel keeps driving, and the only logical part of me left wonders if he has a destination in mind or he's driving in circles to freak me out.

"So," I begin, the first one to break. He won't look at me. "Want to tell me about your most recent killing? Or should I just arrest you now? It might be fun trying to get answers out of you. Depends on how badly I want to pay you back for my concussion."

"Shouldn't you know better, as a detective, to not let the killer move you to a different location?" he throws back.

Oh. Shit. His voice is a ripple of pure sensation over my skin and I feel it inside. In a hidden place where no one else has wanted to dive deep enough to discover. Not even me.

My wrist flicks nervously and I hide the motion by pushing a dangling piece of hair behind my ear.

Since he refuses to look at me, I do the same, staring out the window as the sky darkens and the buildings blur together in a mass of metal and glass. "If you wanted me dead, I imagine I'd be dead already. Unless you like to play with your toys first," I reply.

"I do. But there's no toying with you, sweetheart." He grimaces. "Sorry about the concussion."

I pause to clear my throat before I say something ridiculous. "What's this about?"

"You tell me."

"It seems we both want something from each other. Otherwise you wouldn't have come looking for me at the club." I risk another glance at him. "You *were* looking for me. Weren't you?"

"I might say the same," he purrs.

I need a lead on the hooker killings. Not only because I'm assigned to the case but because picking apart the information, the small clues and details left behind, distracts me from my own bullshit. The bullshit that's as much a part of my psyche as my genetic makeup.

Not to mention the lighter.

The damn lighter found on our fourth vic, the same as the one Blackwell took from me.

A link between our dead woman and Broderick Stevens.

With the same symbol tattooed on Gabriel Blackwell's back.

"How about you tell me more about what you do?" I press, shoving my hands underneath my legs. "How did you get into the business of death?"

His lips are a thin hard line and his gaze hooded, all that black hair tousled and hiding half of his profile. I might as well talk to a brick wall.

"Do you enjoy it? Killing? Do you take pleasure in marking your victims before you end their life or are you nothing but a trained ape doing what your master tells you?"

A muscle in his jaw twitches but otherwise Gabriel gives nothing away.

"The fingers are going to start pointing to you if it gets out about the lighter," I say. And that finally gets a reaction out of him. Well, a clench of the jaw, but still. "Yeah, that's right. A Black Market Syndicate lighter. Your calling card. The dead hookers are marked in your style. Don't think I didn't notice. That's why you wanted to talk to me, right? I won't be the only one who figures it out. If you give me answers now, I might be able to—"

I break off.

To what?

There's no way in bloody hell any of the higher-ups

would make a deal with a man like Blackwell. Not even to get to the bigger fish in the pond. Gabriel is a cold-blooded killer and looking at him makes it difficult to remember that.

Only I, with my shattered mind and my fucked-up moral compass, would get into a vehicle with the reaper. Would lick my lips and fantasize, just a little, about his body.

Not just his body, a small inner voice corrects.

It's his aura. As fucking arrogant as he seemed the first time I saw him, I wonder now if the arrogance is the same kind of face I like to don. Oh, he's got a big ego, no doubt about it, which matches with the rest of him. Blackwell is a *presence*. A fucking force of nature in the same destructive way as a hurricane or a tornado. Leaving just as many casualties in his wake.

Gabriel finally maneuvers the car into the furthest space of an empty lot between buildings, swerving to avoid potholes before slamming on the brakes. Hard enough to jerk me forward and cut off any lingering questions I might want to ask, questions I have no hope of having answered.

I want to curse and ask him what the fuck his problem is. I want to do a lot of things.

I slowly unhook the seat belt, ignoring the sting of pain in my shoulder where it dug deep.

"You're going to have to talk with me eventually," I tell him in an undertone. "Otherwise what's the point of this?"

There's no air in the SUV.

The child locks are engaged on the windows, too.

Gabriel still makes no move to look at me and I switch into instinct mode, falling back into familiar patterns. Reaching for him and running my hand along his leg in a light seductive touch that's sure to get him.

His hand snakes out and grabs my wrist immediately. "I didn't tell you that you could touch," he says gruffly.

My stomach flutters.

"I don't need your permission." In fact, I'm never the one who asks for permission. I'm the one who grants it.

"In this case, you do."

I do my best to jerk away from him but his grip on my wrist is incredibly strong. Gabriel moves with intentional slowness until he's facing me and lifts my arm into the air between us.

"Let go," I command through gritted teeth.

"Ask me nicely. Say please." He smiles and, oh damn, it's like being hit by a bus.

Desire strong enough to curl my toes snakes up through my core and I'm caught in his stare. The intensity of his expression and the full pout of his lips. His smile warms further and the cockiness smothers the rush of lust, thankfully. Frustration pushes against my chest and I trap it while struggling to free myself.

"I don't have to ask you for shit," I reply. Pissed at myself at the slightly breathy quality of my voice.

His neutral expression shifts into a smirk at my frown.

"Blackwell." I fight against him, my chest rising and falling.

"Sinclair. Say please," he repeats.

And that damn thread of obedience inside of me, the one I never give in to and rarely admit exists, tugs at his words. It threatens to kick in and it terrifies me. If I give in to him now, then what else will I cave for?

"You'll do what I say." The words rumble from deep in his chest. "That's what you don't understand. You're not the one with the edge in this case. You're the one who is going to listen, who is going to do whatever it takes to please me."

In his next breath, he grabs me around the waist and hoists me out of my seat. Surprise has me pliable and easy to maneuver as he tosses me into the backseat.

I scramble for the locks before his body is on top of mine. He moves with surprising agility for a man of his size.

"You're not going anywhere until *I* say, sweetheart," he purrs.

The doors are locked. There's no escape.

"I think the hookers I'm avenging have more dignity than you'll ever have." I snarl at him.

I can't place the look on his face. I'm not sure what it means, the expression there and gone in an instant.

"While I'd *love* to explore my dignity in many ways with you...how about we make a deal instead? That's why you're here. Unless you're ready to admit how badly you wanted to see me again." His eyes flicker down toward my breasts.

I'm caged on my back with him between my legs, both of us somehow folded into the back seat and his crotch nestled against mine. His hands rest on either side of my head and my palms press flat against his chest.

I'm in the prime position to gouge his eyes out.

Something in his words stills me.

"A deal?" I echo.

"I'll help you with whatever hookers you're trying to avenge, Detective," he begins. He supports his weight on one arm and strokes one massive hand down my sternum and between my breasts. Goosebumps erupt at the touch. "I've got information you need, connections for you to explore. And in return for my help? You give in to your submissive side. With me."

ELEVEN
gabriel

SHE'S CAGED BENEATH ME, struggling to keep herself in check.

The way her nostrils flare is a hook through me, despite the crinkle in her brow and the furious glare she attempts to throw my way. They all give her away. The fury, yes, but that's an aphrodisiac when it comes from her.

The kicker is the desire for me and how much she hates herself for feeling it.

And if those expressions aren't enough, then it's the way she shifts ever so slightly to tilt her core up to press tighter to me.

Right before she barks back, "Tough luck for you. I'm not submissive."

There's no holding back my chuckle. "You *think* you're dominant, Layla." The way her name rolls off my tongue is intoxicating and just saying it has my dick twitching the way it always does when she's around. Or whenever I'm merely thinking about her. "You just haven't had someone fuck you the way you need to be fucked. I know what will get you off."

"You're disgusting," she says with less oomph than I expect from her.

I jerk my hips to her and push down a little more on her chest. "Tell me I'm wrong."

If she'd shown me fear I would have stopped. I take every tiny change of her face, her body language, her breathing into consideration no matter how my own system demands I take more.

A good Dom understands the strengths and weaknesses of the relationship with a Sub.

It's built on trust.

Layla and I have no trust for each other.

We're building on heat alone.

"Tell. Me. I'm. Wrong," I repeat.

She freezes underneath me but I'm not moving. She's much more delicate than I thought. Her body lithe and almost too skinny beneath me. *Breakable.*

The way I usually like them, but she's got enough meat on her hips to make her a soft cushion. She'd be malleable when I finally thrust into her and easy to toss around. Not exactly a spinner because she's got muscle, too, more than likely from working out for her job.

Fuck.

This angle is bad for both of us because it brings my dick into close contact with her heat. The core of her practically burns through my pants.

With each heaving inhalation, her breasts arch closer to my face. Easy, I think, too easy to dip and grab a budded nipple between my teeth, to bite down and see what kinds of sounds she'll make.

This side of the lot is mostly hidden from the street by the weird angle of the buildings on either side of us. Which gives us the perfect amount of privacy for what I want to do.

"What can you possibly have that I want? It's going to have to be the best information of your life, because I'm the cop here. I don't need you," she argues.

Her eyes are darker than coal.

All lies. She's mastered one hell of a poker face.

She also hasn't answered my demand.

"You said there was a lighter on one of your victims. But I didn't put it there." I toss out the information almost casually.

Information she's not sure whether to believe or not. As if she's not convinced if I'm the real killer or not. Layla goes still and her lips pucker in a way that has me picturing her sliding them up and down my erection.

I'm going to need to drive for hours to get her out of my system at this rate. I had to come grab her from the Velvet Underground to maintain control. I want to win. Want to see her lose and smash through whatever control she believes she has.

And get the information I need for my boss.

That's it.

Plus a deal that might benefit both of us, and once I've helped her, once I've done my job for Broderick, then I'll move on. Sated and ready to put the delectable detective in my rearview mirror.

Why am I not so sure it will work anymore?

Thinking about her and enjoying this is as much as I'm able to allow—it's not what I need.

I can almost see her mind working, gears clicking. "If you didn't put it there," she says slowly, "then who did? What are you not telling me?"

"Ah, so I *do* have something you want. Is it a deal?"

She huffs and rolls her eyes.

"My offer stands for two minutes," I tell her. "Information in exchange for you. Then I'm kicking you out of this car and driving off. You won't see me again. I won't go back to the club."

More lies and these ones are on me. I know myself well enough to know I'll find a way to run into her no matter where she goes.

I know the way she looked at me.

That first night on the stage, I felt Layla's eyes on me from the crowd, watching every thrust into the Sub onstage. Watching every movement I made and then coming to corner me afterward. I know how to manipulate those kinds of looks because I've been doing it my entire life.

I had to stay absent from the club long enough to add fuel to the fire of her interest. To make sure she deserved me enough to have this conversation today and give myself enough time to pull on a few strings.

I don't need to know her to understand she won't be able to resist the temptation to find out more information on her father. And this case.

"I don't deal with drug dealers and murderers," she tells me. Then smiles sweetly. "Sorry. I don't have any intention to explore a side of me that doesn't exist, and certainly not with you."

In answer, I steadily flex my pelvis against hers until the pressure is undeniable. "Then I guess I have my answer. We're done here."

Layla grimaces. The threat is enough to stop her from mouthing off. To have her considering exactly what this partnership between us will entail and have her second-guessing how willing she is to let me go. And my information along with me.

There's too much heat between us for her to make an easy decision.

"You help me," she says, resisting with every inch she has to give and stalling for time, "and *if* we solve the case, you get me one time. One night."

"That wasn't the deal," I argue.

My dick jumps at whatever chance is offered to claim her. *Traitor.*

"Well, it's all you're going to get," she replies.

"And if I decide to take more?"

She's got no answer for me and the air between us thickens further. I brush my thumb against her lips and she goes still, unmoving. The pulse on the side of her neck beats fast and faster. I run my thumb over her lips and her self-hatred rises along with her pulse as she trembles.

Gotcha.

"Remember this feeling, love," I whisper. "Because it will be the only time you get your way when it comes to me and what I do with you." I lean down and nip the side of her neck. "Do you understand?"

Because I'm a bastard, because I'm used to taking what I want, I slide down her body, rearing back to stare down at her. Layla pauses, her gaze hooded. I maintain eye contact and reach down to flick open the button at the front of her pants. Even her breath stills and the only sound in the car is the soft snick of the zipper lowering.

Her whole body jerks when I grab the waistband of her pants and pull them down to her knees with a single jerk, her panties included. A small thatch of nearly black hair points the way down to her already dripping pussy.

Layla does nothing to stop me and I stare at her, a low

growl rumbling in my chest. I push her pants lower, taking every inch I can until they're pooled around her ankles.

"Pick a safe word," I tell her.

She bites down on her tongue and her eyes fill with a combination of desire and annoyance. Her lips open slightly as I push her knees apart at a snail's pace. She's still watching me when I lower my mouth to her, only allowing a small cry to escape as I flick my tongue across her lips. She's molten where I touch her and goosebumps spread along every inch of skin my fingers touch.

She throbs against my tongue as I lap at her.

The softness of her folds intoxicate me and I move my attention to her clit, twirling circles around the nub before biting down on it gently, just enough to remind her exactly who is between her legs. Sucking and swirling it into my mouth like the sweet tip of an ice cream cone.

Her breathing is heavy while I work her and spear up into her core with my tongue, touching her and tasting her, drinking her until she splinters apart for me.

My hands are on her knees to keep her spread for me, for her velvety soft thighs and sweet cunt.

This is as much a test for me as it is for her. How far are we both willing to go?

"You want me to eat you, don't you?" I growl against her pussy.

She's soaking wet and all over my face. Her knees try to move closer, to grip me to keep me in place. I roughly push them back out. My mind is whirling and telling me all the reasons I should stop doing this. Why I need to keep my distance from her because I have a sneaking suspicion this strange, fucked-up creature with her clenching core represents the downfall to everything I know.

Call it gut instinct.

I'm panting, sweat coating my body with the effort to keep from fucking her right here. I don't need a mirror to know my face is flushed.

I bend my dark head between her legs and lick, playing her exactly the way I've learned. I know where to suck. Where to bite. How to get her shaking and close to coming.

The way she is now.

She's let me get this far and hasn't picked a safe word to give me.

No safe word, no orgasm.

I shake my head and stop lapping at her right before she can crash into her release, even though it physically hurts me to stop.

Rising, I slap two fingers against her clit in a punctuation to our time together. "Get dressed. We're done for the night."

She's flushed as well and angrier than a pit viper. "Are you fucking kidding me?"

"One night. Those are the terms you set out and I'm all about fairness, love. I'll keep to the lines you've drawn." I shoot her a shit-eating grin before wiping her wetness from my upper lip and slipping the finger into my mouth. "But you're goddamn delicious."

I let her see her wetness on my face and in my facial hair. Give her the opening to rage against me.

Layla jerks her pants up, one step away from roaring at me. "Get me some worthwhile information, Blackwell, or I'll arrest you and make your life a living hell the next time I see you."

I give her space and reach around to flick the button to unlock the car doors.

"You're a sonofabitch," she seethes.

I shoot her a lazy smile. "If this is the way you get when

you're not allowed to come then I can't wait to see how you react when you do."

She points a finger and jams it into my chest. "You're not touching me again."

"Not only will I touch you again," I say slowly, "but you're going to beg me for it. And when you scream my name until your throat is raw you won't want anyone else."

"*Bastard.*"

Layla is dressed and out of the SUV in the next moment, slamming the door and hurrying off into the night without a backward look. I'm hard enough to cut glass and spend a few minutes alone in the backseat stroking my cock to completion.

It's not a big deal to let her change the rules. She will want me more than once. I'm sure of it.

But...even releasing the reins this much is foreign to me.

Sleep, I think as I climb back into the driver's seat. Sleep will reinforce my ruthless control so that I can deal with the problematic detective.

And hopefully I won't dream about the way she tastes.

TWELVE

layla

THE STENCH OF OLD, sweat-drenched mats combines in intricate layers with cologne, gun oil, and stale coffee. It's home. It's the gym of the 9th precinct station house where I've carved out a career path for myself despite the numerous officials at the police academy who told me I'd never make it. Not with my attitude.

Hit. Hit. *Hit*.

The punching bag is my opponent today because the rest of the guys using the gym are too chicken-shit to go against me when I'm in this kind of mood. Some of them know me well enough to recognize the desperate need to work off my frustrations, while the others claim they've got their own routines to follow. *Cowards*.

I attack the punching bag, one punch after another, my muscles loose and limber, and the constant noise of the gym drowns out my thoughts.

I'm certainly not imagining Gabriel's face on the punching bag.

Not remembering the way he maneuvered me into giving him... I pause, grabbing the bag.

Giving him what we both wanted.

Except he'd held out on me and left me so close to coming I wanted to cry. Or scream. Or both.

And the way he went down on me—

I've never been a fan of oral sex for the sheer fact that none of my partners have touched me in a way I found pleasing. I've kept things mostly above the belt. Not only did I let Gabriel dominate, but he did such a fucking fantastic job with his tongue, I'd wanted more. So much more.

I shove those thoughts aside and attack the bag again.

Gabriel has no place here unless it's behind bars.

I grit my teeth and slam my elbow into the bag hard enough for the reverberations to rattle my teeth.

The precinct, sucking for cash the way we are—my personal opinion is that Ashcroft won't take any of the higher-up handouts like some of the other captains and so our department is being punished—has space for staff to work out in a dingy first floor of the old converted warehouse.

No. It's not the boss who makes sure we've got no money and have to throw things together.

It's because of people like Gabriel. People like him and his boss who run the city. Funding for the police is not a priority for people like that, with their slippery palms. For obvious reasons.

Jerry and his punk-ass partner Clint sidle up to me under the guise of warming up, Clint going so far as to grab his ankles for a deep quad stretch.

"Looks like someone is trying to work off some serious sexual frustration," Jerry teases.

I ignore the jabs and keep working out, moving from

the punching bag to an open space on the stinky mat and doing crunches.

Jerry, who does not know how to take a hint, looms over me and smiles. "What's the matter, Layla?" he asks. "I'm right, aren't I?"

"If you are, then it's a look you know too well," I grunt. Pushing out a breath and focusing on sucking in my lower ribs. "Since it's a look you no doubt see whenever you have sex."

When I'm sick and tired of the two of them staring down at me like vultures with fresh road kill, I push back to my feet and head back to the bag, ready to imagine their faces instead of Gabriel's. Clint takes the bag and leans against it to keep it from being used.

"Apparently the chief's pet got one hot case," Jerry says.

Clint chuckles like a fucking sideshow clown.

"Let go of the bag or I'll resume on your face," I tell him.

Clint goes wide-eyed, and I swear his light-blond hair stands on end at the threat.

"You've got three seconds to go away."

Jerry can't help himself from goading. "Come on, he's just a kid."

"One."

No movement.

"Two."

Clint smiles, but it's nothing like Jerry's grin; maybe the pretty boy thing can turn off, if I push him far enough. Because the look on his face is less fear and more of a taunt, egging me on to do it, to give him a black eye and see what happens. I recognize the coldness.

It's like looking in the mirror for a brief second.

"Three."

I rear back to wail on him just as Devan calls out, "Sinclair!"

His voice echoes loudly enough through the empty warehouse space for everyone to stop what they're doing and stare.

I grimace, ducking my head so that a loose piece of hair hides my face. *Fuck this.*

"How about you run along to your owner now, like a good little bitch," Jerry taunts.

My fist accelerates toward his face, his weak chin practically begging me to do him a favor and add a little character. Suddenly Devan is there, grabbing my forearm to halt the movement.

"Let someone else deal with the garbage around here," he mutters. "It's beneath you."

Jerry blusters and turns a delightful shade of purple at the comment. Before I have a chance to offer a much-needed retort and claim the last word for myself, Devan steers me out and up the elevator toward our office space.

"A fight could really do some good around here," I tell him, yanking out of his hold. "Boost morale or some shit."

"It's not going to do *you* good, and that's what worries me." Devan's strides are so much longer than my own. Today he's dressed like he's about to grace the runway of men's fashion week with a tailored blazer in a camel color that offsets his dark skin. Tight blue jeans taper down to polished black boots, and a pair of glasses decorate the crown of his head.

He's pointedly not looking at me.

Which is never good.

I start to unwrap tape from my hands and I don't need to look down to know I've bruised myself. "When I need your help, Dev, I'll ask for it. I know how to handle those two wimps. They're all bark and no bite."

Except their *bitch* comment has me thinking about Gabriel again and my thoughts circle right back around.

To the man who holds the leash.

To the way he pushes my boundaries.

And the sensation of his tongue sliding inside of me.

"I beg to differ," Devan replies with forced calm.

I'm half a step behind Devan on the stairwell and making sure each footstep is a loud thud, just to piss him off.

He's probably right, though. If I let a thug like Gabriel Blackwell maneuver me into a vulnerable position, then what else am I going to allow? I've been so good until now to only experience sex and anything associated with it on my terms. It's why I'm a Dom.

Blackwell is a killer. He might also be the prime suspect in my case, which makes him my target. Yet I let him pry my legs open and go right to town, to dominate *me* rather than the other way around.

Note to self: call therapist and ask for extra days. I clearly need it.

"You're not even paying attention," Devan is saying when I tune back in.

"Of course I am," I argue automatically.

He glances over his shoulder at me. "Then what did I say?"

We reach the top of the stairs and I take a left, pushing past him. "That's an asinine question and you know it."

"L, your temper is going to get the best of you when you're in real trouble and I won't be there."

"Here's hoping," I retort.

Immediately regretting the cheap shot, I soften. I didn't

mean to say it but I'm too mad to take it back. I'm just like him—my father. The way he used to lash out at me. The way I knew when he drank too much because he started ranting and blaming me for my mom's suicide.

Devan trails me into the office that used to belong to one of the secretaries of the company who owned the warehouse. The Empire Bay police picked it up at an auction for cheap, considering it needed so much work, and except for the gym space downstairs, detectives who chose to were able to claim the offices above for themselves.

It's a shitty place to work but it's ours.

When my partner and I need to work through things and get away from the noise and tangible frustration in the bullpen, we come here.

Today he closes the door gently behind us and I stand in the middle of the room between the two desks. A giant moveable whiteboard takes up much of the left side wall, and on the opposite wall we have a corkboard with pictures from our cases and crime scenes. While I stalked Blackwell at the club, Devan has been busy. He's taken down the information on the board that belonged to our last case and replaced it with everything we've got on the dead hookers, including print-out sheets of their information.

"You've been busy."

I should have been here.

"I also have a lead," he tells me. He perches on his desk and folds his arms over his chest. "Security footage from a nearby Greek restaurant shows our latest vic leaving the place with someone I think is the last man who saw her alive."

I push my guilt so far down it barely exists when I turn to face him. "Have you gone to talk to him yet?" I ask. I already know the answer.

"Not yet. I was waiting for my absentee partner. Good thing I found her right before she exploded."

"I refuse to let you make me feel bad when I'm doing the dirty work on the street," I comment. "You're the one who gets to sit in his nice cozy apartment and go over security cam footage."

"It's a thankless job."

I scoff. "Then don't expect thanks from me."

We've reached a sort of impasse in terms of today's argument but things will blow over in a few hours. Especially when Devan grabs the car keys and jerks his head for me to follow him to the lead's house.

"I've sent the clip to your email," Devan says on our way to the car. "Take a look and see what you think."

I'm still in my gym clothes but throw on an overly large button-up shirt to cover the sweat-stained tank. A quick ponytail adjustment and a check to make sure I've got what I need for my gun before I'm sliding into the passenger seat.

"The time stamp is only a few minutes before the coroner's supposed time of death," I comment, playing the video from my cell. "Is that why you think this is the last man to see our vic alive?" He's large, but even from the video I can tell it's not Gabriel. I'm not sure whether to feel relieved or not.

"That and a few other things," Devan says, unnaturally cagey.

The footage shifts so that the man's face is clearly visible, a greasy-looking Italian mobster thug type who smacks our vic's ass and lingers a little too long outside a tattoo parlor. Men like this, who think that making women uncomfortable in public is hot…make me sick.

Devan drives to our lead's house in a surprisingly nice neighborhood. Here there are cute little storefronts lovingly tended. There are restaurants and churches and, Christ, even a dance studio. We pull to a stop in front of a white colonial type with a single white marble statue in the walkway.

"Keep your cool," Devan reminds me.

And because I'd been a little harsh with him, a little cruel, I let it slide.

"I'm...sorry for earlier," I say.

Devan doesn't respond until we're both out of the car and on the walkway toward the house. Then he clasps my shoulder and replies, "I can take it."

But he shouldn't *have* to take it.

I'm a big girl and I should be able to handle myself and my mental issues. Game faces are on in our next breath, a flow and a dance we've done so many times before, and Devan reaches out to throw a dark fist against the door.

Our lead, twenty-six-year-old Mario Martinello, answers but the door only opens as far as the chain on the lock.

"Yeah?" he snaps.

"If you don't open the door then I'm going to have to break it down." Only Devan can manage to make his threat conversational as both of us hold up our badges in tandem.

The greaseball looks ready to say something nasty to Devan, which he'll regret sooner than later when I break his arm, before his gaze falls on me. He stares me up and down before the greaseball licks his lips and closes the door to unlatch it.

"Fine, sure," he replies lightly. "Anything I can do for Empire Bay's finest."

He steps back to let us inside and slicks a hand over his hair, pushing it away from his face. The motion doesn't make him look any better. If anything, it exposes more of his pockmarked skin, and his smile shows me nothing but cracked and yellow canines.

Devan stops in the hallway, unwilling to go any farther, and Mario gestures for us to follow him into the living room. A black-and-red-checked sofa is pushed up against one of the walls and a giant flat screen television takes up most of the opposite wall.

"What can I do for you?" Mario asks.

Devan slides his badge back into the pocket of his jacket. "We've got a few questions for you, Mr. Martinello."

We roll through the standard questions of where, when, why, how. Doing our best to get Mario to spill without us giving too much away. Eventually, we hit gold and the truth.

"Yeah, Candy was my Sub." Mario looks at me as he speaks. "One of many. You ladies usually don't like stopping once you've had a Daddy like me."

I almost put him in his place, bloodlust rising inside of me and my hands itching for awesome split knuckles as long as Mario looks worse, but Devan steps in.

"You were the last to see her alive," he continues.

I want to disembowel Mario when he laughs. "So that's why she's not returning any of my calls. Hadn't seen her for a while, thought she ran. She was spooked about something." He studies his nails. "Didn't want to go back to our spot, you know? Figured she just wanted a relationship and when she couldn't get me tied down, she took off."

I scoffed, unable to contain the sound. "*That's* your immediate thought? You've got to be shitting me, Mario."

Gabriel has so much more finesse under questioning.

I clench my jaw. No thoughts of Blackwell welcome here.

He runs his tongue over his teeth. "Want me to show

you? I don't mind giving you a little taste. The first one is free," he replies.

I've heard worse. Then again, I've heard better, too.

Devan is irritated. His face gives nothing away but I recognize the little tells he can't help. The skin under his left earlobe always twitches, weirdly, and he's prone to flaring his nostrils when he's not getting as far as he wants to with a subject. "Tell me more about your spot. Where is that, exactly?"

His pen pauses above his notepad. He's the keeper of those things. His handwriting is much better than mine.

"It's a little place known as Whip." He continues to look at his nails like he's actually concerned about his appearance, which he definitely is not. "I like to meet my Subs there. High-class, if you know what I mean."

Which indicates he's scraping the bottom of the barrel.

"Was Candy afraid of something there, then? Is that why you met her outside the Greek restaurant?" Devan continues.

"If she was scared, then whatever it was is deep inside of it," Mario says. "And you won't get information out of the most depraved people there unless you're one of them, if you know what I'm saying." He laughs and shows more teeth. "Whip isn't a place for cops to go, especially if you're entering sacred space without paying."

He's right, and I know it. Mario is finally speaking the truth and we're not going to get much more out of him than we already have. Pushing him will make him clam up tight. "Don't leave town," I tell him as we take our leave.

We're in the car before Devan speaks. "I know you're going to go. To Whip. Be careful."

I stare straight ahead as he pulls away to head back to the precinct. "I always am," I reply.

Knowing that if I'm going to learn anything, I'll need an insider who would be more trusted than me.

Gabriel can get the information for me.

Which means...I really will accept his bargain. One night, as payment for getting me into Whip.

THIRTEEN
gabriel

LAYLA LEFT a message with her friend Taney at the Velvet Underground, a scrap of paper with three words written on it in barely legible scrawl: *It's a deal*.

By the time I head outside to grab the SUV and pull back around to the front doors, she's there waiting for me, a wraith appearing out of darkness. Adrenaline spikes through me the way it always seems to when she meets my eyes, and my cock strains at my pants like I'm a fucking teenage boy with raging uncontrollable hormones.

I dart my tongue across my lips to wet them as Layla slides into the passenger seat.

Almost as though we'd planned this meeting, even though we hadn't spoken for two days. This woman, this cop, is getting more access to me than I should be comfortable offering. And yet...

"You need me," I say right away. I knew she'd come around.

Arrogant.

Yes, I'm arrogant. I've earned that right.

But I understand my kind of arrogance, the pitfalls and

the benefits, and use it as skillfully as any weapon. It's different. My ego is the kind where the follow-through makes the big head believable.

Tonight she's dressed in a pair of pants and a short-sleeved button-up shirt that leaves her muscular arms bare but covers up every inch of cleavage. The outfit emphasizes her curves and the graceful line of her neck.

How does a woman who looks more prepared to pack lunches for a school field trip give me such a rush?

She's carrying a jacket and slides her arms into it once she's settled. She ignores me, though, taking the time to buckle her seatbelt.

"If we're going to do this, then you'll need my number," I tell her.

I've destroyed the last burner phone and given the new number to only one person: Broderick Stevens.

Now two.

Layla wordlessly reaches into the pocket of her jeans and hands me her cell. I type in the number and hand it back to her when I'm done sending myself a message from her phone.

I'm in there as Big Daddy.

She'll hate it when she sees it.

Once this business is handled, I pull away from the curb.

"A lead told us that one of the victims was scared and left one of the other sex dungeons, somewhere on the West Side. She never went back. Have you heard of a place called Whip?" she asks.

I go still, forcing my foot to go easy on the gas rather than gunning it. I've heard of Whip before, yes, and it's not for the faint of heart. It makes the Velvet Underground look like a daycare center. Whip isn't the type of place normal people go. It's for people who like pain, *really* like pain, who lose themselves to drugs and care about nothing except chasing the high.

"So she went too hard with someone and got spooked?" I ask lightly.

It happens. Women—and men, for that matter—who think they want to explore something only to realize they've made a huge miscalculation. Stepped too far over the line and the water is deeper and colder and burns. More than they ever imagined.

"The guy thought she wanted a relationship with him, and when she didn't get it, she disappeared." Layla's tone tells me exactly how ludicrous she finds the statement. "He deserves a kick in the face. Might happen, down the line, if he can't stay out of trouble."

"Typical wannabe," I say under my breath.

"Not one of yours, then?"

I chuckle and reply, "Don't be a bitch. You know he's not part of the Syndicate."

"It seems I don't know anything," she murmurs.

"Then trust me when I tell you. The organization is widespread but he's not one of ours."

"It tells me something is up at Whip, to my understanding. He made a reference that if there is something at the place that spooked her, it would be deep enough where whoever got the info had to be one of them to receive it." Layla talks out loud, working through her theory and finessing it. "The answer is there. You understand?"

"I'm not stupid," I reply. "I catch your meaning."

She taps her fingers against her knee. "He also mentioned that a cop won't be able to gain access to it. Not the way—"

"Your continued presence at the Underground is anathema," I interrupt. "You do realize that."

"Jade knows I won't cause her trouble as long as she doesn't drop it in my lap." Layla seems content with her excuse. "I'm going to need someone to get me access to the inside at Whip. To see if I can scrounge up any more leads based on our new information."

The pieces fall together and my stomach gives a hard jolt. "Ah. So you'd like me to take *you* up on stage and give you the same treatment you watched me give the night we met. Is that it? Because that's the only way you're going to get a foot through the door."

Before Layla has a chance to answer, I reach out and run a finger down her arm. Electricity crackles between us and I circle her nipple with my finger. She pulls away. Not before I notice the way said nipple pebbles.

"I don't think so," she replies tightly. "I'm not comfortable in the spotlight."

"Even if you go in and request a private room, the gatekeepers are going to peg you." I reach out and flick the end of her dark ponytail.

She seems to have barely heard me. "What?" Her voices rises. "I'm in street clothes."

"You have the same stick-up-your-ass posture as all cops." I take a deep breath and look over at her.

Her dark eyes are wide and full of uncertainty.

"You won't get in the door without being tossed out on your ass or worse. There are people in there who will no doubt want to make you pay for any trouble they've had with the law in the past."

An unfamiliar urge lifts its head from inside of me. I want to stop the car and gather her into my lap, tell her that

I'll take care of it. Tell her that I'll do anything she wants as long as she drops this idea of going to Whip.

But I don't.

Because if her leads have pointed her in that direction, then I need to be there as well.

And in my experience, vulnerability is rarely the right answer.

"Layla," I say, softy enough that she's forced to lean toward me to catch my next words. "What else do you suggest?" I wait for an answer. When I receive none, I continue with, "I'm going to walk in with some detective who everyone *knows* is a detective, and fuck someone else, get the information, and walk out again with a detective? It's not a great idea. You'll need to play the part, and the best way to do so is to go in there as a performer."

She glances over at me, her brow furrowed. "I mean, obviously we'd be stealthier."

If she has any qualms about being there with me, she lets nothing show.

"No one is that stealthy. Have you been to Whip?" I shoot her a sideways look and see her shake her head once. That's a no. "These people are looking for a reason not to trust. And that's on a good day. You'll have to work twice as hard, and even so, the stick up your ass will give you away in a second."

She spits poison at me. "You don't know me."

I press my foot down hard on the accelerator. "Trust me, sweetheart, I know your type."

"If that's the case, then I'm sorry for you."

Her voice drops and when I stop at a light, I see her weighing her decisions. It's the perfect chance to study her. In profile, Layla is even more beautiful than straight on.

Probably because her scowl packs much less punch when looking at her sideways.

"You've performed there before." It's less a question than a statement.

She's staring at me now.

"Sweetheart, Daddy Thor has been on many stages. The Velvet Underground just gives me the best choice for pussy," I tell her.

Her eyes flash with irritation. "I'd guessed that, but it hits differently hearing you say it," she says.

Her attitude is almost enough to make me miss the fact that there is something flickering behind her eyes. It's there and gone in a blink as she shoves it down and once again dons the apathetic poker face.

She'd gone tense.

"At least you know you're getting a seasoned partner for your first taste of the limelight. Come on," I croon. "Look me in my eyes and tell me you haven't thought about being fucked on stage." *Fucked by me.* I don't add the last part until I'm good and ready, mostly because I want to savor her reaction.

She scoffs but there's hesitation in the sound. "You say you know my type," she goads. "Why don't you tell me?"

I open my mouth to answer but she barrels ahead.

"I won't come in, then. I'll stay here. In the car," she adds for clarification. She turns her head slightly to face me. "I'm not going to pretend to put on a show with you."

Honestly, I'm surprised.

"Have you ever hung back from anything in your life?" I know she hasn't because I do know her type. The ones who are so emotionally damaged they dive into risk without a thought for the consequences. Except something about her is different, and maybe it's because she chose to protect people with that badge of hers. I've done my studying on Layla Sinclair and from what I've seen, she goes after the deadbeats the same way I do. She takes on the cases that no one else is willing to touch and does her best to get justice for the victims.

Her personal life?

I don't know much about her history outside of her dad's murder but something must have happened to her to make her this way. Or multiple things.

Once she has a lead on this case, when it becomes the kind of case destined to connect her to information about her dead father, she won't let anyone stand in her way. And she'd never let someone she didn't fully trust run with it.

Until we get to that point...

"No, I haven't," she answers sullenly.

I shift toward her, wondering how much of this is just her need to be contrary and how much is a legitimate hesitation. "You just want to wait in the car, then?"

I pull up in a dark parking lot with the marquee for Whip lit and glowing red across the street. Unlike the Velvet Underground, this place lives loud and proud out in the open. The sign pulses like a giant waving banner pointing the way to a rave that promises the time of your life.

What is it about this place that makes her hesitate?

She goes pale, every muscle in her body tensing.

I'm temporarily distracted by two people walking up to the front door, leaning hard on each other and laughing as though they're already high. The man wears nothing but a pair of tight leather pants practically painted to his skin, and the woman's bikini is so small she might as well have nothing on at all. She's thin, too thin, with bruises on the back of her arms in the shape of fingerprints.

I huff out a breath and turn back to Layla.

"Well, enjoy sitting in the car. I can't promise I'll come back with any information you'll be able to use but at least I'll get a little rush from whoever I take onstage."

Pocketing the key, I get out and it's only a matter of moments before Layla hurries out as well, falling into step beside me. She marches ahead with the heels of her boots clicking dully against the pavement, striding like she's ready to march into battle. Good.

She's going to need that armor regardless of what happens.

FOURTEEN
layla

I HAVEN'T EXPERIENCED this kind of fear, the kind I can taste in the back of my throat and along my tongue, since I was a child. The red neon of the sign is exactly the same as the convenience store sign, the dull red light illuminating the stiff lines of my father where he lay broken on the street.

I wasn't supposed to go looking for him.

I was supposed to stay at home.

But I was a child, and when he didn't come back, what was I to do?

I disobeyed and left to search for him.

I found him.

And my life has never been the same.

And yet walking toward the doors to this godforsaken place beside Gabriel triggers a terror I'm powerless to face.

Or flee.

Every instinct is telling me to turn around and get the fuck out of here, and I have to plant my feet to keep from turning and bolting back out to the street. The man at my side, with his solidity, has to physically crowd me to keep me moving forward.

It's not him I don't trust. It's myself.

It's everything about me that's being triggered to the point where my palms go clammy and my head spins. I know that once I walk fully into this place then I'll have no control, the same way I had no control that long-ago night.

The sex isn't the problem.

The eyes on me won't be a problem.

Willingly handing over my future, my safety, to someone who might drop the ball?

No.

I'm not sure about any of this but I know logically that I have a part to play. I've just aligned myself with Gabriel Blackwell, and I'm about to prove it in a very real way. And a single look from the bouncer inside the door to the club says Gabriel is not only known, but *well* known. Here. Everywhere.

The fear is a tangible bitter taste on my tongue and there's no forcing it down or pretending it doesn't exist.

This is the type of club even the hardened players avoid. Gabriel is right on that front.

The only clientele are those fluent in death or those too stupid to know better, like Mario Martinello. The Subs he must find here…it has me thinking about what kind of women our deceased hookers used to be. What brought them to this place and kept them here?

What made one of them scared enough to never come back?

So what do I do, now that I've walked into the club, heading for the stage? There's the role to play, yes. There's the information I'll gain once this leg of the game is complete.

My breath catches and my chest feels overly tight, making it difficult to draw air into my lungs.

This place brings new meaning to the word *filth*, I note once we're on the main floor. Red strobe lights do nothing to cut through the gloom. It smells like sweat and sex and cheap liquor. Not even the good kind of cheap, either. The decor looks gathered from garage sales and thrift stores. Anything that can be cobbled together with no eye for comfort, only a place for an ass to land or a person to grip when they're bent over. The people here are colder than anyone I've seen at the Velvet Underground, their eyes empty and their smiles merciless. They're people who seek to use others and those who resign themselves to being used.

I have to decide which one I am tonight.

How much power the decision will grant me.

And what kind of lessons I've learned in my life that will help me get through this.

I stare around at the sea of faces until they all blur, and my gorge rises. A low stage marks the front of the club, with those red flashing lights illuminating its emptiness. There's no one up there yet, only a steel chair with a flat black seat.

This is a place where sadistic sick fantasies come alive and hope goes to die. And Gabriel wants me to get up on that bleak stage with the threadbare drapes on the side and let him use me? Just to get these people to trust me?

The thought of releasing control to anyone freezes me in place and I can't take another step forward.

I can't do this.

"This was a mistake," I whisper.

I'm about to whirl and get the fuck out of here when

Gabriel grabs my arm and hauls me toward his hard chest. "You had your chance to back down." He leans in close and I feel his breath caressing my ear. "You decided you were a fucking badass, Layla. So be one. Don't let these people or this place make you feel like anything less."

He's not going to let me back down. Not now that we're in the door. The patrons in the dark pay us no mind and the music is low enough for me to hear the slap of flesh on flesh. The muted cries of people in the throes of passion.

I clench my teeth together. "You're a dick."

"I never pretended to be otherwise." He looks as amused as he sounds, although his hold on me softens. He leads the way up to a black bar where the bartender, a man with a scar across one entire half of his face, pours out a round of shots for the both of us.

It takes me way too long to realize that Gabriel is holding up two fingers with his opposite hand, prompting the shots. I'm out of it, to the point where this will be less about gaining information and more a battle of wills. Me against myself, because Gabriel gives no shits.

He only wants me pliant. Doesn't he?

"If it helps, I don't mind making your unwillingness obvious when you submit to me in public." He grabs a glass and chugs back the shot before the bartender even finishes pouring. "It might even enhance the act."

And for a little courage to steel my nerves—it's just sex, why would I be nervous?—I grab one as well. The liquor is adequate enough to trick my system into clearing my head. Not the same kind of stuff I buy when I need the buzz and the clarity, but on the same level.

My hand shakes to the point where the liquid inside the glass sloshes onto the bar top but I finish the shot.

"If I only had my gun," I tell Gabriel once I've swallowed.

I left it behind when I set out to meet him tonight.

"You'd what? Beg me to work it into our act?" he asks. His sharp gaze encompasses the room. "I'm not opposed to a little knife play. I know how much you like it."

"Shove off, Blackwell."

"If you want to stop our play, darling, then you're going to have to use the safe word. Otherwise, you'll keep your mouth shut. Now stay here." He points to the floor. "I'll be right back."

It wouldn't have done me any good to keep talking, I think as I watch his retreating back cut through the gloom and smoke in the room. There's no winning with him. And remembering the burn where he grabbed my arm, I *want* to turn my brain off and obey. I'm tired, so tired of constantly fighting for control and never feeling like I'm ahead.

Never getting in front of my demons.

I want Gabriel to control this, for someone who knows what they're doing to take the lead.

I want to run with this.

None of this is personal. It *can't* be personal. Any desire I feel is because my brain knows what we need for the case, and right now I need him. No more, no less. It doesn't stop the swell of lust rising up in his wake.

I finish the last shot and leave his untouched, the liquor burning my throat and my lips going numb in the best way.

I lean back against the bar and watch the place fill up. Most of the clients keep to the shadows but there are those brazen enough to fuck right out there in the open. Not on the stage in the public light but on the benches, the chaise longues. Doors open and close to private rooms and people in all manner of dress or undress flit around. Most of them look part of the shadows themselves. The women are hard, too skinny, dead-eyed. Most of the men are too. Then there are those large-and-in-charge gentlemen who are content to sit and pay someone to work them without expending any effort.

None of them in the same league as Blackwell. Not in looks, in presence, in prowess. None of it. They can't compare.

It kills me to admit that I've been wet since I got in the SUV with him tonight.

But I'm not used to being on my knees for anyone, any trust or willingness to do so died when my mom took her life. When my dad turned to alcohol and emotional abuse.

Will I even be able to perform?

Everyone around us continues to go about their business and I can't focus on a single one of them. The noise of the crowd becomes one roaring beast and my ears are filled with static. My body might want Gabriel, but things can go south really quick if stage fright and very real terror decide to take the reins.

Gabriel is back at my elbow a moment later. "I talked to the owner. We're up next, doll. Told them I had a desperate need tonight and a fucking sexy partner."

I inhale, bowing my head to Gabriel slightly. *Shut it all down.*

"Walk toward the stage. I'll meet you up there. You've got this," he whispers, and a chill skitters along my spine. My breasts tighten and my core drips.

I obey. Even this is a fight, making me feel weak. As if I'm giving away a part of myself. I refuse to look behind me and I'm not sure where Gabriel goes but I make it to the stairs. Up one, then two, three. Onto the stage itself.

A scream builds inside of me, the loss of too many

things in my life growing until it's too big for me to contain inside. If I let it escape, if I start wailing like a banshee, then our charade tonight is over before it begins.

I counted to 100, Dad. I counted to 100.

My inner voice echoes in my ears with the force of a raging tornado. A red light blips through the main floor of the lounge and when I look down at my hands, they're covered in blood. Blood. Daddy's blood is all I can see. Another scream builds in my throat and black dots dance in my vision. My chest is tight to the point where I don't know where I am. Hands shaking, I turn in a circle.

And then suddenly they're steady.

Gabriel has them. Has me.

I take a step back and he catches me by both arms, holding me in front of him, with his green eyes giving nothing away outside of his confidence. It has to be enough. Knowing his control is in check when mine is not.

His mouth covers mine in a kiss of possession and then I'm not sure of anything anymore. He tastes of midnight and sin.

"You don't get on your knees for anyone, Layla," Gabriel murmurs against my mouth. "But you will for me. And you'll like it."

A thrumming pulse goes through me and a small part of me relaxes.

His fingers dig into my arms and I tilt my head back for a better angle, better access to him.

There's no backing out of this now. Not that there had been a good moment to do so.

This is the strangest bargain I've ever made in my life, and considering stopping it just feels flimsy at this point. Not when there is very real heat between us, and a very real desire to keep the contact and to memorize his taste.

Are we taking advantage of each other?

Does it matter if we are?

His kiss sears through me, through muscle and bone all the way down to my soul, the dark and shriveled energy at the center of me. His arm bands around my back and hauls me closer to him until he is my world, and he's consuming me.

I shut it all off and close my eyes, my chest fluttering.

Going through with this is my choice. As uncomfortable as it is, it's all my choice.

Kissing me, he leads me further onto the stage, toward the chair. He drags his fingers along my arms and down to my ribs, my lower abdomen.

There is silence in my head and all I see is him. His hand moves up my throat, squeezing to let me know he's the one controlling my breath. He grabs my jacket and jerks it off, throwing it aside. He strips off my shirt and bra next.

Cool air teases my skin and goosebumps rise. He trails his fingers over the curve of my ass and along my hips.

"Layla. Stay with me. Be with me."

His words are just for me and his voice deceptively kind. An act?

I can't breathe. We've barely begun and already I'm wet and needy. I jump out of my skin when he presses his fingers to the sides of my breasts, his dark chuckle shooting into my core.

"How do you feel?"

I scoff. "Why do you care?"

"Because you're exposed to the rest of the room." Gabriel drags his fingers up to my shoulders and into my hair, his body against mine. His hand clasps around my throat again with the tiniest bit of pressure, a touch that implies his ownership over me.

My toes curl in my shoes.

I go still when he pulls me against him tighter, his fingers dancing along the seam of my pants.

"You're radiant," he whispers in a harsh voice.

What do I even say to him? It's heady to hear him acknowledge the heat there.

"Please, Gabriel."

I'm not sure what I'm asking for but when I try to roll my hips toward him, he turns me around.

"Hands on the back of the chair." His demand isn't one I'm able to fight this time.

I lose all sense of control when he nips me on my shoulder.

"You want them to enjoy the show, don't you?" he asks, dragging his teeth along the side of my neck. "How is it going to feel when I make you come and scream for an entire audience?"

The lights are as hot and red as they can go and makes it impossible to see the people on the main floor, lounging on couches and chairs with their own partners close at hand.

The unspoken laws of the Velvet Underground don't matter here at Whip. The people who walk through these doors know that there is nothing to hold them back here. They are free to pursue their own pleasure recklessly, in whatever forms they choose.

Same stage.

Entirely different rules.

Under normal circumstances I'd want Gabriel to go slow. To give me time to be the one on stage performing rather than the guest. But we have no time. It comes down to trust.

My pulse is loud enough I can't make out the low murmurs across the room once they get a good look at the two of us. There's only me and Gabriel as he guides me toward the chair.

My inhale brings air to my ragged lungs. He wants to draw this moment out and I'm not sure...what *do* I want?

"Now is the time for that safe word."

I barely register his whispered statement before I shake my head. No safe word, no going back. Only him, and only me.

FIFTEEN
gabriel

I AM IN CONTROL.

I've never had to remind myself of where I am. Never. Fucking comes natural. It's been my escape for too many years to count, where I've thrown a new partner down and drove inside without caring how many eyes are on me. Yet when I break the kiss and circle around Layla, shoving her out of the darkness and into the light at the center of the stage, I have to remind myself of the audience.

That there are eyes out there on us.

Because this whole setup feels like it's just for me.

I take a slow breath and move behind her. She's perfectly still beneath me and allows me to keep her hands to the back of the chair while I flip out my knife. I slice the tip of it through the fabric of her shirt until the two edges slowly peel away and reveal the smooth soft skin of her back.

And the clasp of the black lace bra and the clean line of her spine.

I don't give a shit what happens after this. For this one moment, she's *mine*.

The realization hits me powerfully and I hide the gut-clenching reaction by bending to kiss my way along her spine. Her skin tastes like vanilla and cinnamon. She's a sugar cookie waiting for me to devour her.

I want to do more than taste.

I want to keep her protected from the world.

I want to make her come until her anger, the mask she wears to stay safe, shatters. My control is at a breaking point.

"Trust me to take care of you," I whisper next to her ear. "Trust me to keep you steady."

Her lips quirk like she wants to tell me off but the heat makes it impossible. Her usual smartass retorts are nowhere to be found right now. Eventually she lifts her gaze to mine. "I trust you."

I laugh. I want to tell her that's the worst decision of her life.

She's so taut and stiff it's almost impossible to move her body.

"Don't worry about everyone staring at you." I trail my hand down the side of her neck before using the blade to cut through the fabric of her bra. The pieces fall apart and leave her chest bare for the rest of the audience.

When Layla gasps, I twist her up to face me and clasp her chin. Her jaw is tight.

This isn't her. This isn't the fearless one. This isn't the one who knows the consequences and does whatever she fucking wants regardless.

I kick the chair aside and it slams against the side of the stage before toppling to the floor. I sink down to my knees on the stage and pull Layla down with me.

Facing me.

Settling my hands in her hair and forcing her to look at

me as I dip my head to her tits to take a nipple in my mouth.

"Relax," I murmur against her skin as I work the nub of her nipple. "Relax, Layla."

This is heaven. Her skin is soft and golden, her areolas a dusky rose and her nipples pebbled.

This terror of hers...something got to her and I have no idea what. If she'd panicked much longer she would have blown our cover within seconds.

Taking her this quickly hadn't been part of my plan. Not that I'm the kind of man who worries about the mental state of these women in these moments. Anyone who joins me on stage knows exactly what they're getting into. They consent. They're pliant and malleable.

For some reason, Layla tugs at me. This show might be for the rest of the room but in my mind...it's for her. I carefully remove her bra one strap at a time and swallow over a laugh when she gasps.

Keep the pace slow. Keep her calm. Keep her engaged.

I drop my hand over the creamy swell of her breasts, brushing her nipples, and down lower to the top of her pants. Grabbing her by her neck the same way I did when I first met her, I guide her down, her lean body folding so that the top of her head touches the floor and her breasts bounce free. My head drops between them.

I press a kiss to one nipple, then the other, taking it in my teeth and biting down with just enough pressure to have her gasp.

I'm a murderer and a cold-blooded killer. But tonight it's about her pleasure. About her consenting to *let* me pleasure her.

She's trusting me to do this even if she hasn't

mentioned it out loud in those terms. Her being here is the signal I need.

I drop my hand down to finger her pussy through the fabric of her pants, loving the way she jumps. Within seconds I've got her pants undone, sliding them down her hips and forcing her to shift her legs to give me better access to her.

I move my free hand to her ass and yank the material down to bare her to the room. Her chest faces the ceiling, her black cotton panties now visible. Tossing the pants aside, I yank her up to her knees by her hair, forcing her to look at me.

"I want you to suck me." Still gripping her hair, I stand, the movement bringing her eye level with the bulge in my pants. "Take me out and suck me, Layla."

She obeys and reaches out to tug down my zipper, freeing me from my boxers so that I bob in front of her face. I miss the heat of her on my hand, between her legs, but seeing the way her eyes narrow as she faces my cock is heady.

A small piece of her is shut down and locked away, I can see it on her face.

One day, I tell myself. One day she'll do this freely.

What the fuck is that intrusive thought?

I fist my hand in her hair but she needs no guidance to lean forward and take me in her mouth. Those soft lips slide over the head of my cock while her tongue flicks along the underside. She closes her mouth around me and sucks deep. My eyes cross.

There's no thought. Nothing except the pleasure of her. The way she tastes me.

I might have a hold on her but she is the one possessing me, in a way I never thought I'd like. Or want. Every ounce of instinct I possess demands I claim her and my cock thickens in her mouth.

"That's it," I whisper, smoothing a hand down her head to push the hair out of her face. "Good girl. Suck that cock. Look at me while I fuck that beautiful mouth of yours."

She glances up at me and although there are tears at the corners of her eyes, there is something fierce about her. A warrior goddess who knows what she wants—and this is it. She might always try to be on top, even when she's on the bottom, but she knows who she is. Despite the fear, despite everything, she's going along with this because she wants to, and I don't give a shit what other excuses she gives me.

We'll deal with them once we're done here.

She slurps me down so that the tip of my cock presses against the back of her throat, her gags music to my ears. Once she's adjusted to the size, the angle, I pick up the pace and start to fuck her mouth deeper. Faster.

She's fully submitted to me.

Soon pleasure builds to the point where I need to stop before I blow myself too early. I pull her off of me with a growl and pop free from that spectacular mouth.

"I want you on your back, Layla. Lie down. Slide your panties off and open your sweet pussy for me," I demand.

It's pushing things to keep her on the bottom but we have to sell this.

I've got a reputation at this club, one that took nothing to earn but fucking some of the better Subs in here. Layla has her own reputation to anyone she's Dommed before who may be here tonight.

And if we can do this right, we'll get in and solve this shit.

Then go back to our separate lives.

Layla does as I ask, sprawled on her back and maintaining eye contact as she hooks her index fingers into the waistband of her panties. She slowly drags them over her hips, giving me an up-close and personal look at the small triangular thatch of hair, at the sweet lips of her dripping-wet cunt.

She pulls the panties off and tosses them aside, completely naked for me.

Only me.

My dick throbs and I stroke myself as I stare at her. "Touch yourself," I order.

Her entire body clenches, seizing up for a moment.

I drop between her spread legs and knock them even farther apart.

"I want to see you finger yourself and spread that wetness all over yourself. I want to see it dripping down onto the stage. Know that I'm watching you, and because of this your pussy is mine until I say otherwise."

Layla stills for a moment before she slips her fingers along her opening, through her folds. She's spread open for the rest of the room.

Stroking myself with one hand, I watch her touch before I can't hold myself back and add my thumb in, pushing against her clit. Her pussy is pink, wet, glistening, and ready for me.

This is supposed to be a performance but there are no rules here. If I'm not careful then I'm going to cross a line and I'll never come back from it. I don't give a shit.

I shift closer toward her, close enough to press the head of my cock against her dripping sex and dragging myself over her. And I'm fucking unable to resist the urge to kiss her, to press my lips to hers so she feels my wicked grin.

Loving the way she kisses me back. There is no performance there.

She puts herself into the kiss the same way I do.

I can barely breathe when she arches her hips and brings herself closer to my dick.

"Do it," she whispers. "I want you, Gabriel."

And that means more to me than any dirty talk. Any inch of ownership I've gained tonight.

I yank her to me and thrust inside of her. Filling her to the point where her body presses to mine and there is no space left between us.

"Holy fuck!"

She yells it out, her head tipping back and her mouth open.

"There's only me, Layla." I pull out entirely before slamming home again. "Remember that."

Watching her react...it's too much.

Watching her watch me fuck her, her hands clenching the open air above the stage. She might keep her mask of control in place every other waking moment but right now she's not fighting. She's *enjoying*.

I hold her eyes and grab her by the hips to brace her. She arches her back so that those fantastic breasts are back on display.

No show anymore.

Only her.

Only her pussy clenching around me and tightening with each thrust, to the point where I'm in danger of losing more than my mind. I circle my hips in one direction, then another, slowing my movement to the point where she tries to move. Her sobbing exhales are music to my ears and she's no longer coiled tightly like a snake ready to attack.

No, she's moaning, meeting me thrust for thrust, her expression demanding more.

I want to come inside of her. The thought has my balls tightening and my orgasm creeping closer. Right as I'm about to explode, I pull out and jerk myself off, coming all over her tits instead. She watches me finish, panting.

And surprises the crap out of me when she lifts a finger to her chest, dragging it through the hot arc of cum and sucking it between her lips.

Fuck. I'm going to need to jerk off again later tonight.

This one release isn't going to be enough.

Not nearly enough.

We watch each other for a long moment before I push up on trembling legs, shoving my still-hard dick back into my pants. I reach down for her, waiting for Layla to take my hand. Slowly she lifts her arm and clasps her fingers through mine. I haul her up, ignoring the cum on her as our chests press together.

"I'm clean," I whisper, nipping at her ear. "Just want you to know."

She opens her mouth but no sound comes out.

It takes me too long to realize the sounds of applause coming from the rest of the room and to feel the heat of the red lights overhead. Fuck.

The case.

I shake my head, black hair falling across my eyes, and let go of Layla only long enough to grab her clothes. She stands in the middle of the stage with her arms across her chest, not quite hiding but dragging the pieces of herself back into their familiar places.

She lets me shove her jacket around her shoulders. The panties, though?

Those I'm keeping.

I lead Layla off into the wings as another couple takes the stage, this time equipped with leather ropes for bondage play. The way the couple pauses, the way they stare at the two of us, they're interested in having us join them.

I stifle a growl behind clenched teeth and drag Layla up on the tips of her toes for a searing kiss. Loving the way she digs her nails into me as I grab her by the ass, grinding against her and lifting her so that she's forced to wrap her legs around me.

I carry her off the side of the stage, the small moans she makes slowly subsiding.

When I break the kiss, I see the focus coming back into her eyes, and for a split second—

I'm actually afraid of what is going to happen. What the aftermath of this might do to her psyche.

To us.

SIXTEEN

layla

WHEN I TUNE BACK in to the room around me, the air is filled with the constant drone of wet, slick noises. Moaning. Groaning.

Everything crashes around me at once, my senses heightened and raw, and I gasp, coming alive. Shaking off the odd stupor that slipped into place even when I thought I was up for the challenge. My pussy throbs from the unyielding intrusion of being filled.

By Gabriel.

And *holy fuck* had been an understatement, the words torn from me before I thought to keep them contained.

He'd stretched me to my breaking point, pleasure mingling with pain in the most amazing combination.

Gabriel.

I'm covered in semen from neck to navel. Crap. Had I really had unprotected sex with a psychopath? The solid chest I claw against is just about the only thing around that remains unmovable. His arms are an unbreakable band of iron around me.

"I can get us to a room if you can hold on for a few

minutes." Gabriel's voice sounds in my ear as he clenches me to his chest and his lips find mine again.

"I was just fucked. Not shot," I murmur against his mouth, my voice taking on a harder edge than before. "Stop treating me like I'm about to shatter."

"You're too strong to shatter."

"Your faith in me is astounding." His kisses are sweet, though.

Sweet and addictive.

It doesn't matter what I tell myself. My heart still thrums against my ribs like a bird desperate to escape its cage. I've got to calm down. I've got to do something to smooth myself out and get it together.

"I'm *trying* not to get us shot, so shut the hell up and give me a second to make sure the act worked." He nips my lip to the point of breaking the skin and the ache helps center me further. "Act like you're enjoying this." His hand finds my bare breast and he squeezes once. "I'm supposed to be rewarding you for performing for me. The kisses are your tip."

"Unless I miss my guess, you already gave me a tip." I make sure the sweetness of the statement is coated in venom.

And why do I get the sick feeling that this first time between us won't be enough? That I'll want him many more times?

Among the slick sounds of the other couple enjoying themselves behind us, the crowd claps. Several people, a handful, are still applauding Gabriel's performance.

His hand skips lower, sliding along my hip bone down to my ass and between my legs. My pussy clenches at the thought of him playing with me.

Which makes it completely necessary for me to warn

him: "If you try to touch me again, I'll bite whatever part of you is closest to me."

Gabriel nuzzles my ear and whispers, "Good girl. Keep acting. Your performance isn't done yet."

He maneuvers us off the edge of the stage toward the long hallway leading to a bank of private rooms in the back of the building.

"Hold on tight, Layla."

At least I think that's what he says as someone separates from the crowd, heading purposely toward us. I blink at the other woman's approach. A woman with a closely shaved head, eyes lined to resemble a cat, and a jewel-toned business suit with the skirt riding high on her creamy thighs.

Shit, what is Jade doing here? The bottom drops out from under me.

"Well." She pauses for dramatic effect as I fight against every urge to cover my naked lower half. "I never thought I'd see the day when *you* took to the stage." Jade flicks her gaze from my head to my knees as though she can see all the parts of me that throb. "Lovely performance."

Fuck, why is she here? She saw the whole thing?

"You two put on quite the show together," she continues. She crosses her arms over her chest, pushing her cleavage up higher. "I'm impressed."

Gabriel sets me on my feet and adjusts himself inside his pants. I covertly grab my pants from him and let the legs of my jeans dangle over me.

His gaze is anything but polite, bordering on hostile. "I have some unfinished play to do. If you'll excuse us."

Yes, unfinished play. I've bought my ticket to access the information I'll need, my body the currency. Time to move on to the next step. He bands his arm around my waist and tucks me against the safety of his body. The warning in his tone is painfully clear, and anyone in their right mind should do their best to put distance between us and them.

Naturally, Jade doesn't care. She keeps her focus intently on Gabriel. "Let me know if you're ever up for a repeat performance. The Underground would be thrilled to have both of you."

I force a smile to my face. "Glad you enjoyed," I purr to Jade. "I chose the right partner to make my debut." I play along, squeezing him right back. "Truly beautiful cock."

"Yes. I'm aware," she replies tightly.

I lean into Gabriel, the smallest bit of give I'll allow from myself, and the smallest amount of comfort taken from him.

His fingers press to the small of my back to guide me away from Jade and leave her behind.

"She wants you," I whisper to Gabriel.

He grimaces, his lip curled in a silent snarl, and ignores me until he tugs open the door to one of the private rooms. It's occupied, of course, and the four people inside are a tangled mass of limbs.

"Get the fuck out. Now." He barks out a warning to the foursome and waits until they scatter before he locks us inside. By the time he turns to me, his expression is downright hostile. "Are you jealous?" he asks me.

The strange energy between us gives another pulse, stronger than before, and I have to think carefully about my words. I stare at him like I've never seen him, only then realizing he still holds me.

I yank my arm away from him but he doesn't let go. His eyes search my face.

"Of course I'm not jealous," I reply evenly.

His hands caress my shoulders, my neck, my arms. "How do you feel? What are you thinking?"

I grunt, uncomfortable. "There's no one around. You don't need to pretend anymore," I tell him. "You don't have to act like you're actually worried about me."

He scowls at me, his eyebrows drawn down in a dark V of warning. "There's always someone to pretend for," he replies. He breaks away to search the room, and for the first time I take it all in. The soft fabrics, the bare walls. I practically see the wheels in his mind working before he tugs a small hidden camera down from the corner. "Also, you weren't with me on that stage. Make all the excuses you want but you tapped the fuck out. You might consider yourself some hotshot detective, but I can read people, too. I know when someone has disassociated."

He turns the full force of his attention on me and it's enough to make me squirm. Every part of me is hot in a completely different way than I'd been when he slid inside of me.

"I was fine," I insist vehemently.

He tosses my ripped shirt at me to clean up his jizz.

"I'm not an idiot," he snaps back as I furiously wipe myself. "When you agreed to sub with me, that indicates an agreement where both people understand the relationship."

"We don't *have* a relationship."

The cresting wave of fear has finally receded and I'm back in my body, back on earth. I somehow feel both better and worse, in equal measures, than I did before we started.

"We do until this case is done. I don't want you saying I took advantage of you, because we both went into this with eyes open but only one of us was present."

I swipe a hand through my hair, incapable of arguing with him.

My insides twist together and the rest of me needs to move. Needs to do something to get rid of the manic, tense energy inside. The room is too small but the thought of going back out onto the main floor after what happened fills me with dread and a fermenting sense of wrongness.

"Then stop acting like an idiot. Better yet, stop acting like you're this amazing goddamn guy who actually cares about me when it's not true. It's nothing but an act and one that's going to get me killed because I'm an idiot too."

He steps closer and I knock him on the shoulder to get him to move back a pace.

"You enjoyed it." There's something hopeful about him.

"*You* enjoyed it. Just like you enjoy fucking every other slut out there because you can't live with yourself. You're a bastard, *and* a whore. That's why you come to places like this."

Immediately I regret what I said. I know exactly why I snapped. Because I can't deal with it, and although self-awareness has to count for something, it means fuck-all when it comes to healthy ways to deal with trauma.

"Who are you actually talking about?" Gabriel replies in a low tone. "Me? Or you? I've got my shit handled."

"You're a murderer." I scrub my hands across my face as the reality of the situation presses closer. I'm a cop, and I let a murderer pound me. Worse? The murderer is right. I know what it takes to be in a good Dom/Sub relationship, and I'd made a mockery of it with Gabriel. "I never should have agreed to work with someone who—"

Most likely killed my father. Or at least knows who did.

Gabriel's frown deepens to a glare, his eyes going cold,

lethal. "I'm not so fucked up that I'd be after the daughter of one of my marks. Trust that."

Shit.

How does he know?

"I see it on your face." He answers my unspoken question as I shove my arms through the straps of my bra. My shirt is ruined but at least I've got my jacket.

Once I finish dressing Gabriel steps up, *in my face*, using his body to crowd me back against the door. He grabs my hands and slams them up on either side of my head. There's nowhere to go. Nowhere to run. "You want to think the worst of me, Layla? You're probably right. Any shitty thing you can think of, I've more than likely done. But not that."

We're both breathing heavily.

Gabriel leans down like he's going to kiss me and I jerk. The moment shatters and he pulls back.

"You deal with your fucking PTSD later. We need to go back out and enjoy some time on the main floor. Make small talk. Figure out what had our girl Candy spooked."

He squeezes my wrists to let me know exactly who is in charge—forcing me to remember what we'd done—and steps to the side, reaching to grab the doorknob and flick the lock open.

"Get a drink. Go get drunk."

I clear my throat and shoulder-check him on my way past.

Gabriel takes one side of the main floor and I take the other, but not before he grabs my hand and kisses the knuckles. A pointed declaration of claiming, as though fucking me hadn't been enough.

Damn me, but I shiver, electricity jolting through me.

I grab one of the last seats at the bar and gesture for the bartender, a young woman with half of her head shaved and tattooed and a huge bull ring nose piercing. Long blonde hair curls down to her breast on the opposite side of her head.

"What do you need?" she asks, her hands deftly moving between bottles. She pours without thought.

"Something cheap that burns on the way down," I tell her.

She smiles at me. "I know exactly what you want, baby. I've got you covered. Do you trust me?"

I shake my head. "Not one damn bit with anything except liquor."

The bartender shrugs. "Point taken."

I have no clue what she mixes but she hands me a pint glass filled about halfway, brown on brown liquor, and my first sniff is strong enough to burn my nose hairs.

"You're talented."

"Not as much as you." She gestures toward the stage. "Great performance. I might not have a front row seat from this vantage point, but you're a natural."

And I know flirting when I hear it. "As attractive as you are, I'm into men," I tell her lightly, winking.

"Oh, I saw."

"Guess this is my lucky place, though." I cross one leg over the other. "This isn't the first time I've been hit on by a sexy, leggy blonde here. Someone else did the other night and I am flattered. It's always nice to be noticed."

"Yeah?" The bartender leans closer. "Seems you have the start of a fan club, then."

"Her name was Candy and she looked just as sweet," I say, sensing my in.

The bartender considers the name for a moment before recognition dawns. "Ah, yeah. Candy is her name while she's here. Her real name is Mallory. Real sweetheart. A little rough around the edges, if you know what I mean, but sweet."

Something in the woman's face softens when she speaks about the vic. She doesn't know about the murder yet. Which gives me an advantage. If the bartender knows Candy's real name, then she's bound to know more.

"What's this, now?" Gabriel saunters up, leaning on his elbow on the bar top and piercing the bartender with his gaze. "I didn't realize we were in the market for a third, sweetheart."

The woman blanches but grabs the bottle he gestures to with his nose.

I *want* to make a comment about how his charm must be slipping, but I say nothing.

"Here." The bartender slides the shot his way. "Sorry, I've got other customers to ring up. I'll be right back."

"Great," I gripe to him once she's out of earshot. "I was making headway."

"Leave it to me. I've got it handled. Drink your drink." He's too cocky for his own good.

I do as he says before realizing it, downing the rest of the drink then glaring at him. "Please stop telling me what to do."

Gabriel grins. "Make me."

The bartender returns when she sees my empty glass.

"Maybe the three of us can take this to a private room and explore. If you're up for it..." Gabriel purposely trails off.

I watch his throat bob, moving the lines of the tattoo banded around his neck. The dark promise excites me. The bartender? Not so much.

"Maybe another time." She's clearly spooked by him

and does her best to keep a smile on her face as she sets another drink down in front of me. "Enjoy, sweet girl."

I've never been called "sweet girl" in my life. Something about the look on the woman's face has me mentally shifting her from one category to another. From scum I need to interrogate to a person I need to protect. Which isn't good for the rest of this investigation.

She set the drink down on a napkin this time rather than the bar itself. Lifting the glass reveals writing, nestled within the circle of condensation. I down the drink in a couple of gulps and crumple the napkin, shifting closer to Gabriel.

Against his ear, I say, "We need to go. *Now*."

It's gotta be my real lucky day because for once he doesn't try to argue with me. A break. We've got our first break.

We're safely on the road again with my heart beating a million miles an hour before either one of us dares to speak.

"She passed you something," he says. "What is it?"

I pry the edges of the napkin apart and read the lines of text scribbled there before turning it to Gabriel. "It says Docks on Markee."

SEVENTEEN
gabriel

SOMEHOW, Layla has managed to shock me. Three little words and the clarity returns, the situation back in focus rather than my desire for her.

Composing myself before she sees my shock is a struggle.

Too bad for me Layla's got the sharp eyes of a fucking eagle and she sees everything I want to hide. "You know something about it. Don't you?"

I weigh my options, weigh what to tell her. "Docks on Markee is an old place where Broderick used to do business," I reply. "He shut it down because the police got too close, tightening their traps for him in hopes of catching him in the act. They never did."

"Those were the days before he had the money to buy them off," Layla guesses.

I dip my head in acknowledgment. "Times change. The Syndicate adapts." I blow out a breath. "And I should not be telling you any of this."

"Don't tell me you're going soft on me now." She slides

her hand along my thigh and rather than chastise her, I let her touch.

As though it makes up for fucking her when she was checked out.

"Let me guess. You want to go there," I say, somehow managing to sound pissed off. "Didn't you get what you wanted from Whip?"

"I did, but not enough to close my case," she replies. "I suppose you have something better to do with your night. Marks to hunt down and maim and whatnot. Women to thrust into sin. Or does it not count if you're offstage, in the dark?"

I barely look at her. "You have my complete attention, sweetheart. I'm at your disposal until you're sick of using me." She doesn't need to know I'm on the hunt for the same man. "As hard as it is for you to believe."

Do I want to head down to the docks at the edge of Empire Bay? Fuck no, I do not.

What I want to do is take Layla back to her place, or mine, and continue what we started tonight.

I know better than to get close. Nothing lasts. Sex means nothing.

Yet somehow her jealousy of Jade surprised me.

Unfortunately, she'd rather pistol whip me than fuck me again, and our night is far from over. Playtime is done and now we've got to get back to business. The whole reason that brought us together in the first place.

Foot on the brake, I stop at a stop sign and wait for her to give the word. Are we heading to Docks on Markee or not?

Layla considers everything, her gaze distant and her fingers tapping on her knee. She's not the same woman I saw onstage, not the same one I had the pleasure of feeling from the inside. Yet she's so much more than I bargained for when I first saw her in the crowd of the Velvet Underground. Judging me and damning me with her brown eyes.

"Drive," she barks out, dark brows drawn together. "It might be nice to check the place out with someone who knows it intimately."

I chuckle, grinning once before I hide the expression from her. "Your wish is my command."

"And being cute is not a good look on you."

She tugs the zipper of her jacket higher.

"You're the only one who gets to see this side of me, baby."

"You're still a jerk."

I shoot her a sly look. "A jerk I might be, but I'm a jerk who owes you an orgasm or five. Don't I?"

She shakes her head. "Any excuse you find to touch me again, Gabriel..." But she's hiding a hint of a smile while she fiddles with the zipper. "Just focus on the road."

Being back at Markee isn't going to be pleasant or easy for me. I tap my fingers on the steering wheel, a battle waging inside of me. How to proceed and what to tell her. Weighting what I need her to think about me versus how I want her to see me.

Fuck.

I slam on the brakes hard enough to have Layla grinding against her seatbelt. "What the shit, Blackwell?"

"I want you to know—" I begin, then stop.

She glances at me sourly. "What now?"

"I think you should know something about me. I don't tell anyone this, but since we're going forward, we've got to trust each other." Why is this so fucking difficult? "I don't... actually kill all my marks. I offer them a deal, and if they take it, they bolt. If not, then I do what I'm hired to do."

Discomfort is a living thing in my bloodstream as I wait for her reaction and I'm not surprised when Layla bursts out laughing.

"Sure, and I've got a farm for sale on the moon," she jeers. "What are you after? Why are you lying to me?"

"Look." I drum my fingertips on the edge of the steering wheel. "If we're going to explore the shithole parts of town together for this little murder mystery party, then I need your trust. I'd like to have it. Or as much as you're willing to give me."

"It's unlikely you'll get anything out of me."

She's staring out at the buildings ahead, frowning.

I grip her knee to return her attention to me.

"Most of the people my boss sends me out to kill are not deserving of their fate. There are a few rare exceptions, of course." I think back on the one I'd had to butcher the other day. "I offer them a deal. They disappear, or they die. Most are willing to take the deal."

What would she do in my position, if our roles were reversed? How would I feel, learning this about her, in that case?

I don't expect her to agree with me but maybe she can understand.

For a long moment the silence in the SUV thickens. I sit back in the seat, letting her work through things on her own, not willing to be the one to speak first.

"So what do you do then?" She still sounds skeptical. "If they take the deal and run? You still have to supply a body for your boss."

"I find someone to butcher in their place," I say simply. "There are thousands of scum in this city who deserve death."

"Who are *you* to decide?"

"I'm the one holding the knife, but the decision is out of my hands. I don't kill my hits outright. I give them the choice. And if they choose to run, then someone else takes their place. Someone deserving of it."

"You seriously expect me to see you as a noble judge?"

"More like an ambivalent executioner," I correct.

She says nothing and I pull the car off the main street toward one of the side alleys where we won't be disturbed.

I wind up parking far enough away from Docks on Markee that we'll have to walk but it's much safer this way. Harder to escape quickly but less likely there will be eyes on us at this distance.

"So you offer criminals a second chance and...what? What happens if you get caught? Your boss will never forgive you," Layla says finally.

"I kill people that pose a threat to others. And he'll never find out."

We still don't move.

"Because drug lords are so willing to be merciful," she replies.

Slowly I twist around to look at her. "Selling shit on the street that is laced with bad stuff loses people who are willing to pay for it without asking questions. That's the clientele. Stupid people. Doped and laced shit is bad for business, Detective. So I take care of the problem. I take care of the people who are a drain. The sadistic fucks who hurt kids and only care about making a quick buck."

"As long as they're sadistic in the way you think, then, that makes them okay?" She's looking for answers and I'm not sure if she's ready to accept my explanations or not. My chest is hot and tight and the rest of me prickly. "Your kind of sadism is fine?"

I blow out a breath and push out of the car. She does the

same and rounds the hood until we're both standing chest to chest. Then I say, "You are awfully mouthy for a woman without a weapon at the moment."

"And you're awfully cocky for a white dude with a mediocre-sizes dick." She accompanies the statement with a syrupy sweet smile.

"Filthy fucking mouth." I grin at her. "But we both know the weapon I'm carrying, the one that will do you in, isn't my knife. It's my *mediocre-sized dick,* as you so lovingly put it." I grab her, pressing my half-chub against her. Much better, I realize, to touch her. To joke with her, especially when she matches my teasing tone. "Feels mediocre right now. Right?"

She doesn't fight me.

She doesn't pull away.

I halfway wish she would, which is why I shove her against the hood of the car and kiss her. For a moment she's still, with her hands frozen into claws between us. In the next she's beating at me despite the way her mouth opens. Despite the flick and sweep of her tongue against mine.

She fucking loves it. And she hates that she loves it.

Too damn bad.

My stomach flips and my half-chub turns into a raging boner which I grind into the apex between her legs. The tension has been building since the moment I met her, tension without an outlet.

Or maybe not enough of an outlet.

When she's out of breath and keening a little, probably hating the sound she makes just as much as she hates me, I break away and release her abruptly. Loving the way her eyes have grown even darker.

"We need to go watch the docks. See if we can find any activity over at Markee."

Layla's dazed and can only nod, eventually trailing after me with silent footfalls in the dark. I don't need to tell her how to walk, or to be careful. We both fall into our old habits in an instant.

She might be out of it mentally but years of training, the kind that got her to the rank of detective, kick in without prompting. She's stealthy, and the two of us creep close to the walls of the nearby buildings.

This area of town is not for the faint of heart.

It's also much busier than it has a right to be, considering Broderick shut down Markee. I tug Layla into the shadows between buildings where I've perched and watched before, a better vantage point of the area and the wharf in general. Out here the breeze feels extra cold coming off the water. To the point where my nose hurts with each inhalation.

The scent brings to mind bilge water from a cruise ship, not that I've ever been on one. Too many people shitting and pissing in confined spaces plus rotting garbage, and that's the stagnancy of the wharfs.

The rickety stairs lead to the flat roof of a building adjacent from the old Docks on Markee building.

Layla's got her hands on her hips. "I can see this is one of your hangouts."

"Does it just scream *me*?" I want to know.

Some of my old gear is still here, left over from the last time I had to use the nest up here to scope out one of Broderick's marks. A ratty old rattan chair and a pair of binoculars.

Shit, it's been years.

Not since Broderick shut it all down and gave me a raise and a new title within the Syndicate.

"I think you could do with a couple of plants up here." She surveys the space. "Brighten it up a bit."

"Too bad for me I've got a black thumb when it comes to plants. Doesn't matter much to me. I have better uses for my thumbs."

I might be imagining the blush creeping across her cheeks.

"It's weird to be here with you," she says finally.

My brow lifts to my hairline on its own. "Why's that?"

"I've only had one partner. Devan just gets me."

"You think I don't?"

She purses her lips and says, "You think you do. We'll see." She shrugs delicately. "Then again, there are only two people who can stand me. My partner and Taney."

"The girl from the club. With all the crazy hair.

Layla nods.

"How did you and Devan start working together?" I've got to keep her talking. When she's talking, she's not thinking about how fucked up it is for us to work together. Or about what we did on stage tonight.

If she's talking, she's calm.

"We met each other fresh out of the academy. I'd been labeled as having an attitude problem," she tells me. A ghost of a smile flickers across her face and I have to hide one of my own. I'd bet that's putting it mildly. "I'm not sure who they were trying to punish by putting us together. Me, him...or both of us. There are still a lot of deep-seated issues in this city. Some people don't like the color of my partner's skin." She says it simply but the tenor of steel in her voice tells me everything.

She'd mow anyone down for talking bad about Devan.

"We just clicked, though. Tough shit for the haters. He's the only person I trust to really have my back when bad shit goes down." Layla turns to me, her face vulnerable and open.

Something uncomfortable twists in my chest at the expression. To cover my own suddenly raw emotions, I push Layla toward the chair and lean a hip against the cement edge of the building. A stiff breeze from the west brings in the stench of still water and dead fish.

"Do you ever wish you could see the stars?" she asks suddenly. "Like they do out in Montana?"

I shake my head no.

"Why not?"

"Because then I'd be in fucking Montana."

Layla chuckles darkly. "They call it Big Sky Country, I'm pretty sure. Can't be all that bad."

"I might start to get itchy without all the skyscrapers." The thought of wide open spaces scares the shit out of me. Anti-claustrophobic. "The city is all I've ever known."

All Layla has known too, by all accounts, but her expression is wistful.

"Guess you need a constant reminder of your manhood." She gestures with her nose toward my dick.

"I could give *you* a reminder."

"Oh, please." She holds up a hand to stop me. "I've seen enough. *Big Daddy*."

"Seen, felt, tasted..." I trail off, noting the way her tongue darts over her lower lip at the word *tasted*.

It's easy to sit here with her and talk, easy where it should feel awkward. Just as it felt easy to slide inside of her onstage when there should have been a bit of unease, given the charade.

"This used to be a thriving place, you know," I murmur.

Layla is staring at something in the distance and her gaze sharpens. "Still is, from the looks of it. There are two groups of people approaching the old place, from different directions." She points toward one of the groups.

She's not wrong.

I narrow my eyes and focus on our newcomers.

For a while we sit, watching who is coming and going, keeping our thoughts to ourselves.

It's impossible to make out specific faces from this vantage point without the binoculars, which Layla immediately grabs for her own, but at this point none of them are recognizable.

"We've got to get closer," she mutters.

I reach out, tentatively touch her elbow. "What do you see?"

"They're all there assembled under the awning, but why? It's like they're waiting for something. What would they be waiting for?" She's curious now, fully in cop mode.

The entire situation reeks of bullshit.

It takes less time than normal for Layla to wiggle her way down the stairs and along back alleys to a better, closer vantage point. She's good, capable, and energetic. Even after the pounding I gave her onstage.

Makes me wonder what else she can do, and how much she can take.

I grab her wrist and feel her shaking as though she's got too much pent-up energy trapped inside her. "Don't bolt," I hiss out.

"I wasn't planning on it."

As we watch, a bald man with wide shoulders strides into the main room of the abandoned Docks on Markee.

"Good haul," the man says. His hands are in the pockets of his jacket, leaving only his face and neck visible. "Multiple shipments. Nice job, gentlemen."

He bends at the waist to scrutinize said multiple shipments, nodding at whatever he inspects.

He's not one of our guys, that's for sure. Broderick would have mentioned it if he'd decided to put Docks on Markee back in business. I grab the binoculars for a closer look. The shipping crates have no labels. None of the men are familiar to me...which leads me to believe it isn't Broderick at all.

Which means someone else has commandeered the space.

I know a drug exchange when I see one. Those familiar square parcels are organized into several stacks. I tug on the back of Layla's jacket to get her to move back a bit before someone glances toward the window and sees two shadows that don't belong.

We leave slowly, back out the way we came.

Black creeps along the edges of my vision and it takes me a beat to realize that I haven't drawn in a breath in much too long. The bald guy...he has one of those faces I can't place, which isn't good.

His face seems familiar but not one I immediately identify, and no bells of recognition are ringing in my head.

I'm racking my brain to place the guy.

What's his name?

What are his associations?

He's someone important. A major player. I can tell from the way he carries himself. Broderick won't be happy when I deliver this new information.

"I don't understand," Layla's saying from in front of me. She marches along like she has better places to be. Now she's making enough noise to wake the dead. "What does a drug deal at a defunct warehouse that used to be run by

Broderick Stevens have to do with our dead hookers? Candy was clearly killed in a style that mimics yours."

"Very clear strokes from a left-handed grip. And a token lighter. Although they took great pains not to slice through the birthmark on her hip," I finish.

Layla stops dead in the center of the pavement. "How did you know she has a birthmark on her hip?" Her gaze accuses me of knowing more about the case than she's told me, and her suspicion is clear.

"I have my sources," I tell her coldly.

"You know, with all your talk of trusting each other, I really thought..." She shakes her head. "Delusional, that's what I am. You're nothing but a liar. I have no idea why I let myself believe otherwise." She stalks ahead.

I'm about to follow after her when my phone buzzes. I whip it out of my pocket and stare at the screen. It's a number I know better than to ignore.

"Where are you with the case?"

The boss.

"I'm working on it."

I hang up and catch up to Layla, heart racing. "The less you know, the better. Now get in the car. We have to go."

"Fine," she grinds out. "Let's get out of here."

EIGHTEEN
layla

THE LONGER I think about it, the more logically I understand there's no reason to fight with Gabriel because it won't get me anywhere. Fighting with him is easy. It's a cop-out because I would rather have him yell at me than deal with the seething emotions inside of me.

Not cool.

My therapist would call it *projecting*.

There are three things I do well in this world: fuck, close cases, and project.

I want to do all of those things with Gabriel but one of those is dangerous for my health.

He drops me off in front of the Velvet Underground and takes off without so much as a peel-out, his emotions completely under control.

I'm the loose cannon here.

But something about this set-up bothers me, outside of the man himself. Gabriel clearly knows all about the case, many more details than I told him. Which tells me there's a leak.

I've been around this city and its disgusting political

and criminal dealings long enough to know that if he has confidential information on the murders there is no other explanation.

No matter how badly I want to place all the blame on him, I know I can't do that. Unfortunately, besides there being an information leak, there will probably be a data breach as well, our sensitive information visible to whoever has enough skill to look for it.

I've got to go into the office and clean up shop.

* * *

After a night of piss-poor sleep and enough coffee to give an elephant a heart attack, I shower and head in to the office. It helps to channel some of my aggression into productivity.

Devan is expecting me, not bothered by the thunderous expression I wear like a good pair of boots. He's waiting for me at the door with a cup of coffee as black as Gabriel's soul.

"Update," he demands immediately. "How did it go last night?"

I take a quick sip of coffee and scald the lining of my throat and stomach in the process. "This tastes like shit." It's my version of a thank-you.

Devan grins, smile lines fanning out from his eyes. "Better than the slop they have here. So? What are you hiding? Did you come up with anything that will help us?"

"A lead I tugged yielded some dirt, for sure." We make our way to a private conference room and he closes the door behind us to make sure those pricks Jerry and Clint and their ilk don't follow us. "I ended up going down to Docks on Markee last night."

And I proceed to tell him everything.

"Are you kidding me? You're working this alone and you went down to a shithole like Markee without me?" Devan drags a hand through his hair. "L, I get it. You *are* capable. You know how to do your job. But there are some things you shouldn't do on your own just because you can. Like going down to Docks. That is…well, it's not okay."

I know how to deal with an angry Devan. We've pissed each other off too many times to count over the years we've worked together.

He's ticked off now and no mistake.

But more than the frustration and anger with me, he's disappointed. And I'm not sure I can handle him feeling that way. My heart gives a sickening little thump to let me know I care enough about him to need to make this right, immediately.

"I'm sorry," I say, gripping the coffee cup. "It was so last-minute that I had no choice but to—"

Devan cuts me off. "What, L?"

I sigh. "I didn't have time to call you."

"Literally takes a second or two to send me a text. You're working this alone not because you have to but because you want to. That's the difference."

My voice softens. "You're my partner."

He blows out a forceful breath that has his nostrils flaring. "Then start fucking acting like you have one, because this is not fair. Not to me and not to you. You made the choice, L, not me."

I'm uncomfortable in more ways than one, and I'm also out of energy to justify my actions. Excuses have no place with Devan.

I'll apologize all day long and do whatever it takes to

make this right...yet somehow I still haven't told him about working with Gabriel. Not yet.

"I think there's actually a leak somewhere, though. In the department." I take another sip of coffee. "I ran into someone who had more information about the case than they should know."

Devan narrows his eyes. "What do you mean?'

"They knew about the last hooker to die. Candy? Or rather Mallory. That's her real name. They knew about her birthmark." I drop my tone low, unsure if we should be talking about this here. "How can we find out if our computers or our case files have been hacked?"

Devan taps his foot on the floor, all business now. "We work off of an encrypted server, but that doesn't mean a skilled hacker can't access the information. Who knows what kind of filth is being employed by our crime lords these days. The underground has all kinds of skills at their disposal."

"Intelligent filth," I correct.

"It's time for us to pay a visit to IT."

I groan, even though the guys down in the tech department work for the same people we do. They're just creeps. Not in a weird way, like a typical nerd or geek, but because they never leave the dim fluorescent lighting of their little cave and seem to almost talk in code. One of the guys even went so far as to pinch my ass on my way past him during a case.

I gesture for Devan to go ahead of me. "Lead the way, then."

The trip to their underground bunker will give me enough time to finish the coffee, at least.

There are several IT personnel in the office at all times. Today we've got Bill and Adam, with their faces lit by the dull glow of the blue screens of their computers. Both of them turn to look at us in tandem and the effect is definitely at the top of the scale in terms of creepiness.

"To what do we owe the pleasure, Detective Sinclair?"

Bill elbows Adam in the side to get him to shut the hell up. "Her name is Pocahontas. How many times do I have to tell you?'

"Right, because the nicknames are completely endearing and make me more inclined to be pleasant." I shoot them a smile that's anything but.

"Not to mention political correctness," Devan adds sarcastically.

I nudge him with my shoulder in thanks.

"Look, boys, we've got some questions. Would an outsider have access to our system?" I ask.

Adam pushes his glasses up higher on the sharp bridge of his nose. "Elucidate."

"She's wondering if it's possible for someone who doesn't work in the department to have access to our files on the server," Devan clarifies.

Bill looks startled. "It's not supposed to be possible, no. What gives you the impression we've been hacked?"

I cross my arms over my chest, but the way Adam's eyes flick immediately to my cleavage has me adjusting my posture yet again. "A hunch?"

"Good enough for me." Bill spins around in his chair. "I'll check the firewalls."

"How long is it going to take?" Devan wants to know.

"As long as it takes." Bill snaps out the last bit. He's in his element. The two of them dive right into checking whatever it is they need to check.

With that portion of the agenda handled, I turn to

Devan. "Come on. I want to do a little digging in the daylight."

There are several reasons for me to head back to Docks on Markee. One, because I'll be able to see more without any goons popping out of the woodwork and surprising me. Those kinds of creatures are nocturnal. And two, because going back with Devan will help clear away some of his residual frustration with me.

Three? A fresh set of eyes that do not belong to the reaper.

This time I drive down to the wharf. I've spent too much time in the passenger seat lately. Even if it's just handling a vehicle, a little bit of control grabbed back is necessary if I'm going to keep pushing forward.

"I can't believe you came here by yourself," Devan muttered the closer we get to the abandoned docks. "This place is a mess."

"It's no worse than anything we've seen before," I reply, keeping my gaze on the potholes in the road ahead.

"Good thing Kimmy doesn't know about this."

"Why?" I chuckle. "You're afraid your girlfriend won't let you come down here to play? Not the right kind of kids on the playground?"

"She'd worry unnecessarily." The weight of his tone tells me he's done the same for me lately.

"I know, I know," I say without having to be prompted. "I'm a bad partner and a worse friend."

Devan holds up a hand like a shield. "Your words, not mine."

I pull off around the same place Gabriel parked last night, but this place doesn't look any better with the weak sunlight shining through the sick, hazy clouds overhead. Before heading down to the Markee itself, we take a look around the area for any clues. Considering the number of people making their way down to this area last night there's bound to be something.

"So the people I saw entered the building from both sides, but the largest group came from over there." We carefully make our way over to trace the bad guys' path. There's a slight impression of footprints leading back to a set of tire tracks.

"People here clearly don't care about being seen." I crouch to study the tread. "They're not doing shit to cover their tracks."

"We'll check the opposite direction as well." Devan has his phone out and camera open, snapping photos of the tracks. "You take notes."

I nod, reaching into the pocket of my jacket for my own notepad. My cell vibrates and a glance at the screen shows Taney's name. Ignoring it for now, Devan and I start to move closer to the actual building where the deal went down.

"There were several groups but it seems a large bald man was in charge," I remind him as we walk.

"You've never seen him before?"

My gut gives a single shift then settles. "He has one of those faces you want to forget but something about him is sticking at me. Like I've got a thorn in my paw."

"Not why you've been weird today, then."

I glance sideways at him. "I haven't been weird." I've been totally weird. He's right.

"You apologized and you're actively being sweet," Devan corrects. "Yes. You're acting weird. Softer than your normal speed. Something melted you and I'm saying it's a bad thing. I just want to know that you're going to do this job. With me."

I want to correct him yet something stills my tongue. He's right again. I'll be damned if I tell him the reason why, especially since the reason why makes me tremble in a bad way. The skin on the back of my neck prickles with the fine hairs standing at attention. I pause, taking a careful look around and seeing no one. Why do I feel there are eyes on me, then?

Devan must have the same sensation, and from the corner of my eye I watch him place a hand on his Glock and motion for me to quiet.

We're just outside the entrance to Docks on Markee when we both notice the blood splatters in the dirt. And I nearly jump out of my skin when my phone erupts with another cheerful ding in notification that I have a text.

"Fuck it all," I hiss out.

Devan sucks on his teeth and says, "Turn that damn thing off unless you want to get us killed, L. We don't know who else might be here."

I'm scrambling for the phone. "It's Taney, sorry."

"Well, tell her I said hi—but later."

It's not like Devan to go pale, but he's as bloodless and guppy-mouthed as I've ever seen him, looking at the blood spatters.

I'm about to type out a message letting Taney know I'm fucking busy when Devan grabs me and shoves me in front of him. Holds me steady so that my gaze falls on the shoe lying in the dirt. But it's not the shoe he wants me to see.

It's the body, butchered and tucked into the shadows, his eyes still wide with fear and dark blood caked over his wounds.

NINETEEN
gabriel

ANTONI STARES AT ME, his lips pursed like he's sucked on a lemon and actually enjoyed it on some level. His normal expression, I think, suppressing a groan at him being included in this meeting.

He's nothing but a motherfucker and he enjoys being that way, enjoys knowing no one can stand him. It gives him sick pleasure to annoy the piss out of people as long as he's in good with Broderick.

I'm not sure why he has to be here for this, in my boss's office, but Antoni always likes to make himself available.

Hates being left out of the action.

Broderick Stevens is on speaker, claiming a last-minute emergency that kept him out of the office. There's only me, Antoni, and a couple of goons who go by Bruiser and Howard.

Personally I've always liked Howard best.

He says little and always stares at Bruiser, who resembles a coked-out Bob Ross, with a hint of mixed disgust and longing. It's adorable.

"Let me see if I understand the situation correctly,"

Broderick croons. "You're saying Docks on Markee is back in operation, Gabriel?"

Antoni's smirk deepens at the way Broderick says my name.

I tap my foot on the tile to let Antoni know exactly how I feel about him being here. He smiles in return although his lips are still puckered.

"That's exactly what I'm saying," I reply.

"You're sure it's not a mistake?" Antoni asks.

He's begging for a knife between the ribs one of these days. "I don't make those kinds of mistakes."

Golden afternoon light filters in through the closed blinds of the office, and judging from the silence on the other end of the phone, my boss isn't happy about what I found last night at Docks on Markee.

I haven't spoken to Layla since we parted ways last night but my mind returns to her again and again.

Is she in a similar meeting right now?

Is she talking to her boss about the mysterious bald man?

Is she keeping it to herself about our onstage fuck?

Swallowing hard over the lump in my throat, I focus on staring Antoni down while we wait for Broderick to answer.

I'd thought too many times about finding Layla and letting her know exactly where I'd planned to go today, and who I had to alert about what we found last night. Angry with me as she is, she won't like hearing me talk about Broderick or the Syndicate.

This *trust* business has to work for us to get our answers, and rather than both of us covering the same ground, I might as well share. I could be the bigger person here.

Not my usual style but I tried.

I'd shot her a quick string of texts an hour ago before stepping out of my apartment.

"None of this is good news," Broderick says eventually. "How many of them were there?"

Between us, Layla and I counted ten men excluding Baldy, which I tell the boss now.

"And how did they gain access to the building, I wonder?" he muses out loud.

I open my mouth to answer when my cell, on the desktop besides Antoni's, vibrates and the name on the screen gives me away. *Layla*. I have to hustle to knock the cell aside before Antoni puts the pieces together.

He's a dick but he's not stupid.

"And who might that be, Blackwell? Another one of your fucking creep girlfriends?" he teases anyway.

I say nothing, flicking the notification aside to focus on the voice sighing in disappointment on the other end.

"This isn't how I'd hoped today would go, gentlemen. Antoni? Bring him in," the boss says.

Antoni snaps his fingers and Bruiser moves into position, one hand on his gun as Howard pulls open the office door. Horn-Rimmed guy, who handed me the files, steps inside silently.

"What the fuck are you doing here?" I ask.

"I asked him to come," Broderick continues. "He's a valuable part of the expansion of our operation, after all. Now tell us everything from the beginning."

Being taken by surprise always sucks.

I take the time to compose myself, sliding my hands into my pockets and squaring my shoulders before I repeat the story of last night, Layla excluded.

I tell them about the docks in terse, mincing terms.

"A bald man." Antoni scoffs. "There's nothing remarkable about a bald man."

"There is when we don't have one on payroll," I snap.

He steps closer, looming in my face despite the inches of height separating us. "You know everyone on payroll now, Blackwell? Got a thing for faces?" He grunts when I say nothing. "Stick to what you're good at."

Horn-Rimmed says nothing, simply standing close to the exit with his left hand clenched around the handle of a briefcase.

"Do whatever it takes to get this cleared, Gabriel. I want it handled covertly. You understand?" Broderick's tone holds no inflection. I might as well be telling him about a kid's birthday party in a park somewhere for all he cares. "I don't want to have to bring in any extra bodies. Whoever this man is, find him. And let him know that fucking with the Syndicate has consequences."

Horn-Rimmed harrumphs in agreement.

"I'll track down the bald man's operation," I assure them.

"You'd better," Antoni adds.

"This is slower than your normal progress, Blackwell," Horn-Rimmed says. "We expected more from you. We've heard nothing but good things and yet reality does not always equal one's reputation. Does it?"

I glance up sharply at him, wanting to ask who the hell is he to insult me this way.

"I'm a contract killer." There's no clearer way to describe my position. "I'm not a fucking cop. Maybe if you want leads tracked down you should pull on other strings."

"Yet you're the one we hired." Horn-Rimmed heads for the door and pauses only to call over his shoulder, "I hope next time you waste my time, it's for a better reason."

I wait until he's out of the office before addressing the boss on the phone. "This isn't a cut and dried thing. It takes time." I've got a certain skill set I've taken pains to hone, a wheelhouse where I feel most comfortable.

I deliver death.

As fucked up as it sounds, I found a niche, and I've done well enough.

Why does Broderick and his new glasses-wearing buddy want me on this instead of someone else?

"No excuses." My boss is terrifying when he wants to be.

There are no excuses to give and even the hard truth won't be acceptable to him.

His voice is carefully cultivated to curdle the blood when he tells me, "Make this go away."

"I'm doing my best."

"Your best isn't good enough. I don't like having to divert my attention away from expansion. It's not what I want." The last statement is a lash of reproach and I practically feel the wounds across my back, my face. "If this continues, then you and I have a problem. Understand?"

It's an empty threat. I've lasted three times longer than any other reaper he's employed because I'm damn good and my boss knows it, which is why I get paid the amount I do. It's why I have the freedom I do.

A freedom which may not last much longer, a small voice in my head warns.

Things feel sticky now. The longer this takes, the more the foundation beneath me becomes compromised. I take risks only when I understand the cost.

These costs are unknown.

Broderick hangs up, the call ending with a decisive click.

I never gave much thought to the future before, taking things one kill at a time. When my time comes to an end, then it will more than likely be at the end of a bullet shot by someone I've pissed off. Or someone the Black Market Syndicate has run over on our rise to the top of this city.

Layla would call me a pessimistic bastard if she ever heard me voice those thoughts.

She'd tell me to pull my head out of my ass and start thinking about what I want. At least, I think she would.

"Where do you think you're going?" Antoni asks as I pocket my cell. "We're not done here."

I shoot him a scathing look over my shoulder. "Are we not?" None of his damn business where I'm going. I leave him in the office without another word, his weak chin flapping when he calls out after me.

My mind is a blur all the way to the car, and I take off, pulling away from the underground parking lot reserved only for Broderick's people. The bald man, his familiar yet strange face...there are steps to take to find him. Scouting out the docks was the first.

Now it's off to the usual haunts to see if I can tug a few strings and find out more information.

Where have I seen his face before?

It's the strangest thing.

He's a piece out of time.

Familiar and yet not, someone with a face from a half-forgotten dream, like someone you pass on the street and immediately forget until you fall asleep. It irks me to no end, and the gnawing pit in my stomach opens wider. I place an absent hand on the area, rubbing in circles. When was the last time I ate? I remember downing a cup of coffee this morning on my way out of the apartment but hadn't been able to stomach the thought of food.

Not after a night of dreams about a certain high-strung woman with rich, chocolate-colored hair.

No matter what it takes, I've got to keep her off of Broderick's radar. The tenuous relationship we've got threatens to bring both of us in front of the firing squad if we're not careful, but the reward seemed greater than the risk when I proposed it in the first place.

Now everything hinges on me finding Broderick's mysterious competitor.

* * *

Seated on the rooftop of a hotel downtown, I stare at the street.

Same kind of perch as my first kill.

Except then I'd been a terrified child. Or as close to one as I'd ever been.

Dealing drugs is not the same thing as murder, even though one can be a stepping stone to the other. I drag a hand through my hair, the memories uncomfortable and itchy.

Mom never criticized me.

Which surprised me right up to the last day I saw her.

She never asked about the things I did and she never ostracized me. She was the only person in my life who I felt comfortable enough to be myself around.

Where I grew up, there were only two choices for boys like me: to join the cartels or to die. I didn't want to die. I wanted to do whatever it took to get out of that shithole and take care of my mom.

Here we are.

And it's just me.

I learned too quickly that taking care of someone meant

nothing in the grand scheme of life. Because shit happens. Everyone you love dies and it breaks your heart because love is a weakness.

Except I want to take care of Layla. Even when she's more than capable of taking care of herself, those instincts I thought were long dead are starting to resurface. She'll hate me if I say anything. If I even give her a hint of the budding feelings that have no place in whatever this fucked-up shit is between us.

At once the weight of years pushes down on my bones and I'm dog-tired. The kind of tired that, if I give in, will only drag me down too far to get back up.

Aside from the exhaustion, there's the small matter of the too-large part of my brain taken up by a woman who doesn't even want to see me. Which makes it even harder to admit how badly I looked forward to seeing her again.

How would it feel, I wonder as I allow myself to fantasize, to come home to someone in my apartment at the end of the day?

Instead of dropping into bed after my shower and passing out alone, I'd find her waiting with her gun on the nightstand and the same haunted shadows on her face, shadows we'd chase away together.

Will she judge me if I tell her about that first kill?

How the man begged me not to shoot and then tried to turn the gun on me?

How I shot him right in the eye? Stood over him until he cooled?

After an hour on this rooftop, I give up the ghost on this search, frustration bubbling and my stomach empty. My cell buzzes.

I'm worried about Taney. She wants to meet at Clydesdale Park. Thoughts?

I stop dead in my tracks, inches away from the edge of the building. That park needs to be razed to the ground. It's a disgusting travesty because there are no real trees, no real playground, and no mother in her right mind would take a kid there. Which is how the scum who never manage to rise in Empire Bay the way Broderick did use the greenspace as their own.

No, don't. Not alone, I hastily type back.

It's way too dangerous even in the daylight.

With dusk approaching and turning the sky a bruised peach and lavender? When there's enough darkness to hide the assholes?

Maybe I should be happy that she's even sending me a text, but at this point the worry encompasses everything. Every sick and depraved piece of me is up in arms imagining her there. My stomach refuses to settle.

My partner is with me.

End of story, then.

She wants me to back off without saying as much.

"Fuck," I mutter.

I'm in the SUV a long moment later, hoping to catch Layla and make sure she doesn't damn us both by getting herself killed.

TWENTY
layla

ONE HOUR SLIPS AWAY before I even have time to blink the grit out of my eyes. We've got a male vic this time, with the same slash marks as the last four bodies. No lighter on him, though. From the looks of the frozen scream on his face he died horribly, the attack a surprise.

I want to believe Gabriel didn't leave me last night only to go back to the docks.

I'd texted him right after we found the body, ignoring his message about his meeting with Broderick and working my way around to his whereabouts last night.

He'd made a dick joke. Once his meeting ended, he made sure to tell me.

Told me he'd gone home and to bed after jerking off thinking about me.

I'd rolled my eyes, but was he telling the truth?

I hope so.

Yet I'm back at the docks taking care of another body, doing my best not to dwell on the way Gabriel has the uncanny ability to worm his way past my walls.

"L? Get out of your damn head," Devan calls. "I need you."

We keep everything we need for collecting evidence in the trunk of our vehicle. After a quick call to the higher-ups, we get to work, securing the scene and preparing to document the murder.

The crime scene techs show up within a half hour. Any horror I might have once felt at being around dead bodies quickly disappeared under the weight of experience. Of years doing this kind of stuff.

Poor asshole, though. No one deserves to die this way. Not in a place like this where the only company you keep once you pass is the fish floating on top of the water with the rest of the scum and detritus.

"Clear the way for the chief!"

One of the crime scene techs straightens and lifts a gloved hand to his forehead like he's ready to salute.

Chief Inspector Henderson knows what it's like to get her feet dirty even though she ascended to her current position many years ago. She tramps through the grime with harsh steps that have the dust and dirt clinging to the shiny tops of her shoes.

"As noisy as the press when I need the secret damn service." She glares at the tech who spoke up. "Stop announcing my presence." Henderson beelines for us. She pulls up short when she sees the dead body. "Well, fuck me. Fucking hell."

If she wasn't my superior I might have cracked a smile at her cursing.

"I know who this is. I recognize the face." She slides her manicured hands, tastefully done, into the pockets of her black slacks. "It's the senator's son. He's a party boy, by all accounts, but he's well-known. His face is all over social media. Huge following on one of those platforms," she finishes.

Devan must have been the one to call in the chief because it sure as shit wasn't me. I step aside to give her some breathing room as she bends over to examine the body.

Chief Inspector Henderson is a middle-aged badass who lets her hair grow out into its natural salt-and-pepper state. No one has ever accused her of being beautiful but her features are striking, handsome. Her rounded no-nonsense chin and wide-set eyes give her an air of dignity.

She's earned her respect, though, through her actions and deeds.

"The press are going to create a damn circus with this shit." She clucks her tongue at the corpse like it's his fault he wound up here. And dammit, but it might be, if he wanted cheap drugs. "What brought him down to this area of town? This is going to be a nightmare for everyone." She narrows her eyes at me, her cap shielding her face from the dull glow of the sun.

"We found him here while following a lead on another case. A blood trail led us right to him," I say.

"Finish up and report straight back to me with whatever you find. I've got to make some calls and see if I can get ahead of this thing. There is no good way to handle it, though." Henderson straightens, shaking her head, tongue clucking. "Shit."

She's pissed off and has every right to be. We've got a senator's dead son in the middle of a case that links him directly to drug deals and dead hookers. That isn't going to look good for the father's re-election campaign, is it?

"Things keep getting more twisted," Devan muses out loud as we finish up. "You think it's drugs?"

"I do," I tell him with a firm nod.

"You got everything you need, L?"

I'm staring at the chief rather than giving Devan my full attention. Henderson has got her cell pressed to her ear and an angry expression twisting her face, speaking in tones too low for anyone to hear.

"Yeah, I think we've got enough info to get the hell out of here." I've got my own cell in hand and belatedly remember that I've got to text Taney back.

I've missed several more messages from her and a handful from Big Daddy.

Sorry, been a crap day, I text Taney. *What's up?*

Three dots in a text bubble show up on the screen immediately but the message is far from what I expect as a response.

Meet me ASAP at Clydesdale Park. I'm serious.

No emojis. Nothing outside of a desperation that comes through even in the text, mostly because Taney never uses punctuation and yet a period marks the end of her sentences. She always tells me that punctuation is passive–aggressive.

No matter how many times I argue that it's simple grammar, she never listens, practically sticking her fingers in her ears and la la la-ing me to death.

I debate showing Devan the text but he's already reading it over my shoulder.

"I'm not letting you go alone because Clydesdale Park is nowhere near the club," he says. "Or near where Taney lives. It's not the place you go to meet your friend for a chat."

"The location *is* seriously odd," I agree out loud.

A niggling sensation tickles the back of my head and my immediate thought is to text Gabriel. Rather than questioning myself, I do, asking him his thoughts on the choice of meeting place.

Devan stares at me strangely but says nothing about my focus being glued to the phone.

It's not a special place for us. The park used to be home to some kind of megastore that went out of business and instead of inviting another business into the space, the city decided to demolish it and set up greenspace for the neighboring apartment complexes. Nothing too fancy to draw in a crowd. Mostly it's grass that's either half-dying or in desperate need of a mow, and a single merry-go-round. Sad, really.

They could have done so much with it, like a community garden.

"If you're not going to let me go alone, then hurry." I stuff my cell in my pocket and stride off toward the car. "I don't want to keep her waiting much longer."

"I'll stay in the car while you meet her but make sure it's within viewing distance. Got it?" Devan falls into step beside me.

He is true to his word and stays in the patrol vehicle, hidden but within viewing distance. Taney hasn't texted with a precise meeting location but I let her know when I'm there and make my way to one of the lone benches along the walking path. There's no sign of her anywhere. I don't like it.

I don't like that I felt the need to text Gabriel on my way here and let him know what's going on. I like even less the stupid text I got back from him about the park being sketchy. Between him and Devan voicing their concerns, it's like being sandwiched between two assholes, and I can't handle both of them at once feeling like I'm someone they need to protect.

I want to talk to my friend and I want to do it on my terms.

I stare at my phone's black screen: no new notifications.

Finally footsteps grow closer and I glance up to see Taney hauling ass toward me. Her normally wild hair is held tight to her head in a bun and her arms are wrapped around her midsection. She's wearing jeans and a pair of flats, her posture hunched forward.

I can't help thinking she's so small. Small and delicate and almost fragile. The same way Devan and Gabriel, AKA the two jerks, must see me.

Except Taney isn't like me.

She doesn't have a gun and she doesn't have all of my mental issues. She started working at the club because she wanted a safe space to be able to explore new things. She's submissive; she'd never hurt a fly and always looks out for everyone else around her, even if it means putting up with my crazy ass or giving half her paycheck to a coworker who needs a cash advance.

She's just like that.

The closer she gets, the easier it is to see the bright spots of color on her cheeks, and her dark pupils much larger than normal.

"Hey." I reach for her immediately and pull her toward me in a fierce hug. She's shaking. "What's going on? Are you okay?"

The sense of something wrong increases when Taney reaches for me.

Her arms go around me automatically and her head falls right into place between my breasts. Without heels she's about the perfect height for me to rest my chin on top of her head and I do so now. Taney is clearly distraught.

"Layla." She squeezes me tightly to the point of nearly losing my breath.

"Your text scared me."

She leans back far enough to meet my eyes. Her pupils are so dilated I see nothing but black circles. "I have to tell you. You can't come to the Velvet Underground anymore. You need to stay away. Please."

"What? Why?"

What does her fear have to do with the club?

She draws in a deep breath, her lips thinning into a harsh line as she steps to the side. "I thought about telling you a dozen times." A sharp prick of alarm runs along my limbs. Taney sounds panicked. "I think that there's—"

A shot rings out in the fading afternoon twilight and in the next instant Taney slumps forward, warm blood soaking through her clothes into mine.

"Taney? *Taney!*" Her name erupts as a screech, terror turning my voice raw. I'm clawing at her as we both sink to the ground.

"Don't go back," she whispers. "Promise me, Layla. Don't go back there."

"No no no. No!"

Taney stiffens, her body an unyielding weight, and her eyes close. She's not breathing. Not shaking anymore, not breathing, not moving—

No. No. No.

No no no.

The word stays on repeat in my head and in reality I'm screaming.

Shock. The part of me trained for this kind of situation knows I'm in shock and that part operates my mouth. "You coward!" I scream into the shadows. "Shoot me! Come back here and shoot me! I fucking dare you."

No one is coming, and all too soon my screams turn into sobs although no tears sting my eyes.

Devan pulls the patrol vehicle onto the grass beside us with the lights flashing. Through a haze I watch him push out of the vehicle, running up to me as if in slow motion. Another hand falls on my shoulder first and before I understand what's happening, Gabriel is there.

And Devan has a gun pulled on him.

Gabriel doesn't move away from me as he addresses my partner, Taney's body between us. My arms are wrapped around her, locked there, every part of me unwilling to let go.

"No, no," I mutter. The words are choked and wet. I push down my own feelings of panic.

"Look, I heard a gunshot and came running. For her." Gabriel's talking about me. Why is he talking about me? "What can I do?"

It takes Devan less than a second to assess the situation. "Stay with her, help her. I'm going after the bastard."

He takes off running toward the direction where the shot was fired, his cell in one hand as he calls for backup and his service pistol in the other.

"Taney—"

I sob out her name but Gabriel is pragmatic. His bright green eyes scour my face and he pries her out of my death grip. "Where are you hurt? You're covered in blood. Layla? Are you all right?"

"It's not my blood," I manage to say. "She's—s-someone shot Taney."

"Put pressure on the wound." Gabriel is all business.

I shake my head. "She's gone." I'm ready to shatter. My ears fill with the screech of approaching sirens. The noise in the background is too loud, the sound of footsteps, people shouting...

He presses two fingers to the side of her neck, eyes narrowed, lips a thin line. "She's not gone yet. She's got a small fluttering pulse and we might be able to keep her that way if you put pressure on the wound. Do you understand?"

Wait...what?

The world tilts on its axis.

I roll Taney onto her back.

All of a sudden Devan is back. "Thank you, man."

In my right mind, I might have been able to recognize the moment Devan put things together. Or note the way his gaze zeroes in on Gabriel's hand on my arm and the way I lean into him.

Gabriel backs off, with his hands up between us as Devan turns to me. I press both palms against the gushing wound in Taney's torso.

"The ambulance is on the way. It's almost here but I couldn't find the shooter. There's nothing. No one." He's at a loss.

The wail of the ambulance siren joins with those from other patrol vehicles. I refuse to leave Taney's side. Instead of obeying any of the EMT personnel, I jump in the back of the ambulance, clenching my friend's hand.

Silently begging whoever will listen to keep her here with me. I can't have one of the only people I love taken from me.

TWENTY-ONE
layla

I COUNT IN MY HEAD.

1, 2, 3, 4, 5...

Count up to 100, my girl, and time me. I'll be back before you're done.

Except very much like my father, Taney isn't coming back and I know it. The doctors are full of hope and good things to say, their platitudes urging me and Devan to say our prayers because she needs all of our good energy. Keep the faith, they urge us.

She's in surgery now.

Devan sits at my side, clutching my hand. All the places on my clothes that were wet from Taney's blood are now dry, caked and stiff and a constant reminder. The low humming in my ears won't abate and the palms of my hands are perpetually damp with sweat.

Devan seems to not mind.

I shift my hand but the grip keeping it in place tightens. Devan won't let go of me. I barely register his presence. But he's still here. Sitting beside me in the waiting room of the hospital, both of us quiet, still, while we wait for updates.

At least he doesn't try to tell me that everything is going to be okay. Or my personal favorite, uttered by a million and one well-wishers: There is a plan. I have to trust in *the plan* and everything will work out, as if there is some divine puppet master making the decisions for the trajectory of every life on this planet.

It's really hard to see the plan when bad things keep happening. It's either there is nothing and no one out there, or the people I love are not important enough to save. Not Mom, or Dad, or Taney...

Devan and I both jump when his cell vibrates. My heart slams against my ribs hard enough to crack them. One look at the screen and he finally breaks away.

"Let me take this. It's Ashcroft," he murmurs.

A call about the most recent murder, I expect. Ashcroft will want and need a report and we'll have to do a press conference tomorrow. I scrub my face. We were supposed to talk to Henderson too...

"Are you going to be okay alone?" Devan hasn't answered or stood yet. His dark eyes search mine.

"One of us has to do our job," I tell him. "Please, go. It's our case and I don't want anyone else stepping in and messing with our progress. Whoever we're on to, whoever we are closing in on...they tried to kill Taney. Do it for her." My eyes burn but tears refuse to erupt and give me relief. "I need a minute."

Devan stares a moment longer and finally nods in agreement. "Sure."

We both know what I'm really asking for. I've never had to beg Devan to leave me alone. Until now.

He's looking at me like he's afraid to leave me, like I might do something crazy when no one is looking. I've made it this far, I want to assure him. I've gotten to this point in my life no matter how many dark impulses and thoughts from the abyss attack me at any given moment. I'll be fine. I'm going to be fine.

The numbness of my insides means I'll be fine.

Devan presses the screen to answer and immediately strides out of the waiting room to talk to Captain Ashcroft somewhere more private.

In less than half a heartbeat, Gabriel drops down into the seat just vacated, appearing the instant Devan is out of sight. I blink at him.

"What are you doing here?" I ask, my tone leaden.

"Isn't it obvious?"

He slides close enough to be there should I issue the invitation but with enough space that I don't feel smothered.

"What's the news?" he asks.

"Nothing yet. They're still working on her." I keep bracing myself for the surgeon to come in.

"She had a message for you?" Gabriel pushes, not unkindly. "She wanted to talk to you about something?"

"Yeah, she did." His voice soothes the rough edges the numbness doesn't, and I find myself relaxing toward him a few inches. "She told me not to go back to the club."

I'm not looking at him.

The bitterness rises up inside of me like bile and burns wherever it touches.

"You mean the Velvet Underground."

"Exactly."

I don't know why I'm not really surprised to see Gabriel here. I rock to the edge of the hard plastic seat until my feet press flat to the floor. Bracing for the flashbacks that always take me when there's a loss of this caliber, this magnitude.

He makes some kind of sound in the back of his throat

and when I focus on him from my periphery he's staring at the wall ahead. Until he notices my attention and turns to me.

"Layla...I don't know what I can say to make you feel better." He flashes me a lopsided smile he doesn't mean. "I know how to threaten and kill. Comfort? It's not on my resume."

"I'm the same way."

Unconsciously I shift closer to him, as though the warmth of his body will thaw my chill and pull my fractured pieces into a coherent picture again.

He's careful not to touch me. He doesn't say anything now and his silence is a comfort. There's no expectation for me to fill the void with words. Only a comfortable companionship as Gabriel stares ahead at the blank gray wall, the rest of the people here going about their business. Death is their job the same way it's mine, except they're tasked to keep it at bay and I'm tasked to find the culprit.

Instead of the flashbacks, though, or me giving in to the spiral my psyche craves, I lower my guard and lean against him. Because him being here, no matter what I tell myself, does mean something.

The heat of his body seeps into me and I use it to warm my own.

The walls I've kept up between us have done nothing but help me stay safe. Help me stay one step ahead of more heartbreak because when you let people in, they leave you. It's that simple. Death takes everyone eventually, but for people in my life, friends or family, death comes so much sooner.

Gabriel becomes the only thing I feel and know while I wait. An anchor to life when I just want to...float away.

"You don't have to stay here," I manage to say eventually. "I'm sure you have places to be, people to murder."

"I'm right where I want to be," he replies.

I let out a shuddering half laugh before asking, "What is it about hospitals that makes them so fucking awful?"

It's so strange to watch him turn to me, to physically see the change in him as he releases his own armor. His shoulders shift forward the smallest bit, his muscles relaxing, and the cold haze of his neutral expression starts to melt as he balances his elbows on his knees.

He still hasn't touched me.

"It's how hard they struggle against the inevitable. The delusion that there is some control over what happens."

"My father was an emotionally abusive asshole when he drank." It's not as hard as I always imagined it would be to tell this story. The worst part is that I halfway wonder what Gabriel will think of me once I get it out there. "He never laid a finger on me, not after what happened to Mom, but...times were tough. And he was never the same once my mom killed herself. I don't blame him. Who can come back from something like that? Especially since her mind splintered after her rape."

Gabriel stiffens at the word.

Yet as I continue the story, we both relax, although the tension never fully drains away.

A distraction.

That's all this is.

"He wasn't a bad guy, in his own way. I think, now, that Dad knew something was wrong the night he was killed. He didn't want me involved, and had me count to a hundred while I waited for him to come back. Told me to stay put and he would find me. One hundred became two, then three. Finally I disobeyed him and went down to the convenience store and I...found him."

The scene flashes through my memory strong enough to leave a bitter taste in my mouth. "I stole the lighter before the cops got there," I finish.

"Of course you did." There's no condemnation in his voice.

I like talking to him without having to censor myself. So maybe he isn't really bad at this comfort thing. Not like he tells himself.

I file all these new pieces of information about him away to look at later.

Not as if it really matters, though.

Once this case is solved, then we go our separate ways.

Maybe I'll even be forced to arrest him one day.

But he'll be gone, and so will I.

"What about you?" I ask.

His eyes light. "You haven't researched me? I'd think you would want to know all about Daddy Thor."

I had done a few searches, of course, but I want to hear him tell me himself. From his lips and his experience instead of the meager information gathered on this killer by someone else.

"Distract me," I urge.

I'm the one who touches him first, who stops stifling the urge to rest my hand on his forearm.

"I grew up in drug circles." He bends down and lowers his voice so no one else will hear him, although it's only the two of us here. "Not here in Jersey, but in New York City. I didn't know my father. Some drug addict. Mom worked tirelessly to put food on the table, and when I saw those smugglers and all the power and the money that comes along with the trade...I wanted it." His lips twitch. "Promise me you're not going to take me in for this confession, Detective. All of this has to be off the record."

I lean into him harder. "You know it is."

Seconds later his massive hand covers mine and our fingers link. I should take my hand away. I should move to the opposite side of the room away from this killer.

I really don't want to.

It's asinine for us to trust each other. Yet he sits there letting me cling to him, while we both pry off the scar tissue and expose the rawness of our wounds. Those kinds of wounds that never really heal.

His hand feels so fucking good against mine.

"I got more involved in the drug scene," Gabriel admits. "Started out small-time, selling marijuana and cocaine on the streets, but I hated it. Despite my connections at that point, my mother was cornered and robbed. She gave the thug her wedding ring and he shot her in the shoulder anyway." Disdain drips from every syllable. "She did what she was told and was hurt anyway. I learned right then that charm and street smarts can build a reputation where you get to pay people back for the harm they do to others."

"When did you—"

"Start killing?" He finally looks me in the eye. "A hit was ordered, a competitor who started out small and then began poaching on territory where he didn't belong. I carried out the order even though it started off as a dare. No one thought I'd do it, but I was hungry to prove myself. I'm good at it. Death. I learned to harness my temper into skill which made me a valuable commodity."

"To someone like Stevens," I fill in the blank faintly.

Gabriel turns his body to face me and the weight of those green eyes causes my chest to tighten. I don't miss the heat building in his expression. "Exactly. I'm also a fairly good judge of character. He's a piece of shit but he's got drive. He's stubborn. I knew he'd go far."

It's ridiculous to indulge in any kind of connection with this man. A contract killer who just admitted he delights in murder. Or if not delights, then at least he acknowledges and appreciates that he's skilled at it.

Where does it leave us?

"Detective Sinclair?"

The arrival of the surgeon breaks me out of my thoughts.

I clear my throat, rubbing at my eyes, struggling to focus. "Yes."

Gabriel doesn't rise to his feet but I do and the movement breaks our hands apart. The surgeon is here sooner than I expected. But the way he's shaking his head...

My stomach plummets through the floor.

"I'm so sorry. This isn't the type of news I like to give to people who are already grieving—"

"What?" I bark out. "What happened? What are you saying?"

"We couldn't—"

My own shaking returns. "No. Where is she? I want to see her."

"We couldn't save her. There was too much blood loss," the surgeon continues.

"The bullet caused severe damage to her organs, and the internal bleeding—"

No. The thunder of my pulse drowns out the rest of his words. I'm frozen in place, blinking rapidly.

"Thank you, Doctor," Gabriel says for me. "I'll take it from here."

The room closes in around me because I knew. I *knew* that Taney wasn't coming back. I knew that her friendship with me would take her to some place where I'm not able to follow. I can't breathe.

The claustrophobic feeling is exacerbated when Gabriel closes his arms around me and drags me out of the waiting room toward the elevator. Back to the first floor and the parking lot. I'm dwarfed by his arms, fighting for every breath, and my reflection isn't one I recognize.

Too pale, too wild-eyed, too shaky.

"If you're going to throw up, then wait until we're out of here."

He has to practically toss me over his shoulder to get me out of the elevator.

"Taney."

The voice that comes out of me isn't mine. It's a child's voice. In my head I see the moment I found Dad underneath the glowing red sign of the convenience store, with the lighter displayed prominently on his chest.

Gabriel guides me over to where I parked and I push against him, determined to walk on my own even though I can use his support. The car is there. If I make it, then I'll get home, I'll get my whiskey, my gun, I'll—

Gabriel grabs the car keys out of my hand and I hadn't realized I'd reached for them until he does. I definitely do not feel the way the metal bit into my skin and left a bloodless imprint.

"Give me my keys," I growl.

The world spins around me and the sky overhead is nothing but a blur. The heat of Indian summer has started to fade and the chill of the night air burns against my skin. I welcome the sensation. Anything is better than numbness.

What am I supposed to do? How do I go on without Taney?

She is everything I'm not, full of life and confidence. The real kind. Not the fake crap I peddle.

Not is, I correct. *Was*. She *was* all those things. And I'll never get to see her again.

My throat clenches, closing, hot and scratchy and every piece of me feels poked with needles.

"You aren't driving in this state."

"You don't know me." I wrap my arms around myself although it does nothing to help. "What state am I in, Gabriel? Death happens every day and I'm right in the thick of things. If you think this is any different, then you're fooling yourself."

He snags me around the waist and hauls me close, glaring at me and daring me to try and stop him. Rather than fight me, he tightens his grip.

I'm still shivering when he drags me over to his vehicle, the monstrous black SUV. I'm forced to let him take over and lead.

There's silence, silence all around me. He says nothing when he throws me down into the passenger seat and I flinch. Nothing about the strange hiccupping cough in the back of my throat. No one is more surprised when I actually stay in the seat and let him buckle me in.

Silence all around me.

No more counting.

No more people will come to find me.

TWENTY-TWO
gabriel

LAYLA GOES rigid in the passenger seat and I ignore it, focusing on driving, my hackles raised. Drawing my rage around me at the situation, rage that she's been hurt this way. Rage that all of this leads back to Broderick Stevens somehow, and that makes me responsible.

If I'd managed to catch the fucker responsible for these deaths, then her friend would still be here and Layla wouldn't be fighting to keep it together. She's a hairsbreadth away from shattering and refuses to admit it to herself.

She still says nothing when I pull into the parking lot of my apartment complex and walk around the front of the vehicle, moving quickly. I grab her and swing her out of the seat and into my arms. She takes a halfhearted jab at me which does very little to lighten my mood.

Normally she's got much more fight in her than this, which leads me to believe that she's in shock. Whatever fears she hasn't told me about keep her paralyzed.

There's no better place to take her than mine.

I've got no plan when we make it to the apartment and I click the door shut.

Forget the usual checks. I'm going on a gut feeling that the place is secure as I carry Layla to the shower. Keeping her close, I reach out with the opposite arm to flick the handle on and get the water hot.

By the time I set her on her feet she's stopped shaking, but her eyes are blank and she simply stares at the water.

She's covered in blood and she knows she is. But any spark of life inside her is gone, just as she looked before I took her on the stage the other night. And I know that anything I have to say, she won't hear me. She's not capable of it right now.

It's an even greater risk to peel my own clothes off before I help her out of hers. I let her go only long enough to undo the button on my pants, kick them aside. I follow with the shirt until I'm standing in front of her naked without even the protection of my usual knife.

Her friend's dried blood has stiffened her shirt and makes it difficult to remove. I drop it to the floor, followed by her bra, her pants, her underwear. And without a thought to her nakedness—even the tiny glimpse I allow myself shows small but round breasts, full hips, lush golden skin—I guide her into the shower and step in behind her. She's underneath the spray with her head drooped when I grab the soap and wash her off. Taking the liberty to soap every inch of her hands and arms, her armpits, her legs.

"I'm sorry. I don't have anything for your hair. I'm a simple man."

I run the bar of soap through her hair but she stays silent.

"I'm sorry if it gets tangled," I finished.

The only movement she makes is to reach out to brace a hand against the tile to push back slightly when I start to massage her scalp.

With the shower done and her body clean, I cut off the spray and move to grab a towel for her, dripping across the floor. By the time I turn around Layla is out of the shower, the only move she makes toward my large tub. Her gaze dips down to the porcelain and she runs her fingers over it silently.

A soak.

Yes, I understand.

Without speaking, I turn on the faucet to start filling the tub with hot water.

When it's about a quarter of the way full and steaming, she climbs in and sits with her arms around her knees in the water. Fragile. It's startling to see her this way. She's unwound and the pieces of her scattered. The pieces of whatever mask she cobbled together to cope with her mother's suicide and her father's murder.

It's something no one should have to deal with, not if there's any grace out there. I might say the same for my own upbringing but I've made peace with it.

For the most part.

"I'll leave you to soak. If I can trust you."

She shifts to look at me. "Please. Stay."

It's a lot for her to even ask such a thing. How can I refuse her? It's such an intimate thing, though. I push against my inherent discomfort at getting this close to anyone, let alone a woman. This woman who is so much more than capable of digging her way under my skin and staying there. She'll either compromise me to the point where I never recover or she'll ruin me entirely.

But her lower lip trembles once before she locks it up. And what other choice do I have?

"Gabriel?"

I tune back in and climb into the tub behind her, rubbing her shoulders again because that seemed to help her before.

It's long moments before a coil inside of her seems to snap loose. Layla moves, shifting out her legs to lean back against me. I wrap my arms around her, her back against my chest and my dick snugly pressed to her ass although there's no desire for sex right now.

Only this fucking strange, uncomfortable intimacy.

"I don't have many friends," Layla murmurs. "Even the word *friend* might be a stretch. Taney and Devan were the only people I've had any sort of consistent relationship with, and now she's gone. Where does it leave me?"

I stay silent and trail my fingers along her arms to help dissolve some of the tension.

"She died because she tried to warn me about something. Something about the club." Layla hiccups, swallowing hard over the sound with a vengeance.

"She died because someone shot her. It had nothing to do with you, Layla."

She curls up closer to me. Too small, too delicate. "Everyone I love goes away, Gabriel. They disappear when they're too close to me."

What should I do? How do I help her when I've felt that way all of my life? I've managed to make a life for myself where not only do I not get close to people, but letting them anywhere near becomes a liability.

"Small talk...isn't my thing. But you're wrapped so tight, you're going to get yourself killed hunting down closure to this case, on top of losing your friend."

My fingers wander, of their own volition, and she lets me touch her.

This, I think as I trail a soft touch up to her pubic mound. This I know how to do. This is all I'm good for—a physical relationship.

I trail down her leg to the ankle, massaging lightly before I make my way back up her inner thigh. Spreading her wider to give me better access to her sweet little cunt. She's already wet for me and I work a finger inside of her, crooking it and stroking her inner walls until she moans.

It's a sound of obedience.

One she hardly realizes she's made until it breaks off into a whimper and her muscles clench around me to keep me in place. I slide a second finger in to join the first before stroking against her swollen clit with my thumb.

"Make me come, Gabriel." She's not used to begging. "Please. Finger me, fuck me, make me forget."

I want to so badly.

I shake my head. Taking further advantage of her might be my usual mode, but part of me knows it's unforgivable. "Right now you need rest."

"Unless you trust me to play with my gun and drink, then sex is the only escape I know. I want to escape with you," she murmurs.

Despite my good intentions, I have too little control left. I tighten my circles around her clit to give her a little more friction and time the movement with the thrust of my fingers. She's even wetter now, panting, and a few more strokes has her breathy moan catching and her pussy clamping with her orgasm.

The water has gone cool and both of us shiver as she comes down from the edge. I grip her chin with my opposite hand and gently turn her face to the side to kiss her. I need to taste her. I need to bury myself in her and keep her here with me.

My ability to protect her depends on me being able to keep my reputation. But right now, with her?

I'm just a man. Too scarred on the inside to be anything better than what I am.

Kissing Layla is like opening up a vein and shooting lava into my system.

She is hotter, sweeter, more alive than any kind of drug or alcohol.

I'm used to submissive women bending to my whims and trusting me with their pleasure. Yet there's something about Layla that separates her from the usual type. Maybe because she's fashioned herself as a Dominant. She's never played in the club and only cultivated her individual scene with whatever partners she deemed appropriate.

I've kept to the stage.

Layla is the only Sub I've ever brought back to my home.

Which means something. Something big. But I'm not in any way able to interpret the twisting sensation in my heart at the realization.

I break the kiss and rise slowly to my feet in the tub, towering over her. My dick jerks in anticipation and I'm already hard and dripping precum down the length of me.

She lets me draw her into my arms and carry her to the bed, resting myself between her thighs. There's enough space for her to reach between us and give my dick light strokes. At least the fire is back in her eyes. Whatever had been turned off in the shower, inside of her, is on again.

I draw my hand down her flat stomach to part the folds of her pussy and flick against her clit once again. "You want to be fucked raw, Layla?"

She presses her breasts against my arm. "Come on. Are you chicken? Afraid you can't make me come again with your mediocre cock?"

"Pretty soon I'm going to have to punish you if you keep calling it mediocre."

"Maybe I deserve a little punishment."

I draw my middle finger through her wetness before pressing the finger to her mouth. "Taste yourself and tell me what flavors are there," I demand.

She peels her fingers away from my cock and does as she's told, sucking on my finger. We both know there's nothing mediocre about my cock. Not when her pussy is still clenching with need.

She sucks on me the same way she did my dick and her eyes go molten. "What am I supposed to taste?" she asks. "What answer do you want?"

Anything that will show a little bit of grief has faded from your eyes.

"Just remember your taste now. Because once I fuck you, you're going to taste like *me*. And nothing is going to erase my flavor from your body."

I grab my dick and stroke myself, spreading precum over every inch of me.

Her gaze drops to my erection and she lets out a ragged laugh.

I keep stroking myself as she sucks on my finger, drawing this out. Finally I bring the head of my cock down and slide it through her folds.

Her hands are on my shoulders when I press her back into the mattress with my body.

"Fuck me now, Gabriel."

"Not yet." I pin her in place and arch my hips to rub the

underside of my cock against her clit, thrusting slowly but never going inside of her. She arches closer and I grab one of her legs, hooking it over my shoulder so that she's forced to adjust her hands. The smallest movement and I'll be inside of her.

I'm ready to beg her to stay with me.

And my body does what my mind can't—

"Please, Gabriel. Fuck me."

I drag my cock up her folds. I'm so hard it's difficult to do anything except touch her. Rational thought isn't possible. "I like it when you say please. Even if you aren't obeying. I told you to rest." The head of me nudges at her entrance and she tries to angle herself to force me into her pussy.

She feels safe with me. It's a win. A win to see her let down her guard even a small amount.

Her eyes light and she opens her mouth to no doubt argue with me.

"Your pussy is mine. *You* are mine."

A vicious thrust and my cock is inside her, buried to the base of my length. She tenses, her breath held and her body stretched full.

She takes me to the hilt, and I stop only long enough to give myself the space to drag in a breath before I pull out. Her eyes go wide when I slam home again. Layla's legs wrap around my waist, her hips arched to deepen the contact.

The pace is rough, punishing. Frantic. I wrap my hand around her throat and squeeze gently to remind her that she's here with me.

She's mine.

Whatever fucking happens, in this moment *she's mine*.

Sweat glistens on her skin, drips down my back. Her

nails gouge long claw marks along my shoulders and down my spine.

I tighten my grip around her neck and watch her eyes darken in pleasure. There is only breath and the slap of skin on skin. The two of us together. The muscles of her sweet pussy grip my cock, the friction devastating, pure damnation. The sensation drives me to the point of oblivion. I reach between us, fingering her swollen clit, using her own moisture to keep her lubricated.

Then I drop my head to hers, stealing a kiss. Sliding my hand to her temple, I wrap her hair around my fist to expose her neck and kiss my way there.

"Come inside me."

"Are you sure you want..." I trail off, my balls tightening at the thought of doing exactly that.

"I'm on birth control," she pants as she reaches overhead to grip the headboard and ride out my punishing thrusts. "IUD. You said you were clean. I want to feel you. Fucking come in me, Gabriel. Do it."

As the lady wishes.

I won't say no to her, not when I *want* to shoot my cum all over her insides.

I jerk, my orgasm crashing over me and my dick tensing as I let loose inside her warmth. My balls tighten in the sweetest ecstasy and my eyes roll back, and I'm grunting out my completion.

Later, when she's sleeping, I breathe. Finally really breathe. As if the air is hitting my lungs for the first time in my life.

I might be an asshole and a murderer but this small amount of trust she's placed in me staggers me.

I want to do everything in my power to keep my pledge

to her. To protect her no matter what happens or what price I'll have to pay for it later.

Sleep hits me hard.

Which is surprising, because sleep is always a chase, a hard one, and much harder lately.

Until Layla.

TWENTY-THREE
gabriel

WAKING up with a woman in my arms is new for me.

Not altogether horrendous but a bit uncomfortable. This is my sacred space. The massive bed with dark sheets becomes my safe place when the rest of the world is out of their goddamn minds.

She's delicate in her sleep. Small and insignificant to anyone but me. Instincts I've done my best to demolish rise inside and push to the forefront. Everything about Layla undermines my carefully built life.

I allow myself a few seconds to watch her even breathing. She looks fine, but what will happen when she wakes?

She'll create chaos.

She'll turn the world on its head.

Arms stretching overhead, I suck in a deep breath, filling my lungs and willing my body to wake up. All in a single wave. There is nothing gradual about this. The slight movement wakes Layla and she bolts upright, her hair looking like a rat's nest around her head.

"What time is it?"

"Early. The sun isn't even up." And we're both trained to operate on a deficit when it comes to sleep.

"Doesn't matter. I've got to go. I have a press conference today," she says.

"You don't even know what time it is," I argue, fighting the urge to drag her back to bed and fuck her again. And again.

"Devan will have texted me. Where's my damn phone?" Layla bolts from the bed, standing naked in the room and turning in a circle looking for her shit. "Gabriel—"

"It's probably still in your pocket. Your clothes are in the bathroom. I haven't touched them."

We haven't needed clothes.

She rushes into the bathroom and groans. "Oh my god. Look what you did to my hair. You ruined it."

It's a good thing she's not here to see my grin. I'd get a slap across the face for sure.

"Bed head is a very good look for you, sweetheart."

"Now I'm going to have to fix it. It will take me forever." There's silence for a quick second, probably while she's rooting around for her phone, then an indignant squawk. "Fuck. The press conference is scheduled for ten. Not to mention there's a billion messages from Devan saying I left him at the hospital."

"You've got time."

I lean back into the pillows, staring at the ceiling, my breathing even. Blissfully fucking even.

She comes back into the bedroom holding her clothes between two fingers with a healthy distance between them and her body. Shit. I should have destroyed them. Should have done something other than let myself be distracted because now she's getting a look at her friend's blood in the cold light of day. Dried, brown, stiff.

She avoids looking at them and drops them at the foot of the bed. I assume she's about to roll out another aggressive tongue-lashing, a way to take her mind off the loss, when instead she says, "There's been another murder, you know. Right after we left Docks on Markee the other night. I went back with my partner. This one is a big shot."

I thought it might be hard to take her seriously as she stands there with her breasts jutting out, but even without clothes, she's all business.

"What do you mean, a big shot?" I push into a seated position, the sheets draped over my lower half.

"Senator Wilson's son," Layla replies.

I freeze. The bald man in charge of the drug exchange graduating to murder isn't really a big surprise. But what in the fucking hell was the senator's playboy son doing there?

That raises the stakes too high for comfort.

Layla arches a brow at me. "Are you going to let me go?"

I shake my head to clear my thoughts. "You're a big girl. You know how to handle yourself."

I can't tell if she's disappointed or not.

She moves to the edge of the bed, cat-crawling across the top of the sheets until she's in front of me. Then she drops back to her haunches.

"This...is weird," she admits.

I grunt out a laugh. "You said a mouthful."

"You've told me about your kills that aren't kills."

"You've been more vulnerable," I supply.

She pushes a hand through her mass of dark hair, her eyes soft but wary. "It's not a position I'm used to. It's more than I've done with people before. I'm not really sure how to act and I know I'm going to make a complete fucking mess of things."

"If you think I'll be any better, then you're delusional. My history is a joke, sweetheart."

My heart constricts when she reaches out to place her hand over mine. "The sex was more than sex."

She wants me to say something here, to disagree with her. She's right and we both know it, and still the words get stuck somewhere on their way up my throat because admitting it feels too large for comfort. It feels like a step in a direction where I won't be able to backtrack if necessary. A direction where I'm not in control of anything anymore. Not my life, not my future, not my safety. None of it.

Yet the thought of having sex with anyone else at this point turns my stomach.

She trusts me.

I trust her.

"Hell of a honeymoon phase we're in," I say blandly. "Isn't it?"

She stares at our combined hands and then shoots me a sweet, ethereal smile that I don't trust one bit. Layla flicks her tongue across her bottom lip. "People like us don't get a honeymoon phase. It's unnatural, and pretty soon I'm going to do something to sabotage it whether I know it or not."

"No, we don't get our honeymoon glow, so we have to settle for great sex."

It's a fact of life and one we've both had drilled into us repeatedly by circumstance. It doesn't matter how often you try to fool yourself into expecting good things. The bad always comes to pass. I'm terrified to tell Layla that she might be the only good thing I've had in my life, and this fucked-up combination of the two of us only works because of that. She's just as mental as I am. There's no coming back from that headspace once you're in it.

"What would you do if I asked you not to hold the press conference?" I go out on a limb. "Would you be able to stop it?"

"Why do you want me to stop it?" A simple question.

The fact that she's asking me without flying off the handle says something. I'm not the kind of man who leans into faith, or hope. I know better than to trust that when things are going well they'll stay that way.

And neither of us is fool enough to think that this entire situation won't blow up like a tornado.

"I don't think it will be good for you or your precinct to have Broderick's spotlight on you. And that's exactly what will happen if you go through with this press conference," I tell her, smoothing her hair back from her face.

She shakes her head. "Doubtful I'll be able to do anything. I'm not the one in control of those things and it's going to look suspicious to my captain and chief if I mention it."

Her eyes narrow as she stares at me. The expression on her angular face is open but she's withholding judgment on me. Or my motives.

"A press conference, with these murders, means attention. Attention is never good," I tell her.

Especially when the inner ring wants this quiet. Taken care of under the radar the way things in our world are always done.

I trail a hand through my hair. "Fuck."

I'm falling for her.

That's why I'm nervous. If anything happens to her then I won't be a man anymore. I'll be a beast with nothing but fangs and claws and thirst. I won't stop killing until I get everything back under control.

Neither one of us can stop the press conference since it's already called; I know that. Now I've got to hurry.

"I'll lend you some clothes." I press a brief kiss to the end of her nose before sliding my legs over the side of the bed and heading for the closet. "I like the thought of you wearing my things."

"Oh, like some kind of brand?"

"No, my *cum* inside of you is a brand. I just think you'll be adorable in clothes as big as a circus tent on you."

She blushes sweetly and I release a long deep breath, trying to relax.

"Seems like you're ready to make your escape. Where are you going in such a rush?" she asks.

"You've got crap to handle on your end, and I've got mine." It's a polite way of telling her to let me handle my business, and to trust me to do it.

I throw on a black-on-black ensemble. I'll quickly check the club, to continue my research and try to find something of worth to lessen the blow of the press conference. If I can get ahead of the media attention then the boss will be appeased. Not happy, but there's fuck-all I can do about his mood swings.

If Taney told Layla not to go back to the Velvet Underground, then that is exactly where I'll look first.

Nothing about me screams avenging angel. I'm not about to do something drastic to right the wrongs of Taney's death. But...she meant something to Layla. Something vital.

Whoever fucks with the detective fucks with me now. And I'm not sure which one of us will rain down the worst shit.

My clothes dwarf Layla. She holds her arms out to the

side and the fabric folds around her. "You want me to go out like this?"

I grab her by the ass, dragging her against me and grinding my cock to her front. "You see what you do to me?"

"In these clothes." She's skeptical.

"In any clothes, but I really like you wearing nothing at all."

She lifts on her toes and kisses my chin. "Keep talking like that and you're the one who will need to be punished."

I shoot her a wolf's smile. "You're welcome to try."

"We'll be here all day if I start, and neither of us has the time to spare."

The clothes might be ridiculously big but she strides ahead confidently after I drop her off at her place. The Velvet Underground won't be open yet, not until tonight. Jade will be there regardless. She's always there. Although there's no chance in hell I'll fuck her again, maybe we can come to some sort of different arrangement.

I call her cell while I'm outside and wait for her to answer. She does on the third ring.

"Gabriel." My name is a soft purr on her lips. "To what do I owe the pleasure?"

"Let me in." There's no need to tell her where I am. She's got cameras all over the inside and outside of this place. She would have known about me from the moment I pulled up.

"Have you come to play with me again?" She lets out a string of laughter that feels like claws on my back for all the wrong reasons. The laughter says I had a taste of her and I'm back for more, a cat lapping at cream it can't resist.

"I'm not interested in playing," I growl. "Now open the goddamn door or I'm going to break it down and use your teeth for a new lock."

Jade hangs up on me.

Fucking bitch. In every sense of the word she's a fucking bitch and I've let her get away with acting the part because I enjoy her stage. It gives me the spotlight I need and an outlet on those dark days, those stressed days.

Rather than waiting for her to open the door, I stride forward and I slam the heel of my boot into it. The flimsy lock she has in place gives up the ghost after another kick and soon enough I'm striding down the hallway into the bowels of the Underground.

Jade is more than likely in her office so I take the steps two at a time. This door is open and she's waiting behind her desk with a soft expression. Soft and kind as though she hadn't just hung up on me.

"Gabriel," she says with a smile.

"Cut the shit."

I tether the anger, sliding my hands into my pockets. The knife is there, and at the small of my back is the holster with my gun. Both are at the ready if she decides to make this meeting more difficult than it has to be.

"Tell me about Taney," I start.

"*Taney*." Jade taps her chin with her index finger. "The name isn't ringing a bell. Is she one of your playthings on the stage?"

It's all a game, and the block is Jade's move. Time for me to parry with one of my own.

"It's adorable that you like to act as though you don't know who I'm talking about. Considering she's on your books as an employee."

I see it. The look on Jade's face, the kind a person wears when they're determined not to get caught.

"Is she? We employ a lot of people here and not all of them are noteworthy," she replies.

Delightful.

"If you aren't here to play with me then there is nothing for you right now, Gabriel." She rises to her feet and smooths out the invisible wrinkles of her suit jacket, the glow of the overhead chandelier playing across her bare scalp. "If you change your mind you can find me later."

Not fucking likely.

She must see as much on my face, more transparent than I wish it to be.

Jade snaps her fingers toward someone in the shadows. "Please escort Mr. Blackwell back out to the street. And pick up a new set of door locks while you're at it," she tells him.

Recognition hits me with a punch to the gut when the guy moves into the light, and it takes every bit of presence I possess to keep the surprise from showing. It's the bald man from Markee.

My stomach roils, I feel hot and pissed off, but I hold my hands out in front of me like a shield against Jade. To let her think she's gotten the best of me.

"Fine," I reply smoothly. "I don't want any trouble."

"Trouble is what you look for. You can't fool me."

Her words might be a purr but her tone is cold, harsh.

The drugs are tied to this man. To Jade. And that makes *this* club the connection that didn't make sense before. Not Whip. We shouldn't have been calling the victims hookers. They aren't hookers at all, but Jade's employees.

Fuck me.

The tip from the bartender, Taney being scared...Jade had been at Whip that night as well. Not to enjoy the show but to poach to make up for her dwindling numbers.

Baldie falls into step behind me and maintains a few paces of distance between us. Dammit. Jade is into something and the pieces are only now starting to tumble together. Layla needs to know.

* * *

I flick on the news when I get home, only to see that I've missed the press conference entirely. The news channels are abuzz with the news of the senator's dead son, but no glimpse of Layla outside of a five-second clip where she stares hard-eyed out at the sea of reporters and assures them that the police department is doing their job.

Looking like a dark-eyed goddess straight out of lore.

I grab my cell to send a text to her, when it buzzes with an incoming call.

The boss wants an update.

I click to answer the phone. "I've got a lead," I tell the boss. "The Velvet Underground—"

The boss cuts me off. "I said to make this go away. Didn't I?"

"Yes, sir."

A pause and then, "Well, a press conference where the police mentions our lighters as a prominent piece of evidence, plus a politician's dead son...it isn't just going to go away." His voice is silky and venomous as a snake.

"I have it handled," I assure him immediately.

"I'm not so sure you do."

I swallow over a groan. "Don't insult me. I've been your best man for years."

"Which may be true, but this is taking too long. Time is money, Blackwell. Right now you're not worth what I'm paying you."

"I've got it covered. I'm not sure what else you want me to say."

"Not say, but do. Find out what the detective on this case knows and then eliminate the threat."

The phone clicks and I freeze.

What the fuck does that mean?

But I know. The sick burning sensation in my chest tells me that I know exactly what it means, especially when the phone beeps again and dread fills me. The text comes from a burner phone, a number that sends only names. Names of the hits I'm required to make.

And my body goes numb and my heart cold when I read the name I never thought would cause such a violent reaction in me. At the one name I'd hoped, prayed to an unforgiving god I'd never read. *Layla Sinclair.*

TWENTY-FOUR
layla

ALL THROUGH MY shower at home, I think about Taney.

She died to keep me safe. Someone wanted her mouth closed permanently. When emotion threatens to swamp me, I drop my head to the tiles. If I hadn't had the press conference today, I'd have gone straight to the club, even though it meant she'd died to warn me for nothing.

Not for nothing.

And lying to myself won't help.

Really, if I didn't know deep in my gut that Gabriel is headed to the Velvet Underground, I'd skip the press conference and go myself.

But he will. Without saying anything, he'll go, and he'll get answers.

Finally I cut the water off and start mentally and physically preparing myself for the press. I don't give a shit how my hair looks on an average day but this is different. This reflects on the entire precinct, the chief, and Captain Ashcroft.

It's time to don the only type of battle armor I'll be allowed to have.

The woman in the mirror is familiar only in that the shape of the face is the same. My normally golden skin tone has taken on a pale quality, the purple bruising beneath my eyes giving away that I haven't slept for shit.

If not for Gabriel—

I slam my palm down in the middle of the mirror. Trusting him with anything except my body is a mistake. I've got to convince myself of that fact because otherwise... I'm at risk. In more ways than one. And after Taney's death I'm on the edge of shattering beyond repair.

This is for her, I assure myself as I get dressed.

Closing this case will bring justice not only for her but for all the other poor women mowed down before her.

Thinking of work keeps me centered, grounded, able to push the grief aside enough to make it down to the station. The heels are a little uncomfortable and the arches of my feet ache a bit with each step toward the elevator. A pair of tight black slacks toe the line between business and pleasure, dark eyeliner slicked over my eyelids and my shirt a deep purple.

Shoulders thrust back and spine straight. Professional Layla.

Not a hint of heartbreak on display.

A text from Devan tells me he's already here. The elevator doors open with a ding and I step out into the hallway leading to the 9th precinct bullpen. Noise and the scent of stale coffee greet me.

And then—

"Oh *wow*, Sinclair. Who would have thought *you* could actually look decent?"

The disgusting jab is only the first of many from the

low-life men on the force. They come at me in a never-ending wave somehow disguised as banter.

"Sure. I never dress this way. Like it's a big fucking deal?"

Jerry slow-claps for me and stands up from behind his desk, the ends of his mustache bristling. "Sexy," he says. "You're going to be the new face of the force? 'Bout time you show off that body."

"If you don't stop dicking around then I'm going to file a sexual harassment suit against all of you," Devan threatens. He strides around the corner with a cup of coffee in his hand. "And don't think I won't do it. I'm so sick of your mouths."

I shoot him a grateful smile and head in his direction. Devan is about the only man who most of the guys in here will listen to. Even Jerry listens, grudgingly enough, because none of them wants to get on my partner's bad side. I stifle a chuckle at the way several of the younger detectives look, as though they might piss themselves.

Taney.

My mood sobers quickly.

"Harass her again and you're done. Am I clear?" Devan barks. "Piss-poor behavior for cops. For men."

Properly chastised, although a boot to the ass would be better for them, the room settles as much as the guys and gals are able to settle.

Still, I'm grateful.

Devan waits until I drop down in my chair, hissing out a breath at the ache in my feet, before he shifts over, his arms on either side of my chair to keep me from going anywhere. "Are you okay?" he asks. "You disappeared on me."

I want to tell him the truth, that I've never been okay. Instead I force myself to grin at him. "I'm holding up as well as I can." It's the truth even if it isn't the whole of it. "I couldn't stay in the hospital. After the surgeon gave me the news, Gabriel...he got me out of there."

I won't tell him how many times I've spent reading and re-reading the last text string with Taney this morning or the giant hole she leaves behind in my life. She was always a bright light, there and suddenly extinguished.

Devan will understand if I tell him, of course. We've all had to deal with loss at some point in our lives.

"You should have taken some time off. You didn't have to be the one to take on this press conference. You're holding up, but sooner or later you're going to break," he continues. "No one will blame you if you decide to skip out today. Ashcroft will agree."

"I'll break on my own time. This conference is part of the job and we both know it." I silently beg him to drop the subject.

"Doesn't make it any less my responsibility than yours." Devan groans, releasing his hold on my chair to settle himself on the desktop. He blinks, swallowing his surprise when I reach for his cup of coffee, forgotten next to my computer, and take a sip. "This is still my case. Let me do it for you."

"I've already made some concessions lately with letting someone take care of me," I whisper. "It's my turn now."

Devan shakes his head. "You're not responsible for saving the world, L."

My lips quirk. "Not the world. Just you. And Taney." *I failed on one of those counts.*

I glance at the clock and push out of the chair, forcing down my nerves. I've barely left myself enough time today but the press will already be waiting in the conference room, the captain and the chief with them.

"I'm fine." I smooth my hands down the front of my shirt. "Don't I look fine?"

"You look like shit."

"It's all a part of my technique. Stay here. Keep working on digging through the evidence."

He rounds his eyes at me. "Are you fucking serious? I'm not going to stay here."

"Yeah. Like I said, I have this covered. Do this for me, please, Dev?" I pat him on the hand before making my way down the hallway, my chest hollow. Good thing I had time on the drive over here to think about how I want to play this gig today.

By the time I round the small dais amid the shouting of reporters and incessant flashing of bright lights, I have everything under control, myself included. The familiar anger is back and burning at a low simmer in my gut.

Anger at everything I've lost and the fucking unfairness of this whole thing.

It's a simple matter to keep the spotlight on me, literally and metaphorically. Yes, that's right, I'm the lead in this case. No, I'm working it alone for personal reasons. I'm the only one following leads connected to the senator's son. What about my partner? Bogged down on other cases. Too busy to help me with this.

A flick of my hand has several of the other officers ringing the stage stepping into place to keep Devan from swooping in from where he watches, struggling to understand.

"Detective Sinclair!" One of the reporters fights his way out of the crowd with his hand raised. "Are you having trouble managing this case on your own? Considering the high-profile nature of your latest victim, it stands to reason you'd want as much help as you can get."

I harden my heart, shake my head. "I'm having absolutely no trouble. I'll bring in resources when necessary, but at this point it's all procedure. There is a step by step process to gathering and examining evidence. Rest assured the killer will be captured and brought to justice. Our hearts go out to the friends and family of Senator Wilson. Empire Bay has suffered a devastating loss."

I refuse to give Devan any credit in this case for one simple reason: There's a murderer out there and I can't let another person die. I need to make sure when the gun points at someone, it's me alone. If I keep his name out of the media, we might have a chance of making it out alive.

Devan is waiting in the wings by the time I conclude the press conference and leave Captain Ashcroft to answer any further questions. My partner takes one look at my face before falling silently into step at my side.

"I know what you're doing." His voice is gruff, pained. "And why you didn't run it by me before you went out there."

I shake my head. "I'm sorry."

I've been apologizing a lot lately. And it's never really bothered me before, when I take the lead this way, but it does now.

"You're lucky I don't care about any of that shit."

He seems to get it. I hope he gets it.

"Good."

"What I care about is what you just did to yourself. You're staring down the barrel of a gun alone, Layla. I know things are bad, but are they bad enough to make you want to die?" He asks the question simply.

My cell suddenly weighs a thousand pounds in my pocket. Rather than going through Taney's messages again,

I head to the computer and gesture for Devan to sit down beside me.

"Right before someone shot her, Taney told me not to go to the club anymore. Gabriel is on his way there right now, but it's all connected. She found something, learned something. I think we might be headed for a big break."

Devan pulls up close to me, our voices dropped low so none of the others will overhear. "You've been going to those clubs for ages. You ever suspect anything fishy?"

I've never appreciated his all-business attitude more than I do now.

I shoot him a look. "Do you think I would have let Taney stay there if I thought she'd get hurt? She was a Momma Bear to the end."

"I remember when the Velvet Underground used to be a strip club. Back when you were a kid."

Sure, like he's so much older than me.

"Who ran it then?"

Devan scratches his scalp. "Same woman, I think. Jade something?"

My stomach does a nasty flip. "Well, then she's much older than she lets on. And has been doing this a long time."

So what am I missing?

"Did you have any run-ins with her?" Devan asks. He retrieves his pad and pen from the pocket of his coat and starts to jot down notes on an empty page.

"Nothing. Not from anyone there." I type the name of the club into our encrypted browsers but nothing comes up. No records, no news articles. Which is shocking to me. There should be something on here if she's been in business so long.

I grab the cell to shoot off a quick text to Gabriel, only to stop, a little gob-smacked at how natural it feels to want his opinion on this.

He's always at the club.

He's got to know more about Jade than any of the other people working there. He's one of their star performers. And I've seen the way she looks at him: She wants him. If anyone will be able to dig up dirt on the bitch, it's Gabriel.

Devan is eyeing me sharply, as though he knows more about what's going on than I do. "You need to keep digging," he tells me.

I blow out a breath. "Of course I'm going to keep digging. What do you think this is? My first rodeo?"

"Wow." He rolls his eyes at me. "You're funny when you're in love."

His statement almost knocks me out of my socks. "And you, my fine friend, need to get the fuck out of here with that kind of talk."

"It's the guy, isn't it? Gabriel. The one who showed up at the park the other day." Devan looks like he thinks he deserves to win a prize.

"You mean yesterday?"

"It doesn't matter when. You're arguing semantics with me. Which says everything I need to know." He leans back and laces his fingers behind his head. Looking as at ease as he would if we were on a tropical beach vacation.

"You're absolutely out of your mind." And yet I am intimately aware of everything he's telling me, just as I am whenever I think about Gabriel. "Now quit prying into my personal life and get back to work, my shadow partner. I really can't do this without you."

He salutes me and Devan and I both do our separate research to dig up dirt on the sex club. Eventually my eyes burn and I've got to push away from the desk to stretch.

"I just need a minute."

He nods, too deep in focus, and I head to the bathroom. No, not bathroom. *Caffeine.* Lots and lots of caffeine, because my lack of sleep and that damn press conference gave me one monster of a headache.

Car keys in hand, I course-correct and head to the elevators, stopping only to press the button that will take me to the parking garage.

The doors slide open with a ding and Adam pops his head out, his eyes widening when he sees me. "Oh, shit. Layla." He clears his throat, the sound devolving into a mild coughing fit. "I'm sorry!" His eyes are watering now. "I was on my way to find you."

"You were looking for me?"

"Yeah. I've got info on the leaks."

Well, shit. I grab his arm, hauling him into one of the interrogation rooms and shutting the door behind us, making sure none of the speakers are on. "Do you think you can announce it a little louder? Fuck."

Adam looks sheepish. "I'm sorry."

"I don't want your apologies. You've got information? Show me."

He bobs his head. "I can show you. Sure. No problem." He grabs his cell. "I've got a VPN and some heavy-duty anti-tracking software on this baby," he tells me. He pulls up a screen. "There is definitely no firewall issue that I found during my search and no hacks from the outside. There isn't even an interrupt in connectivity in the weeks since you came into this case. Look."

He shows me a spreadsheet with the information he's compiled. "Can you put it in a language I'll understand?"

"I'm, ah—" Adam breaks off and sweat practically rolls down his face.

He might be nervous but there's no way he's messed this up.

"The leak came from the inside," he whispers.

My blood goes cold. I have enough wherewithal left to clap him on the shoulder. "Good work."

Adam blushes, the color at stark odds with his paleness, and once again I'm grateful for his brains even though I'd never be able to work one on one with anyone this jumpy.

"I've got to tell my partner, but damn good job, Adam."

Gabriel needs to know, too. *My two partners*. One in crime and one working for the law. The killer we're both looking for has a person on the inside here. Or *people*. Who knows how many have been undermining me from the get-go?

Back in front of the elevator, I slam my finger into the button, waiting for its arrival. It's taking too damn long. The stairs. One floor down. I pull open the handle and run right into Clint.

He smiles at me. "It's really too bad you're such a bitch to everyone," he starts. "On camera, you're a fine prize."

"Maybe you didn't hear Devan's threat earlier, little one." I caress his cheek and end with a hard tap. "Say something stupid again like Jerry is training you to do and you'll be sorry."

I push past him, heading into the stairwell.

Suddenly pain explodes along the back of my head, intense enough for me to lose my breath and see black dots dancing.

Then there's nothing but darkness.

TWENTY-FIVE
layla

SWIMMING up out of unconsciousness is no picnic when pain waits for me at the surface.

I come to and the agony in my head is immediate, throbbing from every square inch of my skull, and my heartbeats are too loud. Too heavy. The dizziness isn't unexpected but the chill and the dry mouth are.

Not to mention the ropes keeping me tied to a chair.

Again, not the first time I've woken up tied to a chair.

It is a first, however, for me not to remember how the fuck I got here. I remember the press conference, and doing research with Devan. A need for coffee...

Talking to the IT geek... Thinking about Gabriel...

What happened between then and now?

I peel my eyes open and blink away the grit. This is not the same basement where I'd last woken up with the chair routine. Nowhere close.

The scent of mold, mildew, and dust attacks my nostrils, which leads me to believe I'm somewhere close to the docks. Water damage on the wooden beams supporting the floor above me. Ahead, the open expanse of the warehouse throws every small sound back to me amplified. The dingy windows allow only the smallest slats of weak sunlight through, enough for me to recognize the dust on the concrete floor.

The pieces click together too slowly for my own good.

I'm back at the abandoned Docks on Markee. Sure enough, if I crane my head to the point of breaking my own neck, I can make out the faint blood trail where the senator's son had been dragged. From this vantage point it's almost impossible to see where the crime scene techs had set up, though.

The realization has me tugging against the ropes on my wrists and ankles hard, the rough fibers biting down into my skin with each movement.

"Fucking what the hell?" I groan. My voice is a low garble of sound, my throat raw.

Even speaking hurts.

"I should have had my way with you while I could. Regrets are wasted, though."

The voice registers from the left and I freeze. *Shit*. I hadn't realized anyone was here. I should have.

Out of the shadows stalks Clint, wearing the look I only caught him revealing once. Cold, calculating, the sort of dead-behind-the-eyes deal you expect from a tortured soul. Now the expression is a permanent part of him, etched into his features, and I wonder how hard it must have been for him to pretend otherwise.

He's not the pretty boy new kid right now. I'm not sure if he ever was. How long has he been pretending?

Now I'm staring at a fucking monster.

I force myself to stay calm. "Talking about rape. Very big of you." I jerk my wrist. "How about you untie me?"

He shrugs, his hands in the pockets of his jacket and his

badge still hooked to his belt loop. He'd been at the press conference today, standing with the other officers and watching me give my talk.

"You're not hard on the eyes," he replies. "Especially when you're all made-up. Not to mention how good it would feel to teach you a lesson." There's no inflection in his voice anymore. Not a hint of feeling in the way he speaks or stares at me.

"With your cock? You're a real original, Clint. May I call you Clint? Or would you prefer something like *Asshole*? I'm open to new nicknames." I tug at the ropes again and find them holding firm and tighter than before.

Does anyone know I'm here?

Clint must have used something on me to get me to pass out. Did he move me from the precinct on his own?

"I'd prefer it if you call me *Sir*." His smirk heats and he takes a step forward, hands still in his pockets although there's movement under the fabric of his dress pants, closest to said cock. I suppress a shudder, my stomach roiling sickly at the thought of Clint touching himself in front of me.

"Sorry. I've only been Dommed by one person. I'm not in a real rush to repeat the experience. Certainly not with you." I flash my teeth at Clint.

"Oh yes, I heard about your little performance at Whip."

His words cut right through me and leave frost behind in my blood.

"Heard you got fucked raw onstage. Wish I'd been there to see it for myself," he muses. "I always thought you'd be much happier after swallowing a good dick."

If he comes near me with his, then I'm going to bite it off.

Clint recognizes the thought—I'm too stressed to keep it from showing on my face, I guess—but rather than backing off, he comes closer still. "You just don't get it, Sinclair. None of you get it." He draws a gun out of his holster and points it at me as he flicks the safety off. My insides freeze. "There's no good way to *be* somebody in this town. You can either be a god or a devil. There's no middle ground."

"I'm not sure what I have to do with any of that," I reply slowly.

I've never been good in hostage situations.

My temper gets the best of me and I lose my cool even in training, so my bosses have never let me actually engage in a real-life situation.

Except now it's *my* life on the line, and I'm trying to talk down a psychopath with a gun pointed between my eyes.

Clint sucks on his teeth. "Oh, Layla."

I fucking hate the way he says my name.

"Let me guess," I continue. "It's too hard to be a god, so you decided to go in the opposite direction. You probably have some kind of sob story to accompany the decision, too. That or you've got a serious lack of a work ethic. Did I get it this time, Clint?"

His grip on his gun doesn't falter. He's as steady as I've ever seen him. "Working for Jerry is like working for a goddamn clown. I needed more." Something in those words begs me to understand his motivations.

So Clint is our leak on the inside. Our mole. Christ, I'm stupid if it's taken me this long to get the full understanding of the picture. Clint is connected to the bald man; that's why he's brought me here to this place. He's been the one feeding information about the case to whoever he decided to work for on the wrong side of the law.

"You're dealing drugs?"

He shrugs. "The offers rolled in and I snagged them." Clint crouches in front of me, the gun pressed to my knuckles. He rubs the metal across my skin in a sick mockery of a lover's caress. "I like the merchandise anyway. Why not deal and get high whenever I want? It's a winning situation from all sides."

"So, what, I'm the leverage for you to have a bigger *in* with your low-life drug dealer?"

Clint stops rubbing the gun on me, his eyes darting up to meet mine. He clucks his tongue. "I don't need leverage. I've been with my real people the whole time. All I needed to do was share information here and there. Pathetically easy. You're going to be a bonus. I'll get you out of the way before you become an issue."

"You are such a piece of shit." I spit in his face, the globule landing on his cheek. Clint waits a beat before he wipes it away with his sleeve. My voice drops to a hissed warning. "Let me out of here and I won't kick your ass into the next state."

How stupid am I to have let my guard down around him for even a second. I brushed Clint off as a rookie because he always seemed content to stay in Jerry's shadow. He might have made a snide retort here or there but he never stepped a foot out of line before.

I never looked into him because he never gave me a reason to suspect him.

A perfect position.

And Adam *just* told me the breach came from inside. Rather than using the information to keep myself safe, even in the brief moments since learning the information, right on cue I'd turned my back on Clint.

I struggle against the ropes but the ties are so much

better than I'd have given him credit for. "How did you do it, anyway?" I want to know.

Clint tilts his head to the side and studies me. "Do what?"

"Pass a fucking drug test to even get this far."

He stares at me with surprise sliding over his features at my question. "You'd be surprised at the number of tricks you can pick up if you're observant enough." He rises up to his full height. He's got more than a few inches on me on a good day, but none of that matters.

None of this is a fair fight.

Clint knows better than to untie me.

"A dig at me. Nice one."

"I've had a few saved." He doesn't look particularly concerned at the murderous intent I shoot his way. "You never let anyone get a word in edgewise, Layla. You're always too busy running your mouth. Do you have any idea how many times I thought about shutting you up, one way or another?" He tightens his grip on the gun. "I can finally see what those lips can do."

Just fucking shoot me, then.

"They suck off better men than you," I snap back.

His eyes take on a glint I know better than to ignore. "Did I strike a nerve with you? You're confident for a woman about to suck off the end of a gun." He opens his mouth to say more but the warehouse door bangs open.

My heart gives a thud when Gabriel strolls toward us. Relief is a living beast in my blood until his approach slows. He gives me the barest minimum acknowledgement before running an unimpressed look over Clint from head to toe.

What is he doing here?

"Speak," he barks out. But not to me.

Clint shakes his head and straightens, fumbling with

his gun all of a sudden. Gabriel has that effect on people. "She was about to uncover me and compromise the Black Market Syndicate. I, ah, I let the others know she's here as well. I'm sorry if I overstepped, but since there's a hit on her now anyway, I figured I'd save you the trouble and bring her here."

His words snap me out of my shocked stupor. "Wait." I pull against the ropes. "A fucking hit? There's a hit out on me?"

Gabriel never told me.

He never said a word that I'm on his list. Betrayal replaces any ounce of joy at his arrival. I am dead now. And I know it.

He makes no move to untie me. "What did you tell them?" he asks Clint. "When you checked in?"

"That I'd called you in to take care of her."

"Was she armed?"

"Of course." Clint lets out a hiss of laughter. "To the teeth. I even took her shoes because I figure she'd stab an eye out with those toothpick heels."

Clint pulls my gun out of the back of his pants and hands it off to Gabriel.

Who takes the gun, gives the piece a once-over, and then wastes no time before shooting Clint twice in the chest and once in the head. The world slows again as the rookie crumples, his knees smacking pavement and blood leaking from each bullet hole before he collapses on his back.

My mind spins.

Slowly Gabriel lowers the gun.

"You came for me. You actually fucking came for me." I allow myself a small, hopeful grin.

He really is here to help. But he's quiet, and he's staring

at the corpse. His lips are a thin bloodless line. Finally Gabriel moves toward me. The sound of cars approaching cuts off all but my pulse. Doors shut outside.

His eyes are cold. So much colder than I remember.

Even colder than the first time he had me tied up.

"Gabriel?"

His name is a plea. One I know will go unanswered when instead of loosening my bindings, he makes them tighter.

TWENTY-SIX
gabriel

FUCKING CLINT.

Fucking doped-up mole pussies who think they know better than anyone else. He sent out an alert to everyone and left me no maneuvering room. Left me no time to figure a way out of this bullshit. Layla and I are well and truly fucked now.

Broderick and Horn-Rimmed were only a few beats behind me, their cars already trailing mine when I pulled into the shady alley between Docks on Markee and its neighboring building. Another car door slams from the outside.

Too late.

I'm too late.

Layla is still, her eyes widening in surprise, and I'm not able to stomach how she looks at me as I tighten the ropes.

"What are you doing?" She struggles against me. "Gabriel? What are you—"

I press the gun to her lips with deadly intent. "If you want to stop our play, darling, then you're going to have to use the safe word. Otherwise, you'll keep your mouth shut until I tell you otherwise."

Let her put the pieces together. She had never given me the safe word before we went onstage and I'd taken care of her. How do I get her to trust me now without giving myself away?

"You're not my fucking Dom," she spits out around the muzzle.

Right as the footsteps grow louder and the boss walks into the warehouse.

There is no good way to play this. Not with the countdown starting and so many things hinging on this moment. I pocket Layla's gun and reach out to grab the one from Clint's lifeless hand.

There is also no way we are getting out of here alive if I let her go right now. And instead of trusting me to make these kinds of decisions on the fly...Layla is livid. She should be.

It's smarter to be. I just hope she somehow finds her way to understanding through the haze of fury.

I have to fight back a dark chuckle. I'm a killer and I've proved it right in front of her. But I've also proven that I'll never hurt her. *Come on, sweetheart, put it together!*

"Well. You've beaten us here."

Broderick steps around the corner with his eyebrows raised and Horn-Rimmed at his side. This is the dark god who rules the underworld, except he's got the kind of face one skips over in a crowd. Despite his reputation, he's nothing but a fit middle-aged man with a slender build and masculine features. Today he's wearing a dark suit with a bright blue button-up shirt.

"I made good time," I tell him, nodding my head at Horn-Rimmed.

"Clint called us to say he had a surprise. I certainly never expected to find my little detective friend here." Broderick is baiting me. Especially when he pauses to laugh, rich and deep.

Letting me know that Clint captured my mark for me before I had a chance to get to her.

"She's not yours." I force myself to grin. "But I've got her restrained. She broke free. Fucking killed this loser." I kick the bottom of Clint's shoe for emphasis. Ignoring the hard lump lodged in my chest and pointedly ignoring Layla. "He's not as useful as you thought."

Horn-Rimmed sets his briefcase down on the floor and he and Broderick circle Layla like vultures.

"This pretty little thing has caused quite a lot of trouble for us," my boss croons.

I fucking hate the way he's looking at her.

"I'm not a thing," she snaps. "And fuck you."

"This idiot thought he was a killer just because he squeaked out info from the inside," I add as though she never spoke. "You want something done right? Here we are. He might have got her, but he made a mess of things."

Layla has gone stone cold. Rigid. Watching us. "Fucking bastards. All of you. You're going to get what's coming to you if it's the last thing I do."

I need her to stay quiet. She'll jeopardize everything I'm doing if she runs her mouth, and right now she's too pissed at me to even think things through.

"Careful with your words, sweetheart. Haven't you learned anything at this point? Talk is cheap and you're not in a position to pay up." I laugh.

The laughter only incenses her.

Layla lunges against the ropes and spews off a string of obscenities that makes me proud.

I rip off a piece of Clint's shirt and slide it around her head like a gag. She jerks, fighting me every inch of the way, her glare making it no secret she wants my head.

I say nothing as I shove the fabric between her lips. She gnashes at me and almost takes off part of my index finger.

Spitfire.

Warrior woman.

I'm going to get us out of this.

I read everything in her hateful gaze. It's the absolute opposite of the expression she made in bed last night, falling asleep in my arms. That hint of openness so foreign that it took us both by surprise.

Good, I think, as the boss steps beside me, his face hard. On one hand it really is good because she's going to need to learn to be more careful.

Except a large part of me hates to be the cause of such a fucking stupid lesson. She's already been through too much already. We both have. When do people like us get a break?

When do we get our happily ever afters?

Never.

Except damn me because the brief time I've spent with Layla got me thinking about it. Hoping for it.

I'm too damned for that kind of deal, and this is only a reminder.

The best I can hope for is to find a way to get her out of this. Then she'll be free of me. Free of the quagmire.

I'll think about it all once I get her out of here. No matter how quickly Broderick might try to strike, I'll be faster.

Horn-Rimmed stares at Layla like he's trying to determine where to start on her. "I haven't gotten to play in the field in a while," he tells me. "Or watch you at work."

"Which would you gentlemen prefer? To get in some

hits of your own or to watch what other info she might share with the right persuasion?" I'm careful to keep my tone neutral, to keep any sort of inflection from showing.

But it helps that Broderick pays me no mind. His attention remains on Layla. It takes every ounce of self-control to remain standing in place when the boss smiles and approaches her. He drags his thumb along her lower lip, the shirt fabric tied tightly across the seam of her mouth. Right before he rears back and punches her square on the cheek.

I lose my breath.

The knot in my throat drops painfully down to my stomach as heat spreads along every portion of my being. The boss lands several more punches to her face and her gut. Layla says nothing but tears form at the corners of her eyes and she's gone pale. He hit her hard enough to knock the breath out of her, and inside I'm roaring for him to stop.

Fighting the urge to run forward and throw up an arm to protect her.

The room grows smaller around me because that asshole has one hell of a force behind his fists. He'll do some serious damage to her. He rears back several inches before slamming his knuckles into her stomach.

Layla lets out a wheezing exhale.

She wavers in the chair, slumping forward.

I have no choice but to keep watching, sick to my stomach in a way that violence has never made me before.

But it's too dangerous a game to cave now. The most dangerous I've played and I've got to stay stoic. If we go too far…

It's the small measure of relief I allow myself. If this goes too far, I'll kill the boss and his lackey. It will mean my own death and I'm not sure if I can protect Layla once I go that route.

Broderick is fast. He slams again into the much smaller woman like a fucking truck.

I've never hated him before but I hate him now.

The boss finally stops and leans back, gathering some of Layla's blood on his finger and smearing it against his own mouth. He's out of breath, grinning like a fool.

"Your turn, Blackwell," he tells me. "Show me what you've got. Why you're paid the big bucks."

Christ. Pushing aside every instinct telling me to gut him right here, I step in front of Layla. Not allowing her to see the apology she deserves before I punch her in the side. My knuckles dig into soft skin and ribs. I know I can't hold back.

Two hits, then three.

I'm sorry. I'm so sorry, love.

She'll never forgive me for this. I'm not sure I'll ever be able to forgive myself.

I swing a left hook into her side several inches lower than where Broderick punched her and she lunges forward with a curse.

The fabric stifles her pained groan.

Time slows down.

I pull her up close after the fourth hit and grip the chair in my hands. She's struggling to draw breath through the fabric in her mouth, her chest heaving and her eyes dull with pain. "Piece of shit cops like you make me sick," I force myself to say, my jaw clenched.

Using my body as a shield, I hurry to loosen the knot at her right wrist. So subtly I don't even think she knows what I've done. Right before I tilt the chair with her in it, letting it drop sideways and slam down to the floor. Her skull cracks against the cement and bounces slightly.

"Don't you know there's nothing good in this world to

fight for? Why even try?" I ask her, hoping my performance is convincing.

"Enough." Horn-Rimmed slashes his arm sideways through the air. "I've seen enough."

Layla is bloodied. The skin beneath her left eye is already swollen and red. A few more hours and she'll have one hell of a shiner. The gash on her cheek will need to be tended where I've split it open and I wouldn't be surprised if some of Broderick's punches to her torso result in cracked ribs.

Forgive me.

"I've got more for you," I tell them.

Broderick, that bastard, just grins. "Spill."

Information. Their favorite currency.

"The real thorn in your side is Jade, the owner of the Velvet Underground. She knows that I know she's involved in whatever shit is jeopardizing our operation. My guess? She's been trying to establish a rival drug circuit. She's the one we want," I reply, wiping my bloody knuckles on the front of my pants.

My boss cracks his neck. "Then I guess you know what to do," he says.

"What do we do with her?" Horn-Rimmed asks, gesturing to Layla.

Broderick laughs before he turns to me. "Gabriel knows. We don't have to ask those kinds of questions."

There's no room to breathe. They're leaving her fate in my hands. It's too soon for me to breathe yet. Too soon to think I've won any inch of ground.

"I'll let her bleed a little longer before I take care of things here."

My boss laughs again and his lackey picks up the briefcase as they head outside together. "She won't be any more trouble now," the latter finishes.

I don't relax until I hear the sound of doors slamming and vehicles driving away. We're almost out of this. One more step and then comes the hardest part: getting Layla to accept a new arrangement, as if I haven't just demolished every inch of hard-won trust between us.

TWENTY-SEVEN
layla

"BUT DADDY!"

"Count up to 100, my girl, and time me. I'll be back before you're done."

My father's voice fades in my head and the silence of the open warehouse is welcoming. The cool floor sends shivers through my beaten body and the pain is a dull and constant throbbing. My face feels like I've pressed it into a meat grinder and gone to town.

Holy shit.

My teeth feel loose and I swipe my tongue along first the top row and then the bottom, tangling with the cloth. Breathing hurts, my lungs feel shriveled, my tongue swollen two sizes too large...

I've had the crap beaten out of me before. It happens when you just can't care about your personal safety. I've gotten into plenty of arguments before, not only at the gym but with people involved in my cases, suspects I've interviewed who don't take kindly to me getting in their faces.

I've run after suspects on the street and tackled them, only to have them turn around and retaliate.

Nothing compares to what I just endured.

Being beaten by Gabriel and his boss is in a league of its own. Broderick's ham-handed fists are lethal. He knows exactly where to hit to inflict the most damage with the least amount of effort on his part. I'd fare better being punched with a fucking piece of marble. At least Gabriel pulled his punches—I think—but only by a tiny fraction. Had to be convincing, right? Yeah, my aching ribs disagree.

I jerk, my muscles spasming as my entire system fights against the need to shut down. I'm distantly aware of the voices around me, before the sound of footsteps fade as they walk toward the exit. Broderick Stevens, the leader of the Black Market Syndicate...

What cop wouldn't give their badge for a shot at bringing him down?

He had me here, stared at me like I was an ant trapped beneath a magnifying glass.

Yet as terrifying a picture as he presents, he left me behind with his favorite reaper, struggling against the stars dancing behind my closed eyes. All Gabriel's talk about a safe word...would he have actually stopped if I'd tried to say anything? Doubtful.

Sucking in deep breaths that leave my nose burning and my ribs feeling like hot pokers, I twitch, stretching my fingers, my arms. And unless I miss my guess, my right wrist is moving more than it was before. It's almost like the rope—

It's no mistake. The rope is loose. Somewhere along the line the knot must have come undone. I squirm, jerking and shifting under the binds. My body refuses to cooperate with me and then I move the wrong way, the pain blinding. Bruised ribs. I know the feeling. Hopefully nothing is broken.

If not, it's a small miracle and at this point I have to take what I can get.

The only thing broken here is my fucking pride for trusting someone I knew better than to involve myself with in the first place. Something in my chest tightens and I refuse to believe it has anything to do with my heart. Because I don't get attached to men. *Ever.* Especially not assholes like Gabriel who show their true colors when it's least expected.

The next wave of fire in my torso steals the air out of my lungs but I manage to get my wrist free.

Or at least the knot loosened. A glance up at Gabriel reveals him staring in the direction the men had gone. I pivot the chair as slowly as possible to not make noise as I reach for the tie around my left wrist, then both ankles.

There has to be something close by that I can use to defend myself.

From him.

From the only man I've ever—

No. Distractions, it's only distractions to mentally punish myself more.

He'll be fucking sorry for this.

The bindings loosen completely and I hold back a groan. Clint has to have another piece on him somewhere. I'm sure of it. None of us goes around without at least one hidden sidearm. Where would he have stashed it? If I can get to him, if I can somehow find it, it will be a small nugget of power in my favor.

I scoot closer to the body and grit my teeth against a swell of agony. Car doors slam outside. I hope Gabriel is distracted. He's listening intently, it appears, and then comes the sound of engines revving, then fading into the distance.

What am I waiting for? I should have used the noise to mask any I might make. Maybe there's still time—

A quick glance at him shows he's turned back around, his eyes on me. He doesn't say anything.

He only bends to grab Clint beneath the arms and slide the body across the warehouse, around a pillar and out of sight, where I most definitely can't reach it.

The room tilts, wavering like heat rays in the distance. I'm trying not to move when he comes back. I can't give anything away to let him know that I'm free of my bonds, so I grip the chair hard while he pulls the chair back to its upright position with me in it.

Gabriel slides a hand across my face, pushing hair out of my eyes with a tender touch. He drags the fabric away from my mouth and I catch a glimpse of it, soaked in my blood.

"Did you enjoy the show?" I ask him. My split lip pulses painfully with each movement. "I'm not sure if you like fucking or killing more. Which one is your favorite? I'd love to know."

His silence enrages me.

"If you don't—"

"Shut up, Layla," he grunts. He runs a hand over his face, the annoying superiority back in his tone. "Just shut up. Okay?"

It almost seems like he's waiting for something. What?

He glances over his shoulder, his face strained. He's still distracted. Which means it's my time to shine. I seize the opportunity, dropping the loosened ropes from around my arms and legs and falling out of the chair sideways. Toward the side where Gabriel tucked my gun into his pants. I manage to fumble it out from the waistband and train it on him in the next breath.

The chamber loading echoes through the vast space.

He slowly shifts to stare at me, unfazed.

"Don't think I won't do it." Shit, my voice trembles. My fingers do the same. I'm always so steady but this man unnerves me. "I'll fucking make you pay for what you did to me."

"You think I'm clueless?" he says. "Who do you think untied the first knot?"

I tremble but keep the gun aimed directly at his head.

"Took you long enough to get the ropes off," he comments.

"I was biding my time. Making sure I was in a better position to kill you." I push myself to my feet without blinking. "Guess what? I managed."

Gabriel sighs and he looks so much older than he is. "Then why haven't you?"

My chest heaves. There's only silence, me still pointing the gun at him and Gabriel risking everything to walk closer. I should do it. I need to do it. Shooting him is the only way for me to make it out of this situation intact. He didn't hesitate to beat the shit out of me.

Unless that was just for show. He hit me, but loosened my bonds... That doesn't make sense.

Why am I pausing now?

He stops advancing only when the muzzle presses to his chest, then he wraps a hand around my arm.

"I didn't have a choice. We both would have been dead. *You* were my next hit. I didn't want to tell you because I've been trying to find a way out of this for us."

I want to believe the sincerity in his voice.

It's just so *wrong*.

"You were going to kill me."

He shakes his head, his chest shuddering with his next loud sigh. "Never, sweetheart. Never."

My lower lip trembles along with my fingers, my voice. Crap. "I don't care." Now I sound like I'm going to cry. "Whatever you say, it's all a lie. You're a fucking liar and a murderer."

I might even laugh if I didn't think it would degrade into hysteria.

"If we play this right, we can both make it out of here alive." He's speaking so low I barely make out his words through the pounding of my heart. "Broderick isn't going to let you have your freedom. Not you, not me. Now is the time to be fully honest with each other."

"Stop looking at me like that." I take a ragged inhale and gesture with the gun. Showing him I mean business when my insides are too shifty for me to be still. "Stop looking at me like you feel something for me."

"You have to trust me," he tells me carefully. Despite the risk, he reaches out for me with his free hand, cupping my face. His other arm bands around my waist so that the gun remains between us.

Something tickles at the back of my head, something he said earlier. *Jade*. Jade is the reason why all of this happened in the first place. "Is...Jade still alive?" I ask. "You went to the club today."

"Yes."

It's a simple thing. *Yes*.

And it's time for me to start playing with the only currency Gabriel understands, no matter how my heart wishes it to be otherwise, because I've got to get out of here and change a yes to a *no*.

He'll never let me go.

"Was it ever real?" I wonder out loud. "The feelings between us?"

A muscle twitches in his jaw. "All of it."

My heart lifts with something akin to joy, but what good is it at this point? "I wish I could believe you." I lift on my tiptoes and kiss him.

It's too easy for me to sink into the kiss, to let myself trust in his words like the best kind of delusion. The one where he's not a psycho killer being paid to take me out and I'm not a stupid lovesick fool.

His guard will lower with the promise of sex.

It's always about sex with his kind. Sex and drugs and death. It's about time I start accepting those facts. He's never tried to hide himself or be anything other than what he is. A monster.

He's a monster, and I love him. But I can't hide who I am, either.

A woman with massive fucking trust issues.

"I *see* you, Gabriel."

I don't need to kill him but I do need to get him out of my way. His information about Jade is all I need. He confirmed everything I'd been considering myself.

I deepen the kiss, wondering if he feels the goodbye in the touch.

I see him and everything he's tried to do, and maybe in a different world I really might be able to lean into him and know he'll be there to catch me. As it is, there are too many variables. Too many walls between us. Too many doubts and too little trust.

My throat tightens.

The moment I sense the chink in his guard, I make my move and crack my hand across his face. The slap does nothing to him. It certainly doesn't have him rocking back on his heels. His eyes widen in pain right before I swing the butt of the gun into the side of his head with every ounce of strength left in me.

Too bad for him: I also know where to hit. I know the buttons to push in order to bring my opponent down.

I slam him in the side of the head a second time but he's already crumpling, and in seconds Gabriel falls to the ground.

"I'm sorry. I love you. But don't ever again think you know what's best for me." I step over his unconscious body and head toward the door.

I'll confront that bitch Jade for killing Taney. I'll arrest her and let her rot in prison for the rest of her life.

I'll give Gabriel time to wake and come after me.

And no matter what happens, or how crazy this makes me, I know I'll carry around a hole inside of me where Gabriel started to carve out his place, and it won't matter what I do or how far I run. He'll be there.

I'll have to take care of business before he catches me.

TWENTY-EIGHT
layla

DOCKS ON MARKEE is nowhere near the Velvet Underground. I've got no car, no money, no shoes. Not a damn thing to my name except nerve damage and more trauma. I stumble out into the dim afternoon light, dragging in a breath filled with the scent of blood and brackish water.

Fuck, I hate this place.

Every building here needs to be razed to the ground.

Stop wasting time.

Limping down the street, the warehouse district slowly shifts into row houses and gas stations. There are convenience stores, churches. Once I've put a safe distance between me and the docks, I lift a hand to flag down a passing car.

No badge, either.

Some nice lady in a minivan eventually stops and picks me up. Convincing her not to take me to a hospital is a problem. Telling her where I need to go is a bigger one.

She balks at the idea of going downtown and anywhere near a sex club. To the point where she pulls over at the next street and lets me out of the van with a warning to find Jesus before it's too late.

Still grappling about what to do with Gabriel, I focus on Jade.

Outside of the line of duty, I've never taken a life before, and never ever premeditated. But this woman had something to do with Taney's death. She might have even held the gun herself. Either way, I need to take her out of the picture, and right now, with my emotions running high, I want one thing.

I want to kill the bitch.

I want her to suffer for every punch I received today.

For every tear for Taney.

And with Gabriel down, I'll have one shot at this before he comes for me.

Wincing, I limp my way over several blocks as quickly as possible, with my eyes and ears tuned to any irregularities; there are none. No one follows me when I finally make my way to the front door of the club. There are people on the street enjoying the unseasonably warm weather and going about their day. Not as many in front of the club; this area is reserved for nighttime activity. But she'll be in there.

I'm not in any condition to charge in and take someone down. Especially someone who has clearly been around as long as Jade.

It doesn't matter.

Once I do this there will be no going back, though.

I have half a thought to text Devan and get him and the full might of the force down here but...it's a big but.

The only thing that matters to me right now is stopping Jade. I don't need to actually make it out. The killing calm, that same headspace I've learned to cultivate out of trauma and necessity, slips over me and all outside thought evaporates.

I only need to buy Devan time to come himself. With backup. Whether I'm alive or not when he shows up.

"Hey." I snap my fingers at the chick walking past me on towering heels. She stops, glaring at me, one eyebrow arched. "Can I borrow your phone? I just need to send a quick text."

"Honey. You need more help than that."

"Please?"

I'm not usually the one begging. After some internal debate, the woman reaches into the tiny sparkling purse at her side and holds out her cell. "One text."

It takes no time at all to draft a text to Devan to get search warrants for the club.

The precinct will need them in order to gather intel.

I tell Devan that Clint was the mole.

All out in one shot and I press send. I have no control over what he does with the information.

"Thanks." I toss the phone back to the woman who stares me up and down like I need therapy. Well, been there, done that.

"Honey, get yourself to a doctor," my savior in pleather says before she clicks off down the sidewalk.

I've still got the gun. Hopefully I won't need to use it but I don't trust myself not to. Once I'm inside, how will I react? What will I do?

The back entrance to the Velvet Underground isn't one the regular customers know about. I wouldn't have known either if not for Taney. She had me use it a few times with her, when neither of us wanted to be seen but we both needed some fresh air. Or those times when she tried to quit smoking and couldn't suppress the urge. My heart clenches agonizingly behind my aching ribs.

The door will put me right at the bottom of the stairs that lead up to Jade's office. What then? The part of my brain trained to be a member of a team screams at me to reconsider and wait for Devan. To tell him the truth about Gabriel's hit on me, and what I learned about Jade, and let the 9th precinct handle this.

I grab the gun, my hands much steadier now than before.

Even if there is no *then*, I know what has to be done.

I check the chamber, making sure I've got enough bullets, then take a deep breath and choke on the cough it gives up. *Fuck*. My ribs are in bad shape. Much worse than I thought.

I should wait for Devan. There are a lot of things I should do that press against my mind with phantom fists. I'm too wrapped up in anger and pain to give way to the voice in my head urging me to wait for him. I've got no time. If Jade hears any sirens, she'll bolt.

And with all the information I sent out to Devan, those cruisers are coming for her eventually.

A split second of indecision stills my hand on the black pull to the backdoor. *Don't do this*.

The voice in my head is Gabriel's, which only reinforces my determination. One step inside, and the music from the floor is already banging through my senses. I take one last look outside at the approaching twilight, the darkness of an evening to kick off debauchery. I'm ready.

I was born ready.

This is for Taney and for all those other women who had no choice. Who fell beneath Jade's spiked heels for one reason or another.

I round the stairs with the gun now steady in my hands. The music might be on but there is no one here. Too early. Jade, though—she's always here.

Climbing the stairs, I still see no one, but I'm too close to stop now. *In for a penny, in for a pound.* I kick open the door and step into the room half a second later.

Jade sits behind her desk completely unperturbed. She looks up slowly from her paperwork, her face a mask of apathy.

"Well. You've certainly seen better days, Miss Sinclair." She purposely sets her pen to the side and laces her fingers into a steeple in front of her. "I don't suggest looking in a mirror."

"Unluckily for you, I don't need to look good to kick your ass."

Her grim smile shifts into a smirk. "Is that what you plan to do? Or will you actually use your gun? I'm not a Sub you can intimidate."

"Why did Taney tell me not to come back to this club?" I jerk the gun toward her in emphasis.

Jade pauses before saying, "We both know the answer to that. I wondered when you'd put the pieces together, Detective." She tsks, her lips slicked with red a shade darker than the suit she wears. Her head, buzzed close to the scalp, glows in the light of the chandelier. When I look closer, I can see that the lines around her eyes are deeper, her foundation makeup caked into the creases.

The thought of this woman at Whip watching me and Gabriel has bile rising in my throat.

"A bit slower than I thought you'd be, if I'm entirely honest," she adds.

"Well, not so slow that you made an escape. You're mine now."

A viperous smile teases across her face. "*Darling.*" Condescension drips from the pet name. "I've been doing this longer than you've been alive. Do you really think you've managed to get a step ahead of me? Think, Layla."

I hesitate.

"Have you ever wondered why you are the *only* cop allowed in through my doors? I've always known what you do for a living. It's not exactly a secret. Ask yourself why I would willingly give you free rein when one wrong look at my operation might have you whipping out your cuffs."

"You're right. It's what I am," I bite out. Why had I turned a blind eye to her? Why had *she*?

"No, darling, being a cop is what you *do*. Who you are is the same as any of the sinners downstairs, except you're too stubborn to accept it. You would rather pretend that your sins don't count once you're out the door. And you were so busy pretending that you never gave a thought to mine." Jade's smile hides a murderous secret.

Stone-cold fucking *bitch*.

"The risk I took in letting you through those doors should tell you what you need to know. About the two of us."

A weird tension travels from my lower back all the way up to the top of my skull. While I don't let my guard down, the wariness grows.

"What are you talking about?"

She's maneuvering me in a definite direction. If I move too fast, she won't answer.

Jade sighs, looking at a loss by having to explain things to me. "I saw you liked sex, Detective. Did some research. Found out exactly who you are and where you came from."

"You know nothing about me." My bitterness is clear.

"I know you're a child who lost her father at such a

young age." She clicks her nails on the top of her desk before rising, pressing her palms flat. "Maybe karma was giving me a chance at redemption so what's left of my conscience can rest easy. Not that it hasn't, truly."

Her features twist into a leer at my confusion.

"Explain," I bark out.

"We're all too hasty in our younger days. Don't you agree?" she asks. "Unfortunately for me, I let my men get away with much more than I should have. Accidents happen. I had to be okay with my men killing whoever stumbled across them, just to keep things quiet." She shrugs as if to say it's no big deal. My blood goes arctic-cold. "When you're up against Broderick Stephens, wanting that kind of power, there are always some kinks to work out."

"Don't say it." I want to hear it all but I'm terrified that when I do, I'll hesitate more than I do now.

"Sadly, I will always remember a handsome man." Jade rounds the desk before cocking her hip to the side and leaning heavily on the wood. "A handsome, strapping man murdered by one of my men just outside a convenience store."

Her words land like bombs.

"I figured the unnecessary death could be a test. So I left a lighter." She studies her nails.

"A lighter," I repeat numbly.

"One of Broderick's lighters. I knew having it would be handy one day. A real get-out-of-jail-free card. His murder went practically unnoticed. To all but a little girl who happened to be on the scene and stole my lighter. You still have it, don't you? I saw you using it to smoke a cigarette in the back one night."

I'm shaking, and it's not from fear anymore. Or pain. Fury takes over. "You're lying."

"Oh?" Jade pouts, which only increases my doubt. I hope it doesn't show on my face. "Come now. Your father was simply collateral damage. He died for nothing. Not one reason. Doesn't that make you feel better? He wasn't some drug lord or dealer. He was just a pathetic man. An alcoholic taking care of his dead wife's daughter who isn't even his own blood."

I freeze. I know my mother's story. I know the truth.

But hearing it from Jade's lips?

I lock my arm with the gun still pointed at her. "You shut your mouth," I order.

"Didn't he ever tell you?" She's taking particular pleasure in each biting word, as though the realization will somehow demolish my resolve. "Your mother was *raped*. Beaten and left for dead by some nobody. She kept the baby but killed herself once you came along. Your father—or step-father I guess, whatever he was—cared for you anyway. It's romantic, really. When you think about it." She shakes her head, her gaze pitying. "Think about how many issues it must have caused him."

She just earned herself a messy, painful death rather than the bullet through the brain I'd first considered. And the small part of me that wished for Gabriel before, despite the beating, has grown so that it's the only thought in my head. Vengeance...and the reaper.

I scoff. "If you're done with story time, maybe you can enlighten me on why I should care what you say. Why should I care about your pathetic grab for power? No one knows who you are, Jade. Some two-bit club owner."

She stares at me with her head cocked to the side. My

hits lack the power of hers and we both know it. "That's not true, darling, and you know it."

"So you want to be a drug kingpin when you grow up?" I ask in an attempt to regain some control. "Or would that be queenpin..."

"I want to be *powerful*," she insists. "Untouchable. I'm practically there. I only have two tiny loose ends to tie up. You...and Gabriel."

I tighten my grip on the gun but a solid rock of a body slams into my back.

The man hits me right in the place where Gabriel got me, and I get a glimpse of him from the corner of my eye.

The bald man from Docks on Markee.

A heartbeat later, his hands wrap around my throat, cutting off my air.

TWENTY-NINE
gabriel

LAYLA PAID me back for several of my punches with the butt of her gun and my temples throb as I slam on the brakes, screeching my SUV to a stop in my usual parking spot within sight of the club. Driving had been a mistake. Half the time I'd struggled against double vision.

Please let it not be too late.

The gut instincts that have guided me all my life push me out of the vehicle with the keys still in the ignition, hustling toward the back door. Gun in hand. Knife at the ready.

Hurry.

I take the stairs two at a time and stride into Jade's office in time to see her bodyguard wrap his meaty paws around Layla's neck. Her eyes bulge, surprise making her a second too slow to stop him. Seeing Jade's lackey touching the broken detective I love snaps my last vestige of sanity.

My blood freezes, my pulse thunders in my ears. Arm straight, elbow locked, grip firm, and not caring anymore about collateral damage, I pull the trigger.

The bullet shoots clean through his head, in one side

and out the other. He crumples into a heap. Layla coughs, touching her neck and the red marks in the shape of fingers there. Her gaze shoots to me, and a single arch of my brow is like waving a red flag in front of her.

Still choking, she straightens and throws herself at Jade.

The woman doesn't even have time to grab for her gun. She uses her bare hands on the club owner, from an uppercut to a right hook to a scratch of her nails across Jade's eyes. One of them is roaring, the sound a furious meld of rage and inevitability.

Layla lifts her knee and slams it into Jade's hip. Jade isn't going to go down without a fight, though. Layla swings a punch and slams her knuckles into Jade's nose. The older woman's head snaps back before she retaliates and swipes at the detective's ribs, right where I'd punched her. Layla yelps, clutching the area.

Her injuries are too great for this fight to last, and while she claws at Jade's face, leaving marks, nothing she does is going to be good enough in the end.

And despite all sense, a wave of pride wells up and crashes over me.

Because damn it, Layla is nothing if not a fucking badass and there is not a thing I won't do to save her. Even if she hates me for it later. She'll kill herself to take Jade down. I've got a better plan.

I grab Jade and wrench her arms behind her back.

"My knight in shining armor?" Her voice slurs and blood drips from her broken nose. Her eyes spit poison at me. "Or are you one of the good guys now, *Thor*?"

"You'll figure it out when you go straight to hell where you belong. Enjoy the trip."

Jade laughs. "I suppose you'll send me there."

I shake my head. "Not me."

The barest glance at Layla, and this time she's coherent enough to get it. Her wicked smile is a thing of beauty and her eyes light with fire. Well, the one good eye that's still open, at any rate. The other one has already started to swell shut.

She slams her first into Jade's gut, pivoting her hip to send the full weight of her body into the hit.

I let her get a few good hits in, but as Layla reaches for her gun, I knock Jade out, catching her before she crashes into the desk.

Much to my surprise...Layla levels the gun at me, completely sober.

"Step back and let me kill her," she demands.

"No. You'll never forgive yourself if you do," I tell her.

"She killed my father. She's behind everything. Didn't you hear?" Her lower lip trembles and she bites down viciously on it. Rather than give in to the meaning behind the tremble, she grins at me. An unnerving grin like the first glimmer of moonlight on the business end of my knife.

"I heard enough," I admit. My heart aches for Sinclair and everything she's been through. For the family she never had and the shit circumstances she endured. Just like me.

She's too much like me and maybe that's the crux of the matter. If anyone should make it out of this, I'm bound and determined it shall be her.

"I can't let you kill her," I say firmly.

Layla bares her teeth at me. "She killed Taney. She's a murderer. All those women, my father... I want her to *pay*."

"Do you trust me?"

I'm breathing heavily, waiting for her to answer, surprised when she doesn't slam me with an automatic negative.

"I want to."

Jade's body drops between us, a physical barrier that we would have to step over to get to each other. Neither of us moves.

"She deserves worse than a bullet and we both know it," I say. "I can't tell you what will come, but let me handle her and I'll make sure she get what she deserves."

"You just had to come through. After everything." She's at her breaking point and trying not to let me see it, but I know her.

I see her, too. Every cracked and ashen piece.

"Fucking crazy, right? I thought you'd get the memo. With the whole safe word bit."

Layla chuckles, the sound diminishing as automatically sucks in a hiss and lifts a hand to her side, pressing against her damaged ribs. "I was a bit slow. Blame it on being drugged."

The urge to kiss her overwhelms me. To take her face in my hands and smooth away every bruise I helped put there. "We're out of time," I tell her instead. "You need to get out of here. *Now*. You're supposed to be dead."

She finally lowers the gun but still grips it tight. "Oh, I'm so sorry you didn't finish the job." There's no heat in her voice.

"They think I have, and it's a lie they have to believe. I need you to get to your apartment and wait for me there, Layla. This isn't funny. You'll be shot dead by Broderick's men if they see you anywhere on these streets. So careful. Get home, and I'll come and tell you everything. But *this* is over. It's over."

"Why doesn't it feel that way?" she whispers. She lets the gun drop to her side and I gently retrieve it, tucking it into my pants.

The same kind of trust she has for her partner, she's placed in me. God. I do not deserve it.

She sighs. "I hate this. And I want to hate you. I want you to die a slow and painful death, Gabriel Blackwell."

I nod. "I know you do, sweetheart. I know you do."

"Why can't I hate you?"

"I've been asking myself the same question because God knows—" I'm unable to finish the sentence.

Even on a good day I hate myself.

So it's nothing but a surprise when Layla stares at me now with too many mixed emotions in her gaze for us to untangle. Just as it was a surprise when she admitted her feelings in the warehouse.

Sirens in the distance cut through the tension between us.

"We're about to be caught. Get out of here," I order.

Layla wastes no time bolting down the stairs. I drag Jade's body down to the back entrance and my SUV, pulling out just as three cop cruisers stop on the street.

I head straight to the boss's office and dump the body on his floor.

Broderick barely glances up from his books. "Is this a gift for me?" he asks. "Which bitch do you have today, Blackwell?"

"Yes, consider it a gift." I nudge Jade with the toe of my shoe and she gives a low moan, her eyes flickering behind closed lids. She's in for a harsh reality check when she wakes. I can't find it in me to feel bad for her. "Get whatever you can out of her. She's been working for years on a secondary rival drug ring in the city."

"You kept her alive?" Something else comes to life in Broderick's voice.

I nod.

"Nice work, kid." He flicks cold eyes up at me. "And the detective?"

"Gone." *In one way or another.*

"I'll call you when I need you."

A knot in my chest slowly starts to unwind. Dismissed, I leave and head straight to Layla's apartment, having already gotten her address. Part one of this fucking charade is done. Whatever happens to Jade now will be so much worse than anything Layla might have done. Or even me.

I just dropped the woman off in the lap of the devil who will be sure to pay her back for her ambition.

Layla isn't home yet so I pick the lock and wait inside. When she manages to stumble in ten minutes later, I flick the lights on against the oncoming dusk. At least that will work in our favor. So much easier to disappear under night's cover.

Her shoulders drop and she groans, shutting the door behind her. I want to hold my arms out to her. Wait for her to come to me and never let her go.

How the hell will she ever let me touch her again?

Her black eye is now fully swollen shut and dark color has blossomed down her cheekbone and jaw.

"Took you long enough."

She huffs. "Pardon me for being tardy." She points down to her bare feet. "Stepped on some broken glass."

I'll miss that mouth of hers.

"You have two options." I swallow hard, my throat dry. "If you've got the energy left for it."

She gestures for me to continue.

"One: You leave here, and I get a body that can be mistaken for you, dump it in the river and it will turn up eventually. Or two: I kill you now. A hit is a hit, Layla. They won't let it drop. Broderick thinks it's a done deal."

It might be easier if she rages at me.

If she uses those hands on me and claws at my skin the way she did to Jade in the office.

I *don't* expect her to slowly walk past me into her galley kitchen. "Do you want coffee?" she calls back wearily.

This is worse. Much worse to have her be this beaten down instead of angry. Her rage I can handle; I *want* to see it.

I watch her go through the motions but when she hands me a mug and I take a sip, it takes everything in me not to spit out the jet fuel in there. "This is whiskey," I choke in surprise.

She holds her mug out in a mock salute. "Yup."

I force myself to drink the rest of the swill in the mug as Layla does the same. Both of us seem if not content then resigned to the angry silence.

"I'm not sure what you want me to say. You're itching for a fight, Gabriel."

I harden my gaze. "You deserve one. So do I." I want to snap at her and it takes effort to restrain myself. There is no point in forcing her hostility. Even when it would be easier.

"You do. I should kick your fucking balls right up into your throat."

"You're so sure I had nothing to do with Jade." That's what's plagued me since I followed her up into that office. "You know I fucked her."

Layla looks like she's swallowed a bucket full of nails. "I do."

"How do you know I wasn't in on it with her from the start?"

She pauses for a moment before she shrugs. "My gut, I guess. Or maybe it's a delusion. I wanted to believe, even after everything..."

"I had to make it believable." I can't resist the urge to touch her, to run my fingers down her arm, and I swallow my disappointment when she flinches.

"You can be as furious as you want, but Broderick himself put the hit on you. I'm being realistic. If I don't eliminate you, then someone else will step up in my place. Then another. And another. There is no way to escape this unless we do it my way."

"You bastard."

"I am."

That's all I can say. We're at a stalemate and we both understand there is no way out of this outside of my two options.

"Will Devan be safe?"

"As far as Broderick and the Syndicate know, you worked alone. I don't think they care about anyone else right now."

"Devan will never believe it," Layla insists. She turns and heads back into the kitchen except there's no hiding her motives this time. She doesn't worry about the mug and goes straight for the bottle of cheap whiskey, swigging from it directly. "He'll never believe I'm gone. He just saw me."

"He can't know you're alive or he'll be in danger."

I'll never be able to touch her again one way or the other, and the more time we spend in this little kitchen, the more resigned I am to that fact. No happy endings. Definitely not for me.

She might have a shot, though. And she deserves it after everything that's happened to her. After this mess and the life I'm forcing her to throw down the toilet.

"Fine," she tells me at last. "If Devan is safe then I'm out of here. Far away. From you, from them. From all of it."

She's breaking on the inside the same way I am.

Jade had the information on her father, about his senseless death. No meaning. An accident. It's almost worse than knowing the man had been wrapped up in things beyond his control. Worse than a meaningful death.

It only meant something to Layla.

There are no answers for her, which is the most awful thing of all.

"Who is going in my place then, butcher?" She sounds so tired.

"Another hot skank I got caught up with who needs to disappear."

My joke falls flat and Layla can't muster a smile.

"I figured it was something like that."

I don't deserve to have her think anything of me other than what I am—a monster, a killer. The reaper. It's all I've ever been and there isn't anything else for me at the end of this road. Definitely no white picket fence or that kind of future. No kids. No pets. My black thumb with plants extends to every part of my life.

But if I can make this one thing right and get her out of here safely, I will live with the consequences of every other messed up decision and action I've made.

"I'll leave tonight. Drive until I can't, then ditch my car," she finishes.

"I'll make sure you have what you need."

I down the last of the whiskey, my fingers tense when I set the mug next to her on the counter. She pauses, jerks, keeping herself from touching me the same way I am with her. She won't let me touch her. I never will again. It will be my penance for what I've done.

Just...too late for us.

I love you, too.

I leave without another word.

Because I am who I am, and she is who she is, and she's better off without me. The last thing she needs is me around to continue to fuck up her life.

Once I'm outside, I light up a cigarette in the alley behind her building, drawing smoke into my lungs in a way I haven't allowed myself in years. That one emergency smoke in my coat pocket...if this isn't an emergency I don't know what counts.

What a mess. And the only thing that's going to get us both out of it is time. Time, and me doing what I do best: murder. It's no alternative to love but I've never been built for a happy family life.

THIRTY

layla

ONE YEAR LATER...

YOU NEVER START out on your journey wishing for a new life because wishes are bullshit and nothing ever comes of them. The only way to make a difference is to work hard and claw your way out of the gutter.

Fuck, who am I kidding?

Everything I fought to obtain, the answers I so desperately sought that I almost lost sight of myself...all for nothing. All to run away like a little bitch and hide in the shadows.

A new life in a new city halfway across the country from the hellhole I left behind, and I stayed in bed for about four months, barely able to get up. Someone with a degree will probably tell me I'm depressed or some shit like that, but I can't call my old therapist.

I can't call anyone from my old life *because I'm dead*.

"Layla Sinclair" is dead, and the husk I've been hauling around is hollowed out on the inside, so I might as well be dead for real.

My new identity opened up a membership at a gym across the street from a Starbucks. Sometimes after a particularly grueling session I like to treat my new identity to a venti mocha frappe with extra whipped cream on top, because I figure the woman I see in the mirror at the gym likes it. She's all for the sweet things in life and treating herself. No one else in the classes sees the emptiness in her eyes.

The emptiness is still there when I get home.

A new life and happiness still eludes me. But someone like me doesn't really need to be happy. I doubt I could even recognize happiness if I stumbled across it.

The gym helps me work out my frustrations. I throw a fierce punch to the bag and send it swinging back as a dull ache throbs along my knuckles.

Uppercut, left hook. Right hook.

I just need the last person alive who I care about to be safe.

It's the only thing that matters to me.

And he is, thank God. I checked on him through a back-end channel a few times before I realized that doing so put him in jeopardy if anyone ever found out. Devan had mourned the loss of his partner, though. Genuinely mourned, and that kinda breaks my heart.

Then again, with a less intense partner at his side, it seems he's had more time for himself, to relax and do whatever it is he wants to do in the free time not spent chasing down leads for extra cases. Devan and his girlfriend even got engaged.

I pause and grab hold of the punching bag, breathing heavily.

I swear, I never thought he'd be soft enough for marriage. People sure do surprise you.

Devan is happy and safe. He's the only one that matters to me.

Sure, it might cause him some lasting grief, if I mean anything to him like he means to me, but eventually he'll heal even those holes from my absence and be all the better for it. Who needs an albatross around their neck?

After I'm done with my session I unwrap my hands and start wiping down mats at the gym in preparation. Not only does my new identity have a membership, but I've started teaching a self-defense class for women. It's not great pay by any means, but it keeps me active and it's enough to live off of.

I had found more cash than I knew what to do with in the bag in my room. The only bag I'd packed before I left.

He'd put it there.

I scrub down a forest-green mat and add it to the pile with the rest of the clean ones.

For a while, I didn't touch the cash. Refused to use it because of the ties and what it meant. Instead, to get to this place, I'd used the last of what I'd saved myself and rummaged through the car for change before taking off on foot.

I left my wallet behind when I ran, along with my credit cards, license, badge. Everything.

But the bag, along with the cash, contained a new license and a shiny passport with my new name. I have no clue when he accomplished it or the source he used. I don't want to know, and I don't want to use anything he touched.

I had to work hard to demolish my self-constructed walls, to get to a point where I even let myself spend it. I finally let myself feel the freedom his money bought for me.

I take a beat, a breath, and glance at myself in the mirror. The woman who looks back at me is about as far from Detective Layla Sinclair as I can physically get. I've cut my hair off so that the pixie cut fans my face, added a few piercings, and a bright slash of pink gloss shines on my lips. Mascara. Shit, even the sports bra and yoga pants ensemble screams feminine, classy, cutesy.

It's disconcerting and a little gross. It's definitely not me. Or, at least, the old me.

For the first time, there are no anchors keeping me down. My father's death and the mystery of it all is no longer there to press on me. I'm not constantly worrying about Devan, or Taney. Those pieces from my past life are gone. Poof.

Maybe I won't ever find happiness. What the hell would I do with it, anyway? It's not in my nature to be one of those people who take a stroll through a park and stop to smell the roses. Or whatever it is that makes people feel joy. I'll never be one of those social media butterflies commenting on the beauty of life.

But freedom? I've found it now and cut every loose string. I didn't know I needed it so badly.

I finish up at the gym, taking time to personally talk to anyone who comes up to me with questions.

All with a smile on my face.

On my walk home, the sun is shining and there isn't a hint of yellow smog in the sky.

Weird, though, not to have each breath tainted by smog and hot garbage no matter the time of year. Weird to have people who pass me on the street smile and nod their heads in greeting, believing I'm not a threat. There's no more looking over my shoulder or checking every dark alley to make sure no one jumps out at me.

A smaller town—a smaller city, if you can call it that. There are less monsters roaming freely at night and it's no longer up to me to stop them. At least, there are less of them out in the open and known.

For once…it's okay.

The apartment complex is on the newer side, steel and glass with young trees lining the walk from the parking lot. It's mostly full of couples and young families. The place even has a doorman on rotation to make sure that anyone who comes through the lobby is a resident or an invited guest.

No surprises.

I flash a smile at Lars, the doorman on duty as I enter.

"How was your day, Miss Stone?" he asks.

"Another day in paradise," I reply with a trill.

He chuckles at that, because my weirdly chipper tone isn't weird to him. It's just how "Ashley Stone" operates.

I use my keycard for access to the elevator and press the button for the fifth floor. High enough I don't have to worry about anyone climbing up to the terrace and breaking in. Not to mention a pretty nice view of a community garden.

Never in my life would I have imagined living in a place like this.

Now? It's routine. It's normal. *I'm* normal.

Appearances can be so damn deceiving.

I walk into my apartment and palm my keys, no need to check the place. At least, there's never been a need before. Except today there's a small card on the edge of my kitchen island countertop. A card that wasn't there when I left for the gym.

Instinct has me bending at the waist and reaching for the gun I keep strapped to my ankle. Concealed but accessible at all times. I pull it out and cock it, safety off. The same instinct has me pushing aside my worry and stalking through the apartment looking for the break-in. The point of entry. Places where a thief might hide.

"Are you serious right now?"

Those dark tones are less a bullet and more a caress despite the fact that the man they belong to should not be here. I drop my arm to my side.

Gabriel is leaning against my couch in the living room. His arms are crossed over his chest as he stares at me, eyes lit with mirth.

He's...*here*.

How is he here?

I'm barely able to hang on to the gun with my numb fingers.

"It's an anniversary card," he explains. "One whole year of being someone else. How does it feel?"

"I never took you for the sentimental type." I force myself to lift the gun again and aim it at his forehead. "Is there a reason I shouldn't kill you?"

I want to mean it, but seeing him here in person, someone who risked everything to give me this freedom... how can I hate him? Despite what he is?

Gabriel shrugs. "You tell me."

"Why are you here?"

He slowly unfolds himself and straightens to his full towering height. "It's a long story. But I've got my own identity crisis, it seems. Need to be someone else." His look is loaded. "And you need to be someone else again. Ashley Stone has to die."

My stomach drops. "Why?"

I finally have a routine here. It's boring and monotonous but it's safe and it's mine. And that's what I want.

It's what I want.

I want—

One look at him has me doubting everything I've convinced myself of over the last twelve months.

"Just in case," he says.

He comes toward me slowly, prowling, his muscles rippling beneath the overly tight material of his shirt.

"In case? In case what?"

"In case anyone gets the stupid idea to come after us."

Us.

"The badass detective and the asshole killer," he says with a slight grin. "What a pair we make."

He's so close now. Close enough for me to breathe him into my lungs and remember how desperately I've missed him. Gabriel takes the gun from my loose grip and tosses it aside, running his fingers through my hair.

"You always say the sweetest things," I say ruefully.

HIs eyes are glittering emerald chips. "Unfortunately for you, Layla Sinclair, there is only one fucking woman psychotic enough to give me what I need. And I escaped my chains to find her. I'm hoping we can find a new way. Together."

Oh God. Together.

The one desperate hope I've been too terrified to even think about this past year and he's just said it out loud. *Together.*

I always figured it would be impossible to see him again, this relic from my old life and the object of my nightly fantasies.

I clear my throat a little nervously. "What makes you think I'm still interested?"

I'm not sure what I want him to say or how I expect this to go. The fact that he's here is a miracle in itself and there are a thousand questions in my head. How did he break away from Broderick? How did he find me when I've been so good at covering my tracks?

Where does he want to go?

Because damn me straight to hell, but now that I see him again, I know wherever he wants to go I'll follow. To the ends of the earth or straight down into the abyss, just to be with him. I've never been the Starbucks and flowers type. Gabriel Blackwell reminds me why.

His hand travels from my scalp down the line of my jaw, my neck, past my breast and down my thigh as I tremble beneath his touch. He slides his fingers underneath the waistband of my yoga pants and straight to my core, then he dips a finger into me.

"Your body tells me more than your mouth. It always has, sweetheart. You give yourself away every time."

He crooks his finger through my folds, thumb circling my clit, and I shudder.

"Fuck you," I manage to get out. There's only heat behind the words and none of the threat.

At the end of the day...he's still a killer. No matter who we are or where, he is who he is. The question now becomes whether I can accept that or not, when I still think of myself as a detective. A person dedicated to upholding the law and making sure there is some kind of order to temper the chaos.

He touches me slowly, reverently, his fingers exploring for the spots that will make me breathless. I want to see him. To feel his skin and know that he is actually here. Real and solid.

This dark, forbidden creature.

I yank at his shirt but he grabs my wrists, keeping me from touching him.

"Not yet," he murmurs. He concentrates on moving slowly, hooking his fingers inside me. "You're so wet already. Soft, and hot as sin."

I clench around him, whimpering. "I need to touch you."

"Soon but not yet." The steel of his order is hidden in the softness of his voice and I want nothing more than to get down on my knees for him. Only him.

Gabriel reaches down to hook my leg and lift it to gain better access to my core.

I'm just as dark and depraved as he is and I've fought against it my entire life. It gave me a strong moral compass to follow, but what the fuck good is it when it's not what society dictates? When my tastes run a little too psychotic for the norm?

It's time to reconcile with myself.

I'm the judge and jury. I always have been. And Gabriel? He's the executioner.

We need each other.

I'm so done fighting my own nature.

Gabriel swallows, my eyes tracking the movement of his throat. A small glimpse of nervousness and one I find oddly charming. The two of us are tentative with each other for the first few moments, his fingers still working me. It's been a long year that we've been apart.

Which one of us is going to break first? Because I know myself and I—

I sense Gabriel's movement before he lunges at me and we crash together like two starving creatures. All the uncertainty falls away beneath the lust.

He's hard and hot and ready for me.

I work my hands down into the waistband of his pants and wrap my fingers around his cock.

When his thumb strokes my clit harder, my entire being clenches and I go tight.

He leans down to brush his teeth against my earlobe. "I've missed your pretty little pussy, Layla."

And it is so sweet to hear that name coming from that mouth.

"I've missed your beautiful cock, Gabriel," I reply.

Loving the way he growls when I say his name back to him.

"Tell me you haven't had anyone else inside of you." He's demanding in all the right ways. "Tell me you've saved that sweet cunt only for me."

He pushes my pants down, panties with them, and snarls at the first sight of my naked lower half. A low growl of desire I feel inside of me.

His fingers dig into my skin as he dominates me with his body, moving me back toward the couch, forcing me to release my hold on him. I run my hands over the broad plane of his chest, and when his mouth drops to mine, the taste of my whiskey on his tongue, a fire ignites through me.

He maneuvers himself down on the cushions and drags me onto his lap, my legs parting on either side of his hips and my pussy throbbing and desperate for more contact. He presses closer and grabs the back of my neck.

There's no question this time, no fighting over who is going to do the lion's share of the dominating.

He slides his hand along my aching core.

My fingernails scratch against his skin as I grasp for his boxers, lifting on my knees only to give him enough room to get them down to his ankles and kick them away.

He catches hold of my knee and hooks me solid, his erection slipping against me. The head of his cock drives into my clit and a low groan escapes from my throat.

"You're never getting away from me again," he declares.

With my free hand I drag his dick to my core and slowly sink down onto him.

I gasp. "*Fuck.*" Air catches in my chest at the sensation of him stretching me. Filling me, my body forced to adjust to make room for him. "I almost forgot how huge you are."

He takes his time filling me until he's fully sheathed and we stare at each other, every solid inch of him exactly where he needs to be.

"Aren't you going to tell me what to do?" I ask, my breathing ragged.

"You're already riding my cock," he says. "Right now I can't ask for more."

The feeling of being together again after so long...

He starts to move and I cry out at the sensation of him rocking his hips back, the full length of him driving into me. Shockwaves pulse through my system.

Gabriel grabs my wrists and moves them to his shoulders, my nails digging into his muscles. Our bodies move in time and when he takes my lips again, he's hard and demanding.

Wanting *everything*.

Whatever I have to give, it's all his.

And I plan to take all he has as well.

Every savage push of his cock into me. Every whispered endearment.

One of his palms cups my ass to control the pace while the other tangles in the back of my hair. He yanks my head back, my chest arching toward him and his tongue lapping a trail down to my nipples.

There is only heat and life and breath. There's the sensation of him fucking me so savagely I can only close my eyes and hold on. This is ownership pure and simple.

"Give me more," I pant.

Gabriel does not back down from the challenge. His hand moves from my ass to my knee, lifting my leg higher to drive even deeper inside of me. And when the closeness isn't enough he shifts us again and falls on top of me, my back pressing into the couch cushions so that I'm no longer straddling him.

"You want more?" He grips my ass again, my pussy aching from every fresh thrust. Every punishing, ruthless slide of his skin against mine. "I'm not sure how much that pussy can take. But I want you crying, so raw from me fucking you that you come on the spot."

He's not even touching my clit and I'm close. Every hard arch of his hips steals my breath.

"I'm going to be raw because you're so fucking *big*."

Gabriel grins wickedly, his smile wide. "My mediocre cock? Too big for you?" His gaze is thirsty now. "Have you shrunk? Because I thought I fit perfectly in that sweet channel of yours."

The friction is unbearable. He fucks me hard from on top, dominating me with his position alone, and I slip my hand between us to work my sweet spot. I'm moaning again, loudly, the sound drowned only by the slap of our bodies together.

I refuse to look away from him as energy prickles, pleasure bursting through me and my core tightening around his cock in release.

"You still want me to come inside of you?" He's got me pinned beneath him and times his thrusts to such agonizing slowness I see stars.

"God, yes."

I've met every thrust with movement of my own, the savage intensity making me feel alive for the first time in a year. Throbbing. Pulsing around him. Gabriel's mouth meets mine in a final claiming kiss before he comes with his own intense release, emptying himself inside of me.

A part of me sees his arms shaking on either side of my head as he struggles to keep his full weight from crushing me. Sees the tension in his shoulders even though he's still thrusting through the last dregs of his orgasm.

He hesitates for only a brief second before he kisses the area between my eyes. "At least you didn't go to fucking Montana."

A breathy laugh erupts at the joke. "I thought about it. Trust me."

"If you want to, we'll go, Layla," he says, reaching out to clear the hair away from my eyes. "The only place I want to be is with you."

I don't deserve to be this fucking happy.

This isn't real.

But if it's a dream then let me stay here forever.

"I thought you promised me a *screaming* orgasm," I remind him playfully.

The lust in his gaze makes my heart thump. "Trust me, sweetheart, we've got time."

THE END

(And they live darkly ever after!)

Want more hot, sexy, morally gray heroes and badass heroines? Finish the Empire Bay duology with Devan's story in Love After Darkness.

afterword

Thank you to everyone who took a risk with me and picked up my debut novel! *Love After Never* is a beautiful story I am super proud to release out into the world, and I hope that you love Gabriel and Layla just as much as I do. Stick around, there's more to come!

more books by melanie kingsley

The Balestra Family

His Deadly Lies

Empire Bay

Love After Never

Love After Darkness

about the author

Melanie Kingsley is a pen name for a USA Today bestselling contemporary romance author exploring her dark side. She writes gritty, no-holding-back romances that will keep you on the edge of your seat and your sanity. Happily ever afters may be guaranteed but getting there will be a ride to get there. She loves her fur babies and coffee (light and sweet, go figure), travel, and tile match games. Putting her lifelong love of reading to good use, she now spends her time giving morally gray characters their redemption.

Explore the dark and dangerous side of romance with Melanie's more sinful reads. Or sit back and let the passion drive you wild with an escape into her steamy and seductive romances.

www.melaniekingsley.com